About the Author

Born in Trowbridge Wilts., David L. Young has been teaching English and
History for over 30 years. He is fascinated by the English monarchy and the
development of democracy in Britain. His publications include *Communication in
English* and *Tolpuddle*. He is a keen photographer and has had his work exhibited
and published in England, USA and Israel. Today he teaches in Jerusalem and is
married with three children.

GUNPOWDER, TREASON & PLOT

A NOVEL

by

David L. Young

Published 2006 by arima publishing

www.arimapublishing.com

ISBN 1-84549-064-9

Printed and bound in the United Kingdom

Typeset in Garamond 10/14

arima publishing
ASK House, Northgate Avenue
Bury St Edmunds, Suffolk IP32 6BB
t: (+44) 01284 700321

www.arimapublishing.com

For
my wife, Beverley
and my children and grandson, Vered, Nadav, Ya'acov & Oz

and in loving memory of
my parents, Leah & Sydney
and also of
Jack Stock & Baruch Anson

Contents

Prologue

"Mummy! Mummy!" cried the small boy bursting into the kitchen where his mother was taking a break from preparing the family dinner. His eyes were full of tears and the grubby hankie he was using was sopping wet and useless. It just made his blotchy face look even worse. His mother was sitting at the table reading the evening paper. As usual, the front page was filled with the usual litany of car crashes, burglaries and gossip about the royal family, as well as a lurid report about the sexual exploits of an up and coming Tory M.P. Most of the back page was devoted to the uncovering of a terrorist group which had planned to blow up the Parliament building in a small country in Central Africa. The inside pages included news about the interminable wrangling about negotiations in the Middle East, while at the bottom of page one there was the predictable annual article for parents warning their children about the dangers of fireworks on Bonfire night.

She looked up. "What is it Johnny?" she asked as she gathered him to her and tried to calm him down. A few minutes passed before his small shoulders stopped heaving so that he could straighten himself up.

"Mummy," he said, his words punctuated by a few last sobs. "Mummy, Robert Thompson and Alan Smith said I can't celebrate Guy Fawkes Night tonight with them because I'm a Catholic and Guy Fawkes was a Catholic and he was a very bad man and he…"

"Hey. Whoa there. Here, catch your breath and take my nice clean hankie and dry your eyes. Now start again, child. What did they say?"

The small boy took his mother's clean white handkerchief and roughly wiped the tears off his chubby face and started again.

"You know Robert Thompson and Alan Smith in my class? You know, the ones who sometimes let me play football with them in the park?"

"Yes," answered the mother wondering where all this was leading to.

"Well, we were all coming home from school now and they said that I couldn't go to their bonfire tonight because I'm a Catholic and…" and he started sobbing again at the thought of it.

The mother wiped his eyes again and gently ruffled his hair. The small boy took his cue, sniffled once or twice and continued. "They said that Guy Fawkes was a very bad man and a Catholic and he wanted to blow up the Houses of Parliament and kill all the Royal family and that he also wanted to kill all the king's ministers and …and…" Young Johnny didn't recognize the use of full stops and punctuation at times like these. "It's not true, is it mummy? Tell me it's not true." He looked up at his mother's face. She dabbed his face with the now crumpled hankie.

"Well Johnny," she said, choosing her words carefully. "Some of what they said is true, my love. Now let me think. Yes, it is true that there once was a man called Guy Fawkes and that he was a Catholic and…"

"And did he try to blow up the Houses of Parliament and want to kill all the king's men and his wife and his children?" asked Johnny incredulously. "That's what I want to know. I want to be able to tell Robert and Alan that they're liars 'cos I think they're just making it all up."

"Well, my love, Guy Fawkes didn't really blow up the Houses of Parliament, but he certainly planned to do so."

"Did he really? So what happened to him? Why didn't he succeed?"

"The king's soldiers caught him just in time."

"What? Just before he lit the blue touch-paper?" The small boy's eyes were wide with disbelief.

"No, not exactly. I don't really think they had blue touch-paper in those days."

"But why, mummy? Didn't he like the king?" Such thoughts were pure treason to the young and impressionable citizen of Great Britain.

"Well, it's not as simple as that. You see, some of what Robert and Alan told you is true. Guy Fawkes was a Catholic, and in those days…"

"Which days?"

"Oh, about four hundred years ago. Anyway, as I said, Guy Fawkes was a Catholic and in those days a lot of people didn't trust the Catholics in England and so naturally, the Catholics didn't like that either."

"But why? What had they done?" asked Johnny, sounding as if he were about to burst out into tears again.

"Well, my love, most of the people in England in those days were Protestants, that is, they were Christians, but not Catholics like us…"

"What? Like our neighbours, the Longlands and the Smythes?"

"Yes, that's right."

"And the Goldsteins?"

"No, no. Not the Goldsteins, darling. They're Jewish, and that's another religion. But anyhow, the Protestants didn't like the Catholics and they made lots of new laws against them. Like if they didn't go to pray in Protestant churches, they would have to pay a fine."

"How much?"

"A shilling."

"A shilling? What's a shilling? How much is that worth?"

"Oh, about five pence."

"Is that all? That's not much. You give me more than that to buy an ice-cream."

"That's true. But in those days, and remember we're talking about four hundred years ago, a shilling was worth a great deal of money."

"And were there any other laws then, against the Catholics I mean?" Life in those faraway days was beginning to sound dangerous and exciting for the small boy. By now he had completely forgotten his tears and had climbed down off his mother's lap.

"Yes, I'm sure there were, but I can't remember any of them. And then of course, there were other plots which the Catholics wanted to carry out. Like killing the queen."

"Which queen? Queen Victoria? And anyway, you talked before about killing a king, not a queen."

"Queen Victoria? No, my love. Queen Elizabeth. Queen Elizabeth I. She was the queen a long time before Queen Victoria."

"But why did they want to kill Queen Elizabeth? Didn't she like the Catholics either? Did she make laws that they had to pay a shilling if they didn't go to her Protesting churches?"

"Protestant, Johnny, Protestant," the mother said as she smiled and gently ruffled her son's curly hair again. "You see, the Catholics wanted to take another queen, a Catholic queen from Scotland called Mary, Queen of Scots and put her on the throne instead."

"So why didn't they?"

"Well, first of all, Queen Elizabeth had put her in prison so she wasn't free to be put on the throne and secondly..."

"Wasn't she very beautiful, this Mary, Queen of Scots?" Johnny stopped scratching his head and interrupted his mother. "I remember Mr. McGregor, our history teacher, talking about her once."

"Well, they say she was. And anyway, there was this young man called Babington and he fell in love with her and he wanted to rescue her from the castle where she was being held as a prisoner."

"Sounds just like a boring ol' fairy story for girls," Johnny said, disdainfully waving his hand. But then his curiosity overcame him. "But did he succeed in rescuing her, this Babington man?"

"Oh no, Johnny. But that's another story. A very tragic story in which many people lost their heads."

"What? Do you mean they were executed?" the small boy asked, a bloodthirsty note creeping into his voice.

"Yes, my love. But I'll tell you about young Babington and his plot once you've finished your supper. Now go and wash your hands and face."

* * * * * * * *

Chapter One
The Babington Plot

The day was fading fast. Threatening dark grey clouds were scudding in from the west. The wind was becoming colder and more piercing as the man hurried along the dark and narrow streets that made up this part of the city of London. Streets – actually, they are more like mean alleyways, the man thought as he pulled his dark brown cape tighter around his shoulders. Tugging his hat down even lower over his forehead, its wide brim almost blocking his vision, he hunched over and continued his descent down the hill towards the River Thames.

Suddenly he nearly tripped. A fat rat, its wet fur shining from the light of a brothel window nearby, and probably disturbed by the man's quick and urgent clacking footsteps, had scuttled out from a hole and run across the cobblestones. The rat did not breathe a sigh of relief, at least audibly, but it must have realised instinctively that it had just escaped from being crushed by the man's heavy riding boots. It made off rapidly and headed off in the direction of a gutter flowing with debris and dirty water, its squeals being heard until it was out of earshot.

After this interruption, the man kept up his brisk pace until he arrived at the sought after address. Arriving at the back door and panting a little, he knocked sharply twice on the door of the *"Three Tuns"* tavern and looked around carefully over his shoulder. One couldn't be too sure. No answer. He lifted the heavy black iron knocker and knocked again. Louder, this time. Two knocks, pause and then two more knocks. Just as he had instructed the men he hoped would be waiting inside. For a full minute there was no response of any kind. No call of "Who's there?" or the sounds of drunken singing suddenly being stopped. Just the sound of the damp wind whistling up from the direction of the River Thames. He stood there, tapping his foot impatiently on the crude pavement and rubbing his hands together. The man looked around again. Maybe I've come to the wrong address, he thought. After all, there was more than one tavern in this dockside area and the *"Three Tuns"* was a popular name for such places.

Supposing I've come to the wrong one, he asked himself. But no. There was the sign *"Three Tuns"* painted just as he had remembered it, swinging and creaking in the wind. Just as he was about to reach for the knocker again, the door opened. A thin slit of pale orange-yellow light appeared and dimly lit a man's face. Most of this light was blocked out by the silhouette of a tall figure.

The figure spoke. "Who are you?"

"Babington."

"Babington who?"

"Anthony Babington. Now stand aside my good man and let me come in. I'm freezing here."

"Have you any proof?"

"Have I any papers do you mean? No. But I can tell you my father's name was Henry, my mother was called Mary and I was born in Derbyshire. Is that proof enough for you? Now open the door my good man and let me in. It's cold and drizzling out here."

The figure behind the door was not impressed.

"Where in Derbyshire?"

"Dethick."

"What year?"

"What year what?" Babington asked impatiently.

"What year were you born?"

"1561."

"Which month?"

"October. Now step aside my good man and let me in."

"All right," said the man at the door lugubriously figuring it out. "So that means you're about 25 years old and ...

"Hey! What's going on out there? Who's there? Come on man. You're letting in a fearsome draught!" someone called out from inside the dimly lit room.

"It's a man who calls himself Babington," the self-appointed keeper at the door called back over his shoulder.

"Francis Babington? From Dethick in Derbyshire?" the voice shouted back.

"Yes."

"So let him in man. He's the one we've been waiting for."

The man at the door apologized. "Sorry about all the questions friend. I'm new here and I didn't recognize you and it was hard to see you under that hat and cape." He stepped aside and opened the door. "Come in and do not take offence. I was just making sure."

"Making sure of what?"

"Well you know Walsingham's got his spies about and that spider would surely love to know where we are and what we're planning here tonight."

"I know. That's why the last meeting was held somewhere else."

"That's right. Near St. Giles' Field I was told."

"True. Now step aside my friend and let me get near the fire." And Babington pushed past the young man into the dimly lit room. As he unwound his cape and hung it behind the door, he looked around and counted the number of men sitting there. There were twelve. He recognized only one or two of them. John Ballard and one whose name he had forgotten. He had met Ballard fairly recently and knew that he was a fanatic Roman Catholic. He was also a priest. At least he claimed he was. Babington also knew that Ballard had achieved some sort of fame, perhaps notoriety would have been a better description, as one who had claimed that he could successfully exorcise demons. Babington smiled a brief smile of recognition at the supposed man of the cloth who was sitting nearest the door with his back to the wall. Ballard grimaced back, showing two broken teeth in his too-large mouth.

Just then Robert Barnwell spoke up.

"I see you know John Ballard," Barnwell said. "Now let me introduce the other men here tonight. First of all, I'm Robert Barnwell." And half-rising as well as he could in that crowded room, he smiled at the others seated around the long oval table and pointed them out to the recently arrived Babington.

"Edward Abington, Edward Jones, Robert Gage, Jerome Bellamy, yes that's John Charnock sitting a bit behind Jerome, Henry Dunne, Gilbert Gifford, Chidicock Tichbourne…"

"Chidiock Tichbourne, not Chidicock," the young man reprimanded Barnwell.

"I apologize. Oh yes, and he's a poet too," added Barnwell as if that made up for his mistake. "Now where was I? Ah yes. That leaves Thomas Salusbury, John Travers and another John, John Savage" And with that Robert Barnwell sat down and leant his chair back against the wall.

"Well now you know who we are, tell us something about yourself," John Savage said leaning forward. "All we know about you is that you know John Ballad here."

"All right gentlemen, I'll do that," said Babington, automatically moving to the head of the table. "My name is Anthony Babington, and as some of you may have heard me when Jerome Bellamy here questioned me when I arrived. I was born in Derbyshire and like yourselves, I received a good but secret Catholic education and upbringing. About ten to twelve years ago I was sent to Sheffield Castle and stayed there for a short time where I served as a page to Her Majesty…"

"What! Elizabeth was at Sheffield?" a voice questioned him from the back of the room.

"No," Babington said quickly. "Her Majesty, Mary Queen of Scots."

This reply produced sounds and nods of approval. Babington continued.

"After having served Her Majesty for a short while, I left and…"

"Why? Didn't you enjoy serving Her Majesty?" asked the same unidentified voice from the back of the room.

"Oh, I surely did. I count it as one of the happiest periods of my life. To serve Her Majesty, Mary Queen of Scots. She was as beautiful and as charming as all the reports say about her." He stopped for a moment and then continued. "I wonder if she is as beautiful today. I don't know how all this continuous imprisonment has affected her, but then, even though she was still a prisoner, she had more freedom then and was so happy…" and he stopped talking as his mind went back to those glorious days at Sheffield.

Someone coughed and brought Babington back to the present. To 1586.

"So friend Babington. You haven't told us why you left Sheffield."

"I left because I went into Law and studied it for some time. But I must confess that I found it so boring, all those cases about property-rights and torts and all the hundreds of petty details and precedents, that I stopped after a while and went abroad. I remember that was after Father Edmund Campion was executed."

They all bowed their heads as they thought of the terrible racking and bloody death of this most recent Jesuit martyr.

"Where did you go?" someone asked after a suitable pause.

"Mainly France and the Low countries. And it was there in Paris that I met Thomas Morgan."

"I know him!" John Ballard cried out suddenly. "He's the one I met who had been a soldier once, somewhere in the Low Countries, no? That's right isn't it, Gifford?" And he looked around to Gifford for support.

Gifford stopped picking his teeth with a splinter of wood, long enough to shake his head from side to side. Ballard must have muddled him up with somebody else. Gifford then relapsed into his position in the dark corner where he sat slumped in his chair.

"That Morgan fellow, he's Welsh isn't he?" Henry Dunne asked.

"Aye, but he's no less the Catholic for it."

"And didn't he, a few years back I mean, try and raise a rebellion in France for Mary Queen of Scots?"

"Yes. The same man. But he failed and the French put him in the Bastille, you know, their big prison in Paris."

"Yes, we know that," someone said irritably as he half-knocked his ale glass over. "And then what happened to this Morgan fellow?"

Ballard shrugged his shoulders. He didn't know. The only other thing he knew about Morgan was that he knew how to write and forge letters.

Babington coughed, as though to bring the attention back to himself.

"Well, when I met Morgan, he was a free man then and we spent many an evening in places such as these planning on how to get Mary Queen of Scots out of prison. We hoped to re-establish her as the rightful and Catholic Queen of England."

Four or five of the assembled men clapped their hands loudly in approval.

Babington continued. "Our idea was that the queen, Elizabeth that is, was to be killed and then ships in the Thames were to be seized. We would then start a general uprising and all the queen's ministers, especially Cecil and Walsingham were to be killed as well. Then of course, the Catholics would be reinstated again and life would return to the happy days of Queen Mary Tudor. For as you know, since then, all we have done is suffer for our faith in this country. There is no need for me to remind you that the fine for not attending communion services on Sunday has been raised from one shilling to twenty pounds and..."

"Yes," Bellamy interrupted. "And the Catholic Lords in the North have been persecuted and their lands and properties have been taken over by the Crown."

"He's certainly right there," a bass voice added. "The Duke of Norfolk, England's premier duke mark you, was tried and executed over a dozen years ago. And just because he was a Catholic."

"Yes. In 1572."

"So, as I was saying," Babington continued. "The lot of our faith has fallen so low that we are no longer free men, in our homes or even on the streets.

Walsingham's spies are everywhere. Who knows if any of our servants aren't working for him? Our leaders have been murdered and turned into martyrs. Think of what happened to Sir Nicholas Throckmorton...."

"Who? Sir Walter Raleigh's father-in-law?"

"Aye, the same. Even though he served as an ambassador in France for five years, he was often suspected for his Catholic beliefs. And think too of the Ridolfi Plot. Y'know, when that Florentine fellow tried to get Mary Queen of Scots to marry the Duke of Norfolk..."

"And then put her on the throne instead of Elizabeth."

"And what about the queen's chief minister William Cecil," asked Babington holding up his hand for attention. "Or Baron Burghley as he calls himself now. Hounding Allen and Persons for pamphleteering. And if something happens abroad, we Catholics always get blamed for that as well. We were blamed when Prince William of Orange was murdered in the Low Countries of course, and we were also blamed when our Pope excommunicated the queen. So you see dear friends, we can sink no lower. We have sunk to the bottom of the pit. You know, even the Jews, those Christ-killers do not suffer as much as we do."

"'Tis true," someone muttered. "But that's just because they're not allowed to live in England."

"Well that might happen to us as well," Ballard said. "If the queen and her accursed ministers like Cecil continue passing new anti-Catholic laws. Anyway, 'tis enough of that for now. Let's hear more from Mister Babington here."

Babington coughed, cleared his throat and continued.

"A Mister Rookwood, Robert I think his name is, anyway, some of you may know him, a Catholic gentleman from Suffolk told me that he felt that he couldn't celebrate our greatest feast any longer; that is not celebrate Corpus Christi in the manner that it should be celebrated, for fear of government repression. Oh my friends," Babington continued in an impassioned voice. "We have fallen, and the only thing that we can do now is to stop feeling sorry for ourselves and fight back. And this is the reason why we must carry out the plan I talked about with some of you before. This is why Catholic rule must return to this country."

Babington stopped and looked round to study the affect his long speech had made on the assembled men in that dim and smoky room. There was silence. The only sound came from the sound from the flickering candles. No-one noticed Gilbert Gifford scribbling down a few notes from where he was sitting in the corner.

Then Robert Gage raised a hand to attract attention.

"The plan you spoke of last time, that is when we met near St. Giles sounded good. But we cannot do all this on our own. We'll need more money, guns and horses. But most of all, we'll need money."

"Don't worry about that," Babington smiled disarmingly. "We have been in communication with Spain. His Majesty King Philip II, through his ambassador in Paris, Don Bernardino de Mendoza has let me know, that as soon as we have killed the queen, then he, Philip will give us all the support we need. Then we, the Catholics, the followers of the true religion will rule again, and this new Protestant religion will no longer damn the face of this country."

"I'll say Amen to that," someone said.

Babington looked around, smiled and with a flourish, sat down. The others immediately started to talk about what he had said. The hubbub continued for a few minutes and then Robert Gage raised his hand again. Enthusiasm for Babington's ideas meant that no-one noticed him, so he thumped on the table and called for silence.

"All this is very well," he said. "But how are we going to inform Her Majesty Mary Queen of Scots of our intentions?"

Silence descended upon the assembled men. Gifford manoeuvred himself out of the dark corner where he had been sitting and quietly put forward a suggestion.

"Hollow corks."

"What?"

Half a dozen voices repeated with surprise. "Hollow corks?"

"Yes," replied Gifford. "I know the local brewer, you know, the one nearest to Chartley, where the queen is now imprisoned and…"

"But I thought that she was still at that miserable Tutbury place," interrupted Charnock.

"No," said Gifford warming up to his idea. "She's now in Chartley, which I doubt is any better than Tutbury. And it just so happens that I happen to know that the local brewer there is a Catholic."

"So?"

"Well, I was thinking that we could smuggle messages and letters to her inside the casks of ale that he delivers to the Castle."

"But they'll get wet," said Gage, stating the obvious.

"No they won't," Gifford replied. "Because we'll put them in the bung corks which we'll have hollowed out beforehand. They're surely big enough to smuggle in a message or two."

Again silence descended on that stuffy and airless room. They were all thinking about Gifford's idea. It was so simple. It was almost too simple.

"Well I think it's a brilliant idea," John Savage said looking around. "I think that if something can be done to rescue Her Majesty, then surely something must be done. We must rescue her soon, otherwise she'll die in prison. How long has she been in the hands of Elizabeth? How many years is it?"

"Over eighteen," said Babington quickly. "I remember my father telling me about her when I was but a very young lad."

"Yes, and she is not well," added Barnwell. "She has suffered so much in the queen's castles and places of imprisonment. I wonder if that isn't part of Elizabeth's idea. To get Her Majesty to die of illness or something like that. Then she can get rid of her rival through an act of God, as it were, and claim that she was innocent of the whole affair."

"You are right there," Babington added. "They didn't build those old castles for queens to live in. They were more for the soldiers and the simple people who were used to the damp and rough conditions. Certainly not for gentle ladies like our Mary."

And they all bowed their heads and thought about their beloved Catholic Scottish Queen who, in fact, of the men assembled there that night, had been only seen by Babington, and that was several years ago.

"And that's not all of it," Savage said. "I've heard that they keep moving or changing her servants around and then bringing in new ones in their stead. Rumour has it that some of the new ones are really spies who report back to Walsingham. As an excuse, they say that this or that servant was reported to have attended Mass with her and therefore he or she is to be removed."

And thus it was decided. Gilbert Gifford, together with John Savage, would organize the smuggling of the letters to Mary about the planned uprising in the hollowed out bung-corks and Babington would be the leader of the plot.

In his first letter to the exiled Queen of Scots, Babington insisted that she must address her replies to him personally. This appealed to the vain streak in his romantic but somewhat immature nature. Little did he realize that each letter was to be a nail in his coffin, as well as the coffins of several others of the conspirators who met that night and other nights in dark Thames-side taverns and similar places. For among them sat a two-faced spy. Not one of the men who had assembled that night could guess that Gilbert Gifford, the quiet self-effacing man, the one who had suggested how to keep in contact with his master's nemesis, was in fact being paid by Sir Francis Walsingham, one of Queen Elizabeth's Secretaries of State. This devious minister, a lean and hungry-looking aesthete had in fact invested much of his personal fortune as well as virtually all of his professional life in order to protect his queen by stamping out any sparks of Catholic revolution through single-handedly running the best spy network in Europe. It was not for nothing that he was often heard to repeat the axiom, "Knowledge is never too dear."

And so for the next three or four months, Mary Queen of Scots received packets of letters, tightly wrapped in waxy paper, and all concealed in hollowed-out bung-corks. The conspirators, especially Babington, need not have worried about the ale in those casks seeping into the letters. Walsingham, through Clifford, made sure that Her Majesty received legible material.

Babington's confidence in his plot grew and as a result, his letters and plans became more detailed as he outlined them to his adored Scottish queen. Among the letters he wrote, he said that he himself, Anthony Babington, would rescue the queen with ten gentlemen and "a hundred of our followers." How he would carry out this bold plan, he did not say, but it was enough to condemn him if Walsingham ever found out.

And of course Walsingham did.

One evening as Babington was leaving a small Thames-side tavern, four armed soldiers and a sergeant surprised and surrounded him. He was then escorted to Walsingham's house for a preliminary investigation. Fortunately for the young Catholic, he kept his wits about him and only pretended that his Lordship's wine had any affect on him. While looking around the room, Babington noticed his name on an incriminating document which was resting on a side-table. After being released a few hours later by the queen's spymaster, instead of returning to his own house near St. Paul's, he sought out Jerome Bellamy in St. John's Wood, a couple of miles north of the city.

"Jerome, I need your help. I need shelter urgently. Walsingham has heard about our plans."

"How do you know?" asked Bellamy stepping aside and ushering Babington into his rather cramped lodgings.

"I was arrested earlier this evening and taken to his chambers."

"So how did you get away and what are you doing here? Didn't anyone follow you?"

"No. No-one followed me here."

"Are you sure?" asked Bellamy looking out of one of the narrow windows.

"Yes. Of that I'm sure."

"Well tell me what happened."

"That spider questioned me for well over three hours."

"Did he use torture?"

"Yes and no, my friend."

"What do you mean?" asked Bellamy looking puzzled at his fellow-conspirator's apparent flippancy.

"Well he certainly tried to get certain answers out of me, but instead of torture he used wine."

"Wine?"

"Yes. He kept plying me with some heavy red wine, hoping I would get drunk and divulge all our plans."

"But you didn't?" asked Bellamy leaning forward anxiously.

"Would I be sitting here friend, if I had done so."

Bellamy nodded his head as he acknowledged the obvious wisdom of this.

"So then what happened?" he asked.

"Well," replied Babington feeling pleased with himself, "I noticed that the wine he gave me, a type of Madeira I think it was, had a strange perfume to it. And I also noticed that his servant who had also partaken of some of it was becoming quite drowsy, so I just pretended to drink it."

"But didn't Walsingham become suspicious?"

"Maybe. And just then, when he was about to top up my glass, I accidentally knocked it off the table and made a big fuss over having spilt it over the carpet."

"A diplomatic accident?"

"Of course. Anyway, I didn't tell him anything. Of that you may be assured. I just told him that I would like a passport in order to travel to the Low Countries."

"But didn't he ask why?"

"Of course. I told him I wanted it to spy on refugees who wished to come over to England and harm Her Majesty."

"Queen Elizabeth, you mean?"

"Of course Queen Elizabeth. You don't think I would tell him that I wished to protect Mary Queen of Scots, did you? My, you are slow tonight," laughed Babington.

Bellamy laughed at himself and then asked, "But what do you really want a passport for?"

"Well, the truth is my friend," answered Babington taking a long draught of wine that Bellamy had just offered him, "I wish to organize our Spanish friends in the Low Countries and also arrange a safe hiding-place for myself and others if necessary."

"You mean a sort of priest-hole in Flanders?"

"Yes, you could call it that, I suppose. But I don't think it will really be necessary."

"And did that spider Walsingham believe you?"

"I think so. For he let me go and said that he would think about issuing me with a passport."

But Babington was wrong. The spider had spun a strong and particularly sticky web. Three weeks later, after he had allowed the fly to incriminate himself through his easily decipherable coded and intercepted letters, he began to reel in the Catholic conspirators, the 'green wits' as he called them, one by one.

One evening at ten o'clock, the front door of Bellamy's house suddenly burst open and an armed captain of the guard, accompanied by three musketeers noisily entered the room. One of the musketeers, a large brawny type, was busily rubbing the shoulder he had used to force open the door.

"Are you Jerome Bellamy?" the captain barked at the owner of that name.

"Yes," replied Bellamy, thrusting out his jaw defiantly.

"Then I am placing you under arrest for treason and for aiding and abetting someone else who had planned to harm the body of our gracious queen." He turned to the brawny soldier, who had stopped rubbing his shoulder and ordered him to bind the 'devilish Jesuit's' arms and take him outside. Then he turned to Babington.

"Are you Anthony Babington?" he asked in the same harsh voice.

"No. No, I'm J-John...." But then Babington's voice faltered and he admitted to being Anthony Babington.

"Well, you don't match the description I was given. I was told you had long hair, but I see that isn't true. You must have cut it. And what's that colour on your face? Have you been trying to disguise yourself? Well no matter. We'll wash it off later. Men, take him away, but bind his hands tight first though."

And leaving Bellamy's maid cowering in the corner, the small party of soldiers and prisoners left the house as abruptly as they had arrived.

That night Babington and Bellamy were taken to the Tower and there in the dark and dank basement, overseen by one of Walsingham's chief agents, they were mercilessly racked. At first, the two men denied any knowledge of the plot that future history would link to Babington's name. However, by the time the sun crept over the grey walls of the Norman citadel the following morning and by the time the excruciating pain had worked its way through the prisoners' now broken bodies, Walsingham and his men had all the information that they needed for at least two judicial murders.

In fact, the use of torture was unnecessary. Through his exploitation of Gifford and several other spies, Walsingham already had all the damning evidence he needed. What he really wanted was to show was that when Babington and his accomplices would be seen in public, any Catholic would see that it wouldn't be worth crossing swords with Her Majesty's Secretary of State and soon to be the Chancellor of the Duchy of Lancaster.

And so on 20 September 1586, in the first of two terrible sessions, Walsingham's masterly planning reached its grisly climax in an open space near St. Giles, the same place where the initial seeds of this failed Catholic revolution had been planted. After having been dragged to the site of their execution on wicker hurdles, Anthony Babington, John Ballard, together with Barnwell, Tilney, Habington, Tichborne and Savage were led to the scaffold. John Ballard was the first to be led up to the scaffold, and this, as Walsingham had meticulously planned, so that Babington would be forced to become a close witness to his friend's death, before he too suffered a similar fate. Painfully, his torn muscles and ligaments causing him great agony, Ballard climbed the wooden steps and the rope was wound about his neck. There in front of a large and raucous crowd, he was half-hanged and then cut down gagging for air. Then, in front of his accomplices and the noisy spectators, amid his heart-rending howls of agony, he was castrated and disembowelled. Babington, who immediately followed him, suffered the same brutal ordeal. Ardent Catholic as he was to the end, he was heard to murmur, *"Parce mihi Domine Jesu,"* - Spare me Lord Jesus - before returning his soul to the Lord.

After having witnessed this state-orchestrated savagery, the remaining conspirators were taken back to the Tower, to be left to dwell on what they had seen and heard. The following day it was their turn to suffer the same fate. But they were somewhat luckier.

That night, Secretary Walsingham informed his queen about how the chief plotters had died. He spared her no details as she tried to eat some minced capon. Her Majesty, to his puritanical surprise, was not pleased to hear her servant's grisly report and she did not appreciate how he relished telling her the gory details. Walsingham had gone too far.

"I only wanted them executed," she reprimanded him. "I didn't want you to make martyrs out of them, but now that's what you have done. God knows, those Catholics don't need any more saints. Tomorrow, I just want them hanged, and until they are dead, mind you. There will be no need to draw and quarter them while they are still living. Now go!"

Walsingham, his thin lips pressed together, slunk out of the room like a schoolboy who had just been reprimanded for committing a major infraction of the law. He did not say a word.

The following day, the remaining plotters were once again dragged from the Tower to the scaffold on their wicker hurdles. Looking at their pale faces, it was clear that the previous day's violent cruelty had left its mark on them. This time they were hanged in batches until they were dead, and only then were they cut down, castrated, disembowelled and quartered.

Standing at the front of the crowd, a young man quietly watched the grim proceedings on both days, as the royal concept of justice was administered. Later he tried to blot out the bloody pictures and the shrieks of agony from his brain, but he did not succeed. He was a Catholic from York and he had come up to London to visit some of his family. His surname was Fawkes.

Chapter Two
From York to Flanders

There was a heavy thumping on the door.

"Guy! Guy! Get up! 'Tis five in the morning! You have school today. Now get yourself up and be quick about it."

"But mother," the boy called out in protest from under the warm coverlet. He knew he would have to get up, but he wanted to delay that critical moment for as long as possible.

"Don't 'but mother' me young man. Get up and get up quickly!"

A few minutes later a dishevelled nine-year old boy stood in the doorway of the kitchen.

"Now sit down young man and Juliet here will bring you some bread and ale, and if you're lucky, there might be a piece of cold meat as well. Now move yourself. You know, but since your father died last year, you seem to get up later every morning."

Guy sat down and wolfed down the simple breakfast. The routine at the beginning of the day was always the same. Being shouted out that he'd be late for school, getting dressed followed by a hurried breakfast and then being bundled out of the house for school. Luckily the Free school at St. Peter's, York was not too far away from the Fawkes' house and Guy was often joined on the way to school by his two friends Jack and Kit Wright.

"Look, Guy. See what we can do," Kit said as he and his brother put down their satchels and began to cut and thrust at each other with two sticks.

"Isn't that good?"

"Yes, but have you learnt that Latin exercise that we were supposed to?" replied Guy who had actually been quite impressed by his friends' swordplay. However, he was more concerned now at the moment with the thought of the beating his friends would receive at school when their master discovered their abysmal knowledge of the Latin declensions.

"Well," admitted Kit, "Jack knows the Latin a bit better than I do, but fear not, I'll struggle through. But anyway, let's walk a bit faster. I don't want to be thrashed for being late as well."

The three boys continued on their way, passing the white limestone city walls of York. Whenever they passed Micklegate Bar, Jack would always mention how the heads of the Lords of York, Rutland and Salisbury had been impaled there over the gate, following their defeat at the Battle of Wakefield in 1460.

"Just imagine," he would say ghoulishly but grinning at the same time, "seeing their heads dripping blood all over the place. It must have been terrible."

"Well brother, that's what's going to happen to us if you don't quicken your pace," Kit would reply. And they hurried on their way.

One evening soon after, Guy returned home to find the house in great confusion. Half-packed boxes and ropes seemed to be everywhere. As he threaded his way into the kitchen past piles of clothes and bedding, he saw Juliet carefully packing pewter mugs and dishes into a straw-lined box.

"What's happening here? Are we moving? Won't someone tell me?"

Just then his mother came in and handed some wooden trenchers to Juliet.

"Guy," she said, gathering him up in her long skirt. "I have something important to tell thee." And she cleared a space between the boxes and sat down.

"You know your father died last year?" she began.

Guy nodded. He had loved his father. He had been an educated man, and like his father before him, he had worked as a notary public and had later been promoted to become the Registrar of the Exchequer Court. It was expected that Guy would follow on in their illustrious footsteps. In his distant and somewhat academic way, his father had been kind to the boy and had often helped him learn the difficult Latin and Greek exercises by rote for school.

"Well Guy," his mother continued. "Two important things are going to happen to us. The first is that I am going to get married again and..."

"Married? To whom? To that Dionys..."

"That's right my son. To Master Denis Bainbridge. Its true, his real name is Dionysius, but everyone calls him Denis."

To Guy, this wasn't real news. He knew that his mother loved Master Bainbridge and it was only a matter of time before they would marry.

"And what is the other important thing?"

"Well I was coming to that. We are leaving this house and moving to ..."

"London," said Guy hopefully. He had heard of how his cousin had spent his time there and from his stories it seemed as if it was the most exciting place in the whole wide world. Certainly much more exciting than dreary old York.

"London? Whatever for? Now who put that strange idea in your head? No lad, we are moving to Scotton, to Master Bainbridge's house."

"Scotton? Where's that?"

"It's near Knaresborough."

"Knaresborough? But that's miles away!"

"No, it's not lad. It's only twenty miles to the west of York. You know, after Kirk Hammerton, where we once went last year. And we'll have a much larger house there, much grander than this one."

"But what about my friends? What about Jack and Kit? What about school? Will I continue studying at St. Peter's? And what about...?"

"Hush child! All your questions are turning my head. Yes my son, you will continue with your studies at St. Peter's. It's a fine school and your father would have been proud to see you going there. It would be a shame to take you out of there. So trust in my new husband and we'll see about finding a way so that you may carry on there. I'm sure he'll find an answer to that one."

She stood up and took a plate from a box, put it on the table and motioned Guy to come and sit down.

"No doubt you will miss a few days until we have settled down, but with your brains you'll catch up quickly enough. Now let's see what there is to eat. Ah, here's some pottage and barley bread. If that isn't enough, go and ask Juliet to give you some cheese and an apple as well."

Half an hour later, when Guy had finished eating, he looked up to ask his mother a question. But before he could ask, she asked him as always, "Have you thanked the Lord for your meal?"

"Yes, mother," he said, and without stopping he asked her, "Mother, what's a recusant?"

"A recusant? Now where did you hear that word?"

"In school. Kit and another boy, George Fowler I think it was, were saying that there were some recusants in the school. And when I asked what they were talking about, they wouldn't tell me and told me to go away. Even Kit said that."

"Well, a recusant is," began Edith Fawkes slowly, "is a Roman Catholic who refuses to attend the Protestant church services."

"But surely that is against the law, no?"

"Surely it is."

"Then these recusants must be rich people, mother."

"How is that so?"

"Because I heard Kit saying that they have to pay a fine of one shilling for every Sunday they don't go. I wanted to know what he was talking about, but he wouldn't tell me. But now I know," he said with a grin. "And I'll tell him I know."

Then he added, "Do we know any recusants mother? Are they really rich?"

"Yes my son. We do indeed know some recusants. But I'm not sure if they're all rich." She leaned closer towards the boy. "Guy, you know my family name, the name I used before I married your father?"

"Jackson?"

"Yes. Well your cousin Richard..."

"Richard Cowling?"

"Yes, Guy. Well, my sister's son is a Catholic and he is also a Jesuit priest."

"What's a Jesuit? Are they like Catholics, mother?"

"Well, they are and they're not," she replied, biting into an apple. "They are like Catholics in that they believe in Our Lord Jesus Christ and the Holy Trinity. They also see that the Pope is the head of their church, but the Jesuits are much stricter than ordinary Catholics and they have a special society called the Society of Jesus. Now, is that enough to be getting on with? Yes? Good. So off with you and let me get on with the packing. Go and ask Juliet if she needs some help. There's a good lad."

But Guy didn't move. He was thinking. "Mother," he asked scratching his head, through his reddish-brown curls. "How do you know so much about these recusant people? We're Protestants, no? We go to church every Sunday. We..."

"Hush up, my boy. I'll tell you more, later. Now be off with you and see if Juliet needs any help." And she gave him a motherly push in the direction of the scullery before his fast moving brain could think up any more awkward questions.

Later that night, when all the packing had been completed and all the boxes were tightly roped up, Guy's mother called her son into the almost bare kitchen. She motioned him to sit on an upturned box. Before she could say anything, Guy had a question ready.

"Where's Juliet mother? I haven't seen her since suppertime."

"I sent her back home to her folks. We won't be needing her any more. We're leaving in the morning. The carter is coming here at daybreak. But listen. I've got something more important than that to tell you."

"What is it? Is it about the new house? Will I be able to go fishing there? Will I...?"

"Hush up son and listen! You remember you were talking about recusants earlier this evening?"

Guy nodded.

"Well, what I'm about to tell thee is very important." She took a deep breath and continued. "I was a recusant before I married your father, and your new father, your step-father that is, is also one. That means that when we move to Scotton we'll be leading a more Catholic way of life than we have led up to now. Do you understand?"

"Does that mean we'll still believe in Jesus Christ?"

"Of course. But we won't be going to the Protestant church services any more. We'll be attending mass with other Catholics, or even Jesuits, those people I was telling you about earlier."

As Guy was about to say something, she put a finger to his lips.

"But you must keep this a secret son. Do you understand? A secret. You mustn't breathe a word of this to anyone. Not even to Jack and Kit. Is that clear? Many of our people have been killed and burned at the stake for their beliefs, so you see it is very important you don't tell anyone. Is that understood?"

Guy nodded his head.

"You wouldn't want to be burned at the stake like them and become a martyr, would you? There have been too many martyrs as it is. Think of Edmund Campion or of Anthony Babington and his friends who were cruelly hanged, drawn and quartered. And remember son, there were many other Catholic martyrs too. So keep what I've told you now as a secret. Do you promise?"

Guy nodded his head solemnly. This was the first time his mother had spoken to him so seriously since she had told him his father was dying and that he would have to be 'the man of the house.' He knew people took their religion very seriously. Some four years earlier, he had seen two people being burned at the stake and he still remembered how one of them had cried out as the flames had burnt into his flesh. He remembered the smell as well - like burnt meat, and he remembered how his mother had hurried him on towards their destination, somewhere near Clifford's Tower. But most of all, he remembered the grim and tearful expression on his mother's face, and about how she wouldn't answer any of his questions.

That night, that fiery scene came back to haunt him and it was not until much later that he fell into a restless sleep. He remembered wondering how people could bear such pain and agony, just for their religious beliefs. What was it like to die like that? What did these martyrs feel? And above all, was all the pain and suffering worth it? Fortunately, before he could dwell on these questions any longer, sleep claimed him and the next thing he realized was that his mother was shaking him awake as the pale grey dawn invaded the room.

"Wake up sleepyhead! Come on get up. I want you to help me load the wagon. Come on," she gently pummelled him. "We've got a long day in front of us and I'm going to need all the help I can get."

Two hours later, with everything strapped securely on the carter's wagon, they set off for Scotton. They stopped to water the horses at Kirk Hammerton and at Knaresborough, where Guy was allowed to wander off for half an hour and poke around the ruins of Henry III's castle. By nightfall they were settled in their new house and a new chapter had begun in the life of Guy Fawkes.

And so life continued for the young Fawkes in his West Yorkshire village. Despite the fact that Scotton was much smaller than York, Guy was not bored there and soon found himself involved in more intimate friendships than he had dreamed were possible. In addition, he occasionally journeyed to Harrogate or even further afield to Leeds and even more occasionally to London. By the time he was twenty years old in 1590, he was a devout Catholic. He had been heavily influenced by his step-father's family as well as by his school, which despite its outward show of Protestant faith, harboured several recusants who were to become contemporary household names. These secret Catholics included Edward Oldcorne and Father Robert Middleton who was later put to death in 1601 at Leicester. Another Jesuit priest who exerted a crucial influence over the young man was Oswald Tesimond who later, under the name of Father Greenway would write a detailed report of the Gunpowder Plot in Italian. Some say that while living in Scotton, Guy Fawkes married Maria Pulleyn who later gave birth to a son, Thomas. But this cannot be proved. All we know is, that by the beginning of the 1590s, Guy Fawkes was a well-known figure in West Yorkshire, a young man who led "an exemplary life." According to Tesimond's records, Guy left his native Yorkshire and moved south to Sussex where he became attached to the household of Lord Montague, a Catholic nobleman.

One day while Guy was attending to a horse in his Lordship's stables, Spenser, Montague's steward approached him.

"Ho, Guy! This is not a task for thee."

Guy looked up from where he had been inspecting a cut on a horse's foreleg. "Why not?"

"You are much too refined for doing work such as this. I've been watching how you talk and behave, almost like a gentleman I would say. And as your kinsman, I have an idea."

Guy listened carefully. He had already been transferred from working with Montague's father to here and he did not really wish to move again.

"So listen Guy. This is what I've been thinking. I think you should be allowed to wait on his Lordship's table. The work will be far more amenable and pleasant. Think of it before you refuse me. There'll be none of this dirty and smelly working with horses or helping with the pigs. Now what do you think of my idea, eh?"

Guy agreed that Spenser's idea was a good one. And so within a few days he found himself wearing cleaner clothes and attending on the young aristocrat in the great hall of the Sussex country mansion.

One evening as Guy was removing a heavy candelabra from the long dining table, Montague tapped the table imperiously.

"Fawkes!" he called out. "Put that thing down and come here! I wish to speak to you. Now, do you know anything about arms? Well, do you?"

"Guns and swords, sir?"

"Yes, that's what I was referring to. Well, do you?"

"Yes, sir. You see, when I lived in Yorkshire, in Scotton that is, I was considered quite a fair swordsman sir. I also used a gun, an arquebus on occasion too, sir."

"So you know how to fire one of those noisy things then, eh?"

"Yes, sir. I was quite accurate with it too. I could fire a ball and hit the target from about four hundred paces, sir."

"Was that with using a rest for support?"

"Yes, sir."

"Four hundred paces. Hmm. I'm quite impressed. Now, how would it be if you were to use your military talents, if I may call them that, eh?"

"I don't quite understand what you mean sir," replied Guy nervously. He had never thought of himself as a military man.

"Well, it's like this Fawkes. You are a Catholic and so am I. It's also true that the Spanish in the Low Countries are looking for good Catholic soldiers. And they're willing to pay them well too. In addition, I've also heard that you are an upright young man. You don't swear and use foul language and I've heard that you have nothing to do with harlots and the like. Is that true?"

"Yes, sir."

"And you're about twenty years old, yes?"

"Yes, sir."

"Splendid. That's just what the Spanish are looking for. Good soldiers who can shoot well, fight and who don't drink. You know what I mean, don't you? Spenser informs me that you don't."

"That's right, sir. I don't drink."

"And you're not married?"

"No sir." And Guy lowered his eyes for a moment.

"Very good. Then what are we waiting for? I'll see one of my people and see about getting you over to the Low Countries to help the Catholic cause there. They surely need some help. I would go over there myself of course, but I have my estates to manage and my wife and children to think of. But you, my lad, consider yourself lucky. You're not burdened with such things. Well, off you go now and I'll talk with you again presently."

The result of this conversation was that several weeks later, after a stormy crossing of the English Channel, Guy found himself in the Spanish occupied Low Countries. This country, which had formed part of the Holy Roman Empire and was later ruled by the Spanish king, Philip II, had tried to throw off the Spanish yoke in 1581. However, it wouldn't be until 1648, when Spain signed the Treaty of Westphalia, that the United Provinces would be recognized as an independent country.

And now, several months later, in 1593, while sheltering from the drizzle in a Dutch ale-house, Guy found himself sitting next to a tall and burly Irishman who had come in and sat down beside him, completely uninvited.

"And what do you call yourself?" the Irishman asked, his large hairy paw wrapped around an overfull tankard.

Guy shook his head showing he hadn't understood the question.

"Oh, it's the accent," O'Leary laughed. "You English never understand us Irish. You never did and you never will, but I'll try again, and slowly this time. Now, what is your name?"

"Guy Fawkes."

"Fawkes," repeated the Irishman rolling the sound around in his mouth. "Now is that pronounced like the forked tongue of the serpent?"

Guy smiled in agreement, although he did not really like the comparison.

"Ah, well, then I've heard of thee, boyo. You're the young man who is supposed to be good with the gunpowder. Is that true now?" And he breathed a mouthful of stale air into Guy's face.

"If you say so," Guy replied modestly. "And what's your name?"

"O'Leary. John O'Leary from Dublin. And are you in Stanley's English regiment too?"

"I am."

"'Tis strange," commented O'Leary, wiping his mouth with the back of his hand. "'Tis strange to think that most of the men in Stanley's English regiment are Irishmen like myself. Very few of them are from o'er the water. There's about one thousand of us. Now did you know that?"

Guy replied that he didn't, but said that he had noticed that there were indeed many Irishmen about. He in turn had a question for O'Leary.

"Tell me about Stanley. Who is he? Is he a trustworthy gentleman?"

"Ah, Sir William. Well I'll tell you what I know about him. First of all, he's a good God-fearing Catholic, like our good selves here. Secondly, I know he fought in Ireland. In Limerick and Ardagh or Ardee or somewhere like that, and I happen to know that he was made Sheriff of Cork for his troubles. And... no wait. Let me order thee a drink and I'll have another meself and then I'll tell thee some more."

After doing justice to his new supply of ale, O'Leary continued.

"Sir William Stanley. Ah yes. So's after fighting in Ireland, he was sent over here, here to the Low Countries, to the Netherlands. That was about the time of that Spanish Armada thing. Well, he joined up with the Earl of Leicester..."

"The favourite of Queen Elizabeth?"

"Aye, that's right. The same one. And then he and Sir Philip Sidney commanded the fighting at Doesborg and Zutphen and..."

"That's where Sir Philip was killed, no?"

"Aye, right again. And so Sir William Stanley became Governor and was given a garrison of over a thousand men and most of them were good ol' Irish Catholics like meself. And anyway, after that Sir William started to spend a great deal of his time between Flanders and Madrid. And that's where you and I come in."

"How?"

"Because we are part of his English Legion, as he calls us. English, huh! Even though most of us are Irish."

"But what are we supposed to be doing here now? The fighting has died down now, no?"

"Well, about that I don't know. But what I do know is, that for soldiers of fortune like us, something will turn up. It always does. Now do you want another round of ale?"

Guy declined, but the Irishman's prediction proved to be correct. Several weeks later Guy was ordered to appear before his commander, Sir William Stanley. The meeting took place in a small tavern in Flanders. As with many such meetings, the walls of this drinking establishment were dark, the air was thick with the smell of wine and ale, and all the heavy wooden furniture looked well-used. As though it were an unwritten rule, there were few women about, and of those who were present, they would either be serving the drinks or sitting in a dark corner nursing a hot punch on their own. That's as far as it went when it came to Guy Fawkes and the fair sex. On the table in front of Sir William was a chess set; its well-worn metal pieces shining dully in the poor light.

"Come in, Fawkes. I was expecting you. Sit down and have some wine. You must be cold."

"Thank you, sir, but I would prefer some buttermilk. If they don't have any, I'll have some ale, sir."

"Even this Flemish brew?"

"Yes, sir."

After having dismissed the servant, Sir William decided it was time to say what was on his mind.

"Fawkes, before I tell you why I asked you to come here, tell me, do you play chess?"

"Yes sir. I first learnt to play when I was a young lad in Yorkshire. And since then I've played quite a lot here in Flanders. It helps me to while away the time, sir."

"Good. Then let's have a game while we are talking."

Sir William took two pawns, a black and a white one and held them out in his clenched fists to Guy. The Yorkshireman pointed to the right one and Sir William opened his hand.

"White, Fawkes. So let us begin."

Guy moved a pawn forward two squares and waited for Sir William. His commander pushed a black pawn forward and before Guy could react, he suddenly lifted his head and spoke out.

"Fawkes, I have heard report that you are a brave soldier and a leader of men. It says here in this report that I've been given. Here, listen to what it says here. Ah, here we are. Let me read it to you. It says, you are "of excellent good natural parts, very resolute and universally learned." Another man describes you as "a man of great piety, of exemplary temperance, of mild and cheerful demeanour, an enemy of broils and disputes, a faithful friend and remarkable for his punctual attendance upon religious observance.""

Guy held his head down in embarrassment. He was not used to being spoken about like this in such a style. Sir William ignored his discomfort and continued.

"And in addition to this fulsome praise, I have heard favourable reports concerning your conduct at the Battle of Nieuport. You served there under Colonel Bloodstock, no?"

"No, sir. Colonel Bostock sir." And Guy moved another pawn into play.

"Ah yes. Colonel Bostock. And you were wounded, were you not?"

"Yes, sir. But 'twas nothing serious sir."

"And is it true that I've heard that you are an expert, a craftsman as someone said, when it comes to using gunpowder?" Sir William took one of Guy's pawns with a knight.

Guy lowered his eyes modestly and seemed to concentrate on the chessboard.

"Yes, sir," he said at last. "I'm quite good at using gunpowder. And I've had quite a lot of experience in using it as a sapper sir. You know, placing it in underground tunnels and cracks in walls."

"But isn't that dangerous? Can't it suddenly explode?"

"Not if you're careful, sir. Besides, nothing has happened to me so far." And he moved a knight into position to counteract one of his commander's knights.

"Well, I hope your luck doesn't change, for I have two or three important things to tell you."

Guy sat up expectantly.

"Fawkes, did you know that over the past two years I have paid several visits to the Spanish capital?"

"To Madrid, sir? Yes I had heard rumours about that. Some of the other soldiers said that..."

"They were not rumours Fawkes. They were speaking the truth. Now what did they say?"

Guy hesitated and then replied. "They said that you were doing something for the Catholic cause, sir."

"They were right. Now the time has come for me to acquaint you with what I was doing there. And in doing so, I am binding you to an oath of secrecy. You must be completely silent and discreet. Can I trust you on that score?"

Guy nodded, and to relieve some of the tension, moved one of his bishops from the back line. Sir William countermoved by moving one of his bishops forward in the direction of the opposing lines.

"Now listen, Fawkes. Remember, this information is for you only. You are not to tell any of it to anyone else."

Again Guy nodded assent.

Sir William continued. "The reason I travelled to Spain was to offer some advice to the king, King Philip II about invading England."

Guy looked surprised and held a bishop in the air. Sir William continued.

"The idea is for the Spanish to land in England, remove the Protestants and then restore the country to its rightful and proper place as a Catholic realm. This was not the first time that I had spoken to the Spanish king about this idea, for I had done so earlier in 1585 or '86 I think it was, but then they ignored me." He took a swallow of the red wine in front of him, wiped his moustache and continued afresh.

"Then, I advised them to attack London from the west and use the Catholic populations in Ireland and Wales for support. You know, in the same way Henry VII used his western forces to attack Richard III at Bosworth Field. But they wouldn't listen to me nor take my advice. Instead, a year or so later they launched their armada, and you know what happened to that, don't you?"

"Yes sir. It was utterly defeated." Guy moved another pawn forward.

"Well, after that defeat," Sir William said with a certain smile as he moved a castle forward three squares and took Guy's remaining knight, "they were prepared to listen to me. So when I returned to Madrid some two years after the armada fiasco, I had a force of a thousand men with me, most of whom were good Catholic Irishmen." He swelled his chest as he spoke of them.

"Yes sir. I've met many of them in the last few years. You're referring to the English Legion sir?"

"That is correct. In addition, I also went to Rome as well on behalf of the Catholic cause. Did the rumours tell you that?"

"No, sir," and Guy moved a knight to the centre of the board.

"Well it's true. While I was there, I laid plans that Arabella Stuart, who is related to the Scottish royal family through her connections to King Henry VIII's sister Margaret and to the late Mary Queen of Scots of blessed memory, would succeed Queen Elizabeth. And as you may know, she is also related to Lord Strange."

Guy sat there stunned. All of this was completely new to him.

"Had you heard any of this before, Fawkes?"

"No, sir," and Guy moved a castle in an attempt to trap Sir William's queen.

"Ah," said Sir William. "Threatening my queen, eh? Well, that is what we planned to do." He smiled at his own joke. "Remove Queen Elizabeth, eh? Just like I'm going to take your queen." And in a sharp move he moved a knight forward from where it had been lurking behind two pawns and took Guy's queen off the board.

"Now, what do you think of that?" he asked smugly.

"Very impressive, sir. But if I move my pawn like this," he said, moving another pawn to his commander's back line, he reclaimed his queen.

"Yes, you're right, Fawkes," Sir William ceded. "Queen Elizabeth is still with us, even though she is nearly seventy years old. However, I was about to..."

"Excuse me, sir," Guy interrupted "But who is Lord Strange? Isn't he also known by the name of Fernando Stanley? And who is Arabella Stuart, sir?"

"Yes, you are right. Lord Strange and Fernando Stanley are one and the same person. But let us put some order into things. Ladies first. Well, Arabella Stuart is certainly a lady, for she is the first cousin to King James VI of Scotland. As such, she has been considered as a possible successor to Queen Elizabeth. This would be especially good for us Catholics, although of course, many Protestants, especially those surrounding the queen are against this. They say we've had two women on the throne and they don't want another. But that's an excuse of course, as they are perfectly happy with the present queen."

"And Lord Strange, sir?"

"Lord Strange is my brother, Fawkes. I'm surprised you didn't know that. Anyway, he is the Fifth Earl of Derby and on his demise, I am to become the Sixth Earl."

"But isn't he the man who is or was supposed to have written those plays, sir? You know, those plays that some people say were written by that fellow from Stratford-upon-Avon?"

"Who? Shakespeare? No. Some people have even given me credit for those plays, but I can assure you, that is a lot of nonsense. Me writing such plays indeed. That's all I have time for!" And he waved his hand dismissively. "Anyway, we are digressing. Where were we? Ah yes. I took your queen and you replaced her on the throne. So it's my turn now." He moved his king one square to the right.

"You see. My king is moving in to claim his place in the sun. By the way, Fawkes, do you think King James would make a good king of England?"

"I'm not sure," Guy said guardedly. "First of all, we don't know that he will become king of England and we also don't know how he'll treat the Catholic population, sir."

"I have heard, that he being a Catholic, or at least the only son of Mary Queen of Scots, and that she died for her Catholic beliefs, we shouldn't have any problems with him."

Guy moved a knight forward, within striking distance of his commander's king.

"Ah, I see, you don't give up. Very commendable. Now let us leave the past and concentrate on the future."

"Yes, sir."

"What I would like you to do Fawkes, is to leave your present position with the army of the Archduke of Austria..."

"Duke Albert, sir?"

"Yes, and travel to Spain and inform the king there how much Catholic support he will find waiting for him in England. Especially in the north and the west. Is that understood?"

"But sir," replied Guy, finishing off the ale remaining in his tankard, "I haven't lived in England for some time now. How do I know if my information is correct? And anyway, I hardly speak any Spanish. Just a few words here and there."

"It will be all right Fawkes. Don't worry about your Spanish. I'm not sending you there on your own. Someone who knows Spanish will accompany you. And you certainly know more about England than the King of Spain. I can see that you are not stupid. You have a quick tongue in your head and you should certainly be able to help the Catholic cause."

Guy was about to open his mouth in protest, but the future Earl of Derby stopped him.

"Then all is arranged. I will furnish you with some letters of introduction, stating something like you are representing me and two other eminent Catholics, namely Mr. Hugh Owen and Father William Baldwin. I will write that your task is to enlighten King Philip II of Spain concerning the true position of the Romists in England. Is that understood? Remember this. It is a great honour and responsibility that I am placing upon your shoulders, Fawkes. And do not forget. You are sworn to secrecy about all this. If you are captured or if any evil befall you, I will say that I do not know you, have never met you and have never been involved with you in any way. Is that understood?"

Guy nodded his head slowly in assent.

"Good. Now let us proceed and finish off this game of kings. Yes, it's very apt that we should be playing this game now. A game of kings. Or is it a game for kings. King James and King Philip and also perhaps King Henri of France too. I'm sure that he would also love to become involved with all this."

And Sir William Stanley smiled at his own witticism as the two men bent over the chessboard.

* * * * * * *

Guy Fawkes returned to the Spanish Netherlands several months later. He had failed in his mission to persuade the Spanish king to give active support to a Catholic uprising in England. The fanatic King Philip II, the champion of the Counter-reformation, had died and had been succeeded by his weak son Philip III. Before dying, Philip II, now in a weakened position following the failure of his allegedly Invincible Armada to replace the Protestant rule in England with Catholicism, had signed a peace treaty with France. Philip realized that he could not have two major enemies in Europe. Therefore he decided to recognize Henri IV as the true King of France, despite his Protestant background.

On the other side of the English Channel, Queen Elizabeth, aged seventy, had eventually died in March 1603. Her place was taken over by the Scottish King James VI. He had moved south to London from Edinburgh to take control of his now nominally united kingdom and was now ruling under the title of King James I of England.

And so at the turn of the seventeenth century, North West Europe was a relatively peaceful area, that is, on an international level, but within England many Catholics were disappointed with their new king. Being the son of Mary Queen of Scots, the English Catholics had expected him to ease the intensity of their persecution. But this was not to be. As a result, many wild and impractical schemes and plots were laid by Catholic extremists on how to persuade the new king to ease their burden. One of these plans included seizing the king and holding him prisoner until he consented to abolish the anti-Catholic laws, but nothing ever came of this.

The more moderate Catholics were shocked by these plots and rushed to inform the king of their existence. Some of these Catholics were so anxious to disassociate themselves from their more fanatically inclined co-religionists, that Sir Thomas Tresham, a leading Catholic, rushed to court to inform His Majesty that the Catholic community in England was in fact most loyal to their new king. Even the Spanish ambassador in London voiced his opinion and said that the English Catholics were, "in such a timid fear of one another" that the chances of their rising up against the king were minimal.

It was this feeling, of uprising and rebellion, that Guy Fawkes, Sir William Stanley and others were counting on. However, what they did not appreciate or wish to realize is that they were living a life of illusion. The waters of peace, at least on the surface, were now flowing smoothly between England, France and Spain. As a result, when Guy Fawkes returned to the Low Countries from Spain, he returned empty-handed.

One evening, as he was sitting in his room in Brussels, feeling very bitter and disappointed over the lack of help and support he had received at the hands of the Spanish court, he was suddenly disturbed by an urgent knocking at his door. Getting up quickly, he drew back the heavy bolt and opened the door to reveal a short and stocky man standing there. The man was smiling broadly.

"Guy Fawkes?" he asked with a slight Midlands accent.

"Aye, and who might you be?"

"My name is Thomas Wintour, and I'm glad I've found you at last. I've been searching for you for some time. May I come in? I need to talk to you. Urgently."

Guy asked him in and noticed that his unexpected visitor's clothes were slightly frayed at the edges and spattered with mud. Wintour, catching Guy's look said quickly, "I'm sorry my clothes are not of the cleanest, but I have just arrived from England and have ridden many miles."

"From England? But why have you come to see me? But wait. Before you answer me, may I serve you with some food and drink?"

Thomas Wintour nodded his head and a short time later, the two men were sitting around the table eating a simple but satisfying meal of pottage, rye bread and eggs. Guy offered his guest some buttermilk and it was only after his guest felt satiated, did he come to the point.

"First of all. Thank you for the meal. Now let me introduce myself more fully to you. Like you, I believe, I've been a soldier in these parts, in Flanders, in the Low Countries. When I first came, I served as a soldier in the English army. Then we were fighting the Spanish. But as the time passed, I began to realize that it was the Spanish who were right and that the Protestants here in Flanders, those whom we had been called on to protect, were in the wrong."

"Yes," agreed Guy, showing a keen interest in his visitor's story. "But where do I come into all this? Why have you come to see me?"

"Patience friend. That's what I was coming to. Now you're a devout Catholic, are you not?"

"Yes."

"And you have fought for the Spanish here in the Low Countries?"

"Yes."

"And you have tried, even if you were unsuccessful then, to get help from Spain in order to overthrow the Protestants in England?"

Again Guy nodded in agreement.

"And you're an expert with gunpowder?"

"True. But how do you know all this?" Guy asked quickly before Wintour could ask another question.

"Well, we've been keeping an eye on you and we want you to help us with our plans for a future rising in England."

"Who are you, who have been keeping an eye on me as you say?"

"I'll come to that later. Just let us say for the present, that a group of influential Catholic gentlemen, including a Mr. Robert Catesby, of whom you may have heard, have been following your progress out here. You will learn more about these gentlemen later."

Guy was silent for a moment. "Wait a minute," he said picking at a few rye crumbs on the trencher, "You want to overthrow the English Protestants without help from abroad? You want to do this from Spain?"

This was a new development to him. Guy looked at Wintour incredulously, but the latter continued unconcerned.

"Yes. We hope and believe that the Spanish will help us once we have got started. Now have you any more questions? For I seem to have been doing most of the talking here this evening. And yes, I will have another beaker of buttermilk, thank you."

Guy sat back in his chair after pouring Wintour a drink and thought. At last he asked, "So how is the situation for the Catholics in England today? Remember, I have been in these foreign parts for most of the past ten years, and so what I know is chiefly by hearsay."

Just as Wintour was about to reply, there was a loud knock on the door.

"Who could that be?" Wintour asked, already rising from his chair. "Are you expecting anyone?"

"No. I'll go and see who it is and send them away. Go into the back room behind the curtain there in the corner. Quickly!"

As Guy slowly and deliberately made his way to the door Wintour rushed to hide himself. The knocking started again.

Opening the door, just a few inches and keeping his foot firmly behind it, Guy was surprised to see a short tubby woman standing there. He breathed a sigh of relief.

"Good evening sir," she said. "I'm your neighbour from across the street. I saw there was light in your house and I'm wondering if you could lend me a loaf of bread, even a loaf of corn bread will do. We have run out and my husband is hungry and is getting very angry. So please help me sir, if you can."

Within a minute she was gone, clutching half a loaf of bread. Guy and Wintour then continued from where they had been interrupted.

Guy's visitor rubbed his hands and warmed up to what he wanted to say.

"Let me tell you first of all that life in England for Catholics has been less than easy. Do you know, that King James, that turncoat son of our Catholic

Mary Queen of Scots, has even said that he detests the superstitious religion of the Catholics, as he calls it. Those are his own words, mark you. Superstitious religion. And then to make matters worse, he has issued a proclamation ordering all priests and Jesuits to leave the country before March the nineteenth."

"But why then?"

"Because on that day they want to open Parliament. And to make matters worse, several well-known Catholics have been executed, such as Robert Grissold and John Sugar. They were executed at Warwick, you know, where many of our supporters live. In the Midlands."

"But why were they executed?"

"To be an example to others. To show what would happen to you if you were a prominent Catholic. Do you understand?"

Guy did. He shivered as the memories came back. The hangings and the burnings. The choking and the screaming. Yes, he had seen enough executions in his life. You did not forget them. Ever.

Wintour continued. "And while all these good and pious brethren of ours are being tortured and executed, other Catholics, although in God's name they are a shame to the True Faith, are rushing to the king and his ministers like the milk-sops that they are, and protesting their loyalty to the Crown. So all in all, us true Catholics, the real believers, are in a very sad situation, my friend. A very sad situation indeed."

Both men sat in silence for a few minutes thinking about how their endeavours for the past few years had brought them nothing. Then Guy broke the silence.

"Well, what do you want of me?" he asked at last.

Tom Wintour looked up, finished off his buttermilk and pushed his face close to that of his host's. "We want you, Guy Fawkes, to return to England and to help us rid the country of this traitor, this so-called King James and kill his ministers at the same time."

Guy stopped drinking and looked at his visitor straight in the face. He needed time to take in this latest piece of information.

"Now tell me. How is this plan going to happen? What will I have to do? When is it going to take place? And where?"

"Wait a minute. Wait a minute," replied Wintour holding up his hand as if to stop any further questions. "I've been sworn not to tell you anything unless you agree to return to England with me and meet our leader."

"And who's that?"

"Robert Catesby. Have you heard of him?"

"No. I don't think that I have."

"Well," continued Wintour with a note of pride in his voice. "He's a member of my family, my cousin, in fact, and he wishes to meet you most urgently. Now, what do you think of all this?"

Guy's answer was to leave Brussels a few days later and return to London. Following a smooth crossing of the Channel, he stepped foot once again in England in April 1604. After landing at Dover, the two men hired horses and set off as quickly as possible for the capital. Here Guy was to have his first fateful meeting with Robert Catesby, the brains behind the Gunpowder Plot.

Chapter Three
Robert Catesby

My name is Robert Catesby. My friends call me Robin instead of Robert and that suits me well enough. I suppose that I'm a lucky fellow, because I know a lot of good people whom I can call my friends, but at the same time, I must add, that life for the Catesby family wasn't always so good. One of my ancestors, Sir William Catesby, who lived about two hundred years ago, was one of the chief advisors to King Richard III. You know, he was the king who they say murdered the two princes in the Tower, but actually I think it was Henry VII, but that's another story. Well, as Richard was not a popular king, it follows that his closest advisors like Sir William and his friend Sir Richard Ratcliffe were also tarred with the same brush. Thus it was, that this disgusting piece of doggerel was sung about them:

> *The Cat, the Rat and Lovell our dog*
> *Rule all England, under a Hog.*

Lovell of course, was Richard's third advisor and he was luckier than my forebear and Sir Richard. Sir Richard was killed trying to defend the king at the Battle of Bosworth Field, while Sir William was hunted down as one of Henry VII's enemies and executed at Leicester a few days after the battle. Lovell managed to escape all this and two years later joined Lambert Simnel, the Pretender to the throne, and ended up challenging Henry VII's right to be king, near Nottingham. These rebels, as you may know, lost and Lovell was either drowned trying to escape across the River Trent, or that he died soon after.

But I digress. I was born in 1573 at Lapworth, Warwickshire, in the Midlands and I was the only surviving son. I believe I was born there, for there my father, who was also called Sir William, preferred to live instead of at our other country house near Ashby St. Ledgers in Northamptonshire. My father though was less lucky than I, for he spent a long time in prison on account of his being a prominent Catholic. This Catholic religion has caused us much trouble in the past. I clearly remember that when I was an eight year old, some of the queen's soldiers came to our house to arrest my father. He was prepared to go quietly, but my mother wrung her hands and cried out to the soldiers not to take him. One of them called her a "damned Jesuit" and the others just laughed. Then they bound my father's hands and pushed him onto some old farmer's wagon and took him away. Then they tried him in the highest court, in the Star Chamber, together with his brother-in-law Sir Thomas Tresham and Lord Vaux. In fact, not only did they try them for being Catholic recusants, but also for having hidden Father Edmund Campion from the authorities. But my father was luckier than some though, for he wasn't executed but was released instead. But afterwards he had to pay a huge fine and then was sent back to prison again.

My mother Anne was also a Catholic, and through their marriage, my father became related to some of the major Catholic families in the land. These included my mother's family, the Throgmortons as well as the Treshams, the Vauxes and the Habingtons and of course, the Monteagles. Naturally we kept our Catholic worship and practices a secret, and this certainly made life very difficult for us on occasion. This was especially true when Lord Cecil and the other Secretary, Walsingham, tried to catch us out, for example on crimes of treason and the like.

When I was thirteen, that is in 1586, I entered Gloucester Hall at Oxford to start studying for a degree, but I left before I completed it, because to do so would mean that I would have had to take the Oath of Supremacy, and you know what that means. If you don't, let me explain. It means that you have to swear an oath that says that you acknowledge that the king or queen, meaning Queen Elizabeth in this case, to be the Supreme Head of the Church of England, which I as a believing Catholic could not do. It saddened my friends at Oxford when I left, but my parents and my family understood why I had acted so and respected and supported me for standing up for my principles.

After I returned home, I led a pleasant life, alternating between our two country homes, having and attending parties and balls and spending much time hunting. Even though I say it myself, I was a good horseman and I continued to have a very pleasant social life. This happy period of my life continued for several years. Then, when I was nineteen, I married Mistress Leigh, Mistress Catherine Leigh that is, and my life became even better.

I was very happy with her and in fact, by having married my sweet Catherine, I also obtained a dowry which came to two thousand pounds per annum. Of course, this was not the reason that I married this lovely lady. Ironically, my wife was from a noted Protestant family, and so, apart from obtaining such a fine dowry, I also rendered myself more respectable in the eyes of the authorities. They no longer regarded me as a dubious recusant, which in fact I was. That is a recusant, but certainly not dubious.

Unfortunately, my wife died two years later, that is, in the same year that my father and my first-born son William died, and so for me, 1598 was the most terrible and tragic year of my life.

So looking back on these past few years, living the life of a Catholic gentleman was always a mixture of happiness and sadness. It was also a period of dangerous excitement, for it was during this period that I had to hide Father Henry Garnet as well as other priests from the authorities. This I did in one of our houses, or if I couldn't do that for any reason, I arranged them hiding places in other people's houses. I remember that among other people, we hid Father John Gerard after he had managed to escape from the Tower of London by climbing out of his cell. Somehow he had obtained a rope and succeeded in evading the guards. But anyway, we were prepared to do all of these acts because first and foremost we were honour-bound to help our fellow Catholics. I also did it because it showed that the ancient name of Catesby was still an honourable one and a name that still could be counted upon.

The next important period of my life happened during the last years of the reign of Queen Elizabeth. As the queen grew older and older, (and remember - she was about sixty-five years old at this point), she began to suffer from all sorts of illnesses. Some of her physicians said it was just old age and others said she was like this because she was feeling sad, you know, seeing all her old friends dying off. Anyway, whatever it was, her ministers, especially Lord Cecil and Walsingham decided that if it became known that the queen was in poor health, then the Catholics would exploit the situation and rise up and try and reclaim the throne. To forestall this, the government arrested several of the leading Catholics, including my good self and sent us to the Tower of London. There I met the Wright brothers, Jack and Kit from York and I also met Francis Tresham.

Luckily our conditions in the Tower were not too harsh, and with a little money we were able to purchase extra food and warmer clothing, which was necessary to keep out the damp. However, the worst part of all this was not knowing how long we would be incarcerated, and also not knowing what would happen to us once the queen died.

Fortunately for us at least, she didn't die from her illness, and when she recovered we were released. In a strange way, some personal good came out of all this, for it brought me into contact with such noble and stalwart fellows as the Wright brothers as well as with Francis Tresham whom I have just mentioned and several others. But I'll tell you more about them later.

However, I was almost returned to the Tower on a much more serious charge a few years later, in fact, for having aided and abetted a treasonous action.

It happened like this. In February, the queen's favourite courtier, Robert Devereux, the second Earl of Essex planned to take over the court, as well as the City of London including the Tower. This handsome, dashing and persuasive man, who was also called Robin, was extremely angry with the queen, and perhaps even more so with the powerful Cecil family whom he considered had more influence at court and with the queen than he did. On this last point he was probably right. Unfortunately for Essex though, he hadn't learnt from his past experiences. Even though the queen had pardoned her "dear Robin" for abandoning his post as Lord Deputy of Ireland and hurrying back to London without permission a couple of years earlier, he was still considered as a man of great importance. In fact, when he rushed back to court, "to be by his queen," he said, and even bursting unannounced into her bedchamber at night at Nonsuch in Surrey, the queen was not really cross at all with her favourite. And when he fell ill a couple of months later, it was Her Majesty who sat by his bedside and acted as his nurse, you know, wiping his brow and feeding him stuff like jelly.

But if the truth be told, the queen had really had her fill with Essex, and soon after she caused him not to receive all sorts of monies that he considered were due to him from the business of customs and taxation on the sweet wine monopoly. That really hurt the financial situation of the impetuous earl and as someone has described it, he gathered about him a private army of "swordsmen, bold confident fellows, discontented persons and such as saucily used their tongues in railing against all men."

One of those saucy men was me. On Sunday morning, February the eighth 1601, we all met at Essex House and took the four officers of state who had been dispatched to enquire into our affairs, as hostages. Then Essex and I, together with about two hundred others galloped into the City. Essex, who was at our head, raced ahead on his great horse shouting, "For the queen! For the queen! The crown of England is sold to the Spaniard! A plot is laid upon my life!" He led us up Ludgate Hill and along Cheapside, but the crowds did not join us as we had hoped. Seeing this, Essex tried to return home, but instead, found his way blocked off by the soldiers of the Mayor of London. In the noise and confusion, I tried to sneak away but I was captured and held for some time. In the meanwhile, Essex had succeeded in returning to his house but was forced to surrender that evening. In fact he had no choice. For the Lord Admiral threatened to blow up the house with Essex, his family and his servants in it, if he wouldn't surrender. Essex gave in and was taken away. He was then tried and found guilty and a week later was executed at the Tower. As it says in the Bible, "How are the mighty fallen."

I was more fortunate than my leader. Like him I was put on trial, but the judges thought that because I had played such an insignificant part in all this I should be let off and just have to pay a fine of four thousand marks. If the truth be known, I was really worried at one point during the proceedings because an officer of the court read out a report about me which said,

"Mr. Catesby did show such valour and fought so long and stoutly as divers afterwards of those swordsmen did exceedingly esteem him and follow him in regard thereof."

While I am the first to admit it, it is flattering to hear reports of your own bravery. But it is less so, if it means that you will meet a traitor's end, that is, of being hanged, drawn and quartered. For believe me, that is something I never wish to experience. Not that the paying of the fine was such a minor punishment either. To do this, I had to sell my manor at Chastleton to a neighbouring wool-merchant. However, I still had my other properties, so in contrast to the other Robin, I came out of this affair relatively unharmed. forever in just living the life of a country gentleman, enjoying myself while my Catholic friends were trying to further the cause of Catholicism in England. So in 1602 I banded together with Monteagle, Father Henry Garnet and Francis Tresham and as a result we dispatched Thomas Wintour and Kit Wright to Spain. The aim of their mission was to obtain arms and financial assistance from the Spanish court and then bring about the overthrow of the Protestant regime in England. We received many promises, but the truth is that the

Spanish were not really prepared to commit themselves to anything more than just promises.

By 1604 the situation for the Catholics in this country was very grim indeed. We felt even worse when the new king, James I, stated that despite of a promise made earlier that he would ease our situation, he would now make it worse and persecute the Catholics even more harshly than even Queen Elizabeth had done. This we could see was very easy for him to do as he had kept Sir Robert Cecil on as his chief minister. And then to make matters worse, the king made a proclamation stating that he utterly detested all Papists. In addition, he said that all the Protestant bishops had to see that all the Catholics were severely punished.

And if all that wasn't bad enough, he also proclaimed that all the Catholic priests must leave the kingdom, in the same way that Edward I had ordered the expulsion of the Jews from England three hundred years earlier. And just as we were trying to see if something could be done about this, about two months later the king went and supported a law which decreed that all Catholics, not just the priests, would be considered as excommunicates. Even Queen Elizabeth had rejected the passing of this law, saying that it was much too harsh. This was not just a question of religion, for it also meant that we God-fearing Catholics could not openly deal in trade, make wills or enter into all manner of legal deals which are so important to our society. This meant that we would be treated as some sort of outlaws. It also meant things like those who owed us debts or rents were no longer legally obliged to pay us and that we were not allowed to seek any redress from the proper authorities.

By this time, I was feeling that our lot was so intolerable, so extreme, that some action, anything that was equally extreme had to be taken. However, before doing anything, I sent my Catholic friend and ally Thomas Wintour to Flanders to meet the Constable of Spain. This was just before he set out to conclude a peace treaty with

England. I have here before me on my desk a copy of the instructions I gave to Thomas. On it I wrote that he was to

"inform the Constable of the condition of the Catholics here in England, entreating him to solicit His Majesty at his coming hither that the penal laws may be recalled, and we admitted into the ranks of his other subjects. Withal, you may bring over some confident gentleman such as you shall understand best able for this business and named unto me, Mr. Fawkes."

Later, Thomas informed me that the meeting with the Constable had not proceeded as we had hoped and that Sir William Stanley and Hugh Owen, two prominent Catholics in the Spanish Lowlands were equally pessimistic about the chances of receiving any Spanish help. They said that this was so since Spain really wanted to end the state of warfare with England as it was costing her too much money. The only good thing that resulted from Thomas' journey to Flanders was that he brought back with him this Guy Fawkes fellow. He is reported to be a brave and stalwart soldier as well as being a devout Catholic. In fact, I am now about to leave my London house here at Lambeth and go and meet Thomas and a couple of other fellows at the *"Duck and Drake"* inn. I have an idea and I want to share it with them. I hope they approve of it, but I am not sure, for it may sound a little too extreme.

Chapter Four
The Meeting at the "Duck and Drake"

Sunday 20 May 1604.

The *"Duck and Drake"* is situated near the Strand, just over on the opposite bank of the River Thames from Robert Catesby's Lambeth house. It did not take him long to get there, and when he arrived he saw that Thomas Wintour and Guy Fawkes were already waiting for him downstairs. After a warm handshake with his friend and kinsman Thomas and another for Guy, the three men went upstairs to meet in a small room at the back of the inn. Thomas had already asked the innkeeper to set it aside for them, saying that he needed such a room "in order to conduct an important business meeting in great privacy."

As they were sitting down, there was a knock on the door and the innkeeper appeared.

"Pardon me, my masters, but I was wondering if you would be wanting any drink or something to eat. The ale in this house is of the best and is not diluted at all."

After a hurried discussion, they agreed that the innkeeper, or actually his daughter, "a pleasant looking lass, I can assure you, gentlemen" would bring them a flagon or two of mild ale together with some cheese and apples. As the innkeeper was about to descend the narrow back stairs, Catesby called out to him, "If two other fellows come asking for us, please show them up to this room. Otherwise, my good man, we are not to be disturbed, as my friend said, we have an important business deal to discuss. Thank you."

The innkeeper saluted and left. As soon as he had closed the heavy door behind him Catesby turned to Thomas.

"Couldn't you have got us a room at the front of this inn? I want to know if we have been followed, or if there are any government informers about."

Thomas put his hand on Catesby's shoulder. "Don't you worry, Robin. No-one knows we're here and anyway, the room at the front was already taken. The owner of this place uses it to store some of his things and I didn't want to make too much of a fuss about this meeting. So calm yourself and let us proceed with what we came here to talk about." And saying that, he looked around at Guy Fawkes who gave him a nod of support. A few minutes later, the innkeeper's daughter, a pleasant looking lass, as her father had proudly described her, knocked on the door. On hearing a shouted call to enter, she did just that, somewhat apologetically. She had a pretty and plump face with two neat dimples and smiled shyly at the seated men. She was wearing a white cap, which failed to hide or control her tumbling ginger curls, and left as soon as she had placed the tray of food and drink on the table. Catesby cleared his throat and was about to begin when there was another knock on the door. At a sign from Catesby, Guy stood up and moved a chair away from the door where it had been wedged up underneath the handle. He opened it slowly and saw two men standing there.

"Ho! Isn't that Guy Fawkes?" asked the taller one as he stepped into the room. "'Pon my oath man, you have indeed grown fatter. Must have been that good life you were leading back there in Flanders, eh? All those delicious Dutch cheeses," he joked, and poked Guy in the ribs. "But fear not man. I would recognize you and your copper head anywhere. So how are you, you old soldier? Stopped fighting so you could come back to England? Well I'm not sure that that was a good idea, but 'tis surely good to see thee again after all these years," and Jack Wright put his arms around his old school-chum from York.

After a short exchange of good-natured banter in reply from Guy, the other man entered more quietly. It was obvious to see that he was of a much more nervous disposition than his companion.

Guy returned the chair to its position under the door-handle and sat down with the others.

"So, my friends, now that we are all here, let us introduce ourselves," and Catesby continued. "Since all of you know me, I will keep quiet and..."

"Hear, hear," interrupted Jack Wright with a smile.

"So, Jack Wright," Catesby replied with a matching smile, "I propose you say something about yourself. After all, not everyone here knows you, or your sense of humour."

Jack leaned back in his chair and began.

"Well, the first thing I want to say to this esteemed company, is that Percy here," and he pointed to the other latecomer, "Thomas Percy to be exact, is my brother-in-law, since this valiant gentleman married my sister Martha some time ago."

"Wait a moment," interrupted Guy, that means that everyone in this room is related to each other, that is, except me."

"True," replied Thomas Wintour. "But I have known you from our schooldays in York, so that almost makes you family, no?"

Guy smiled and Catesby indicated that Jack should continue introducing himself.

"Well," continued Jack. "As I said, I know all of you through school or family, but the last time I was busy with something exciting, that is, when I could use my sword with Mr. Catesby here, and with my brother Kit of course, was when we took part in that Essex Rebellion affair."

"What? Were you involved in that too?" asked Guy. He wanted to learn more details.

"To be sure I was," replied Jack proudly, and turning to Catesby asked, "Don't you remember how we put up such a grand fight on Ludgate Hill?"

"Aye man, I do that," replied Catesby mimicking Jack's Yorkshire accent. "But we both paid a heavy price for that one, did we not?"

Jack nodded his head in agreement, thinking of the thousands of marks he'd had to pay as a fine, as well as the time he had spent being locked up in solitary confinement afterwards.

Bringing him out of his dismal thoughts, Catesby clapped him on the back. "Fear no more my friend. We aren't beaten yet. Just wait 'til you hear what I have to say."

This was too much for Thomas Percy. Suddenly he stood up and slammed his heavy hand down on the table causing the flagons and trenchers to jump about. "All we do is talk and plot, talk and plot!" he shouted. "The time is ripe for..."

"Hush man!" called out Catesby, clapping his hand over Percy's mouth. "You'll give us all away if you shout like that. You never know who might be listening, so have a care," and he removed his hand.

Percy wiped his mouth and had the good grace to look apologetic and said in a more moderate and deliberate tone. "I'm sorry Robin. I truly am. I wasn't thinking, but truly, we must stop talking and start acting. The plight of us Catholics worsens by the day. The king banishes our priests and passes laws against recusancy, and all we do is just sit here and talk of failed plots and of Essex's miserable rebellion. That won't get us anywhere. I for one have had enough of this. I want some action." And his voice began to rise again until he caught a warning look from Catesby.

Lowering his voice again he continued. "We must rid ourselves of this accursed king and his equally accursed ministers once and for all. Don't you all agree with me?" and he looked around in appeal to the other four men in the room.

Jack Wright stood up to reply. Just then there was a double knock on the door and on receiving a signal from Catesby, Guy pulled the chair away again. He opened the door to find the innkeeper standing there.

"Is everything all right with you sirs? I just heard some shouting and I thought there might be some trouble. You never know who is using your rooms now, do you? Might even be some terrible fellows plotting revolution, eh?"

Catesby moved over to the innkeeper and placed a reassuring hand on his shoulder. "Don't you worry yourself about that noise you heard, my man. We were just having a somewhat noisy discussion about a certain business venture. And no thank you, we won't be needing any more food and drink yet. We will call you when we do. Thank you." And he gently escorted the owner of the "*Duck and Drake*" out of the room.

Catesby then indicated to Jack to continue speaking, but as he was about to do so, Guy interrupted him.

"Percy? Thomas Percy? Aren't you related to the Percy family of Alnwick in Northumberland?"

"Aye, that's right. I'm a distant relative of the Earl of Northumberland, and in fact he made me the Constable of Alnwick Castle near the Scottish border and..."

"And didn't this selfsame Earl send you on a mission to Scotland a few years ago," interrupted Thomas Wintour. "On a mission on behalf of us English Catholics?"

"Aye, that he did, but nothing ever came of it, and so that is why we are gathered here."

"Why? Because of that failed Scottish mission?"

"Well in a way, yes," replied Percy cynically. "This time I want to make sure that we're not just sitting round a table in a dimly lit room, talking. That's not what we're here for I hope. So let's listen to what Robin here has got to tell us. We've wasted enough time as it is," and he relapsed into silence.

Guy nodded his head to Catesby who continued. He looked at the four men in turn. "Jack, Henry, Thomas, Guy, this is what I want to say..."

"Wait a minute," said Guy holding up his hand. "I must apologize for interrupting you again Robin, but from now on I want you fellows to call me Guido and not Guy. This is the name the Spanish Catholics and the others in Flanders called me and I rather like it." He looked around. No one said anything. "All right then. Then that's settled. Please continue Robin."

Catesby smiled. He was pleased that Guy, now Guido, was feeling comfortable among his new-found friends. He continued.

"My plan is very simple. All I am saying is that we should devise a way of blowing up the king's Parliament... "

"With him inside?"

"Certainly."

"That's your plan?" asked Jack quietly.

"That's it," replied Catesby equally quietly. "And in that way, we shall rid ourselves of all of our enemies with one blow."

"And then what?" asked Jack.

"Then we lead a Catholic rising, but a serious one this time, not like that Essex affair or the one that Anthony Babington hoped to lead and then..."

"And who will succeed King James? His son?" Guido asked. "Or will we not have need of a king?"

"No," replied Catesby. "We won't have need of a king. We will have a queen instead."

"A queen?" asked Wintour and Percy together. "And who might that be?"

Catesby leaned back in his chair, a smug smile on his face. He looked like the man who had found the solution to every problem.

"The queen would be," and he looked around at their expectant faces. "The queen would be Princess Elizabeth."

There was silence in the room. Outside, one could hear the noises and voices of the City as it went about its business.

"Princess Elizabeth," sneered Thomas Percy at last. "But she's nowt but a lass," he said relapsing into his North-country dialect out of sheer surprise.

"Aye, she's barely nine years old. And anyway, how are you going to get hold of her?" asked Jack.

"That should be no problem," replied Catesby calmly. "She lives apart from the Royal family..."

"Aye, in the Midlands."

"True. And where do we have most of our Catholic supporters, the major Catholic families outside London?" countered Catesby.

"In the Midlands," stated Percy flatly.

"True again," said Catesby. Again with the smug smile of the prize pupil who had just answered all his teacher's questions correctly, he sat down.

"So we make her queen?" queried Guido.

"That is so," continued Catesby. "Then we arrange a marriage between her and the Spanish prince in order to strengthen her position in the Catholic world."

"The people will love that idea," remarked Percy somewhat dourly. "I can just see the London mob rejoicing with that one."

"What do you mean, Percy?"

"Well, listen to reason, Robin. The last time we had a Spanish prince or king over here to marry an English queen, it failed. It failed so badly that he returned to Spain leaving the queen on her own. Now do you understand me?"

"You mean Queen Mary and Philip II?" asked Catesby. It was more of a statement rather than a question.

"Aye, I do," replied Percy. "And I want to tell you something else, friend Robin. You are an educated gentleman. Do you not remember from your studies of history how child-kings have failed to rule successfully in this country? Think of the kings like Richard II, Henry VI and even Queen Elizabeth's own brother, Edward VI. Until they were old enough, they were always surrounded by counsellors of one sort or another. Counsellors I might add, who counselled more for their own good and not always for the good of the country. Think on that, my dear friend. Think on that." And looking around to the others for support, he sat down.

But Robin was not to be beaten.

"But don't you see, Percy and you other fellows. That was well over fifty years ago. Things have changed. The country wants the Catholics back. And in power. I just know it. And also," he added, becoming more and more enthusiastic as he continued, "this time we'll get support from Spain, that is once we have rid ourselves of this Scottish monster of a king and all those who cling to his shirt-tails."

"And what a king," said Wintour, sneering. "A king who dribbles all the time into his food and wears thickly padded garments all the time through fear of the assassin's knife."

"Well, wouldn't you be scared if you had been the target of some assassin's knife twice before?" asked Jack.

Percy didn't look convinced. "Well," he said dourly. "The Spaniards haven't helped us much in the past, neither Philip II and nor his son Philip III."

Jack and Guido nodded their heads in agreement.

"Yes," countered Catesby. "But that's because we have never showed them a sign, a light in the darkness. By blowing up the Houses of Parliament, they will certainly see a light. In more ways than one, I might add. It will serve as a beacon for all the Catholics in England and in the Low Countries."

They all sat back and considered what Catesby had said. Individually they all agreed that by executing Robin's plan, a light would certainly be lit. But the question was, what would happen afterwards? Thomas Wintour, who had not said much during this debate now pushed his hat back on his head, and then pushed himself nearer the table.

"Cousin Robin and friends," he said slowly. "I have not said much up to now because I have been thinking, been brooding if you like on what Robin here has told us. All I can say is this. If Robin's plan succeeds, then we shall be blessed by all the Catholics in England..."

"...and abroad," added Catesby smiling.

"But if we fail," and here he looked slowly and ominously at each of the four conspirators around the table, for that is indeed what they had become. "If we fail, then we will be giving our enemies so great a reason to do us harm, that our present situation with its anti-Catholic laws, fines and threats of exile and banishment will seem like Paradise. It will be so bad that the people will beg the king to bring back the happy days we are living through today. We ourselves will be executed as heretics and burned alive and nothing, nothing I say, will save us."

After this speech, they all relapsed into thoughtful silence and none of them looked at each other. It was as if a bucket of cold water had been thrown over them, washing away their heat and enthusiasm for Robin's idea with one great splash. However, their leader seemed unaffected by their feelings and in his passion he bounced back.

"Listen. Listen all of you. What you are saying makes sense enough. But it also means," and here he enunciated every word very slowly and clearly, "we must not fail. We have to succeed. I think that you understand that this disease, this persecution of us English Catholics is so great and so terrible that it requires an extremely sharp remedy."

Guido and Jack nodded their heads, half in agreement. But they still were not sure. Percy and Wintour were still slumped in their chairs deep in thought. Catesby was beginning to feel that he was recovering lost ground and continued as passionately as before.

"Listen, my friends. What does a surgeon do if the foot of a man is green and rotten? He cuts it off. Surely this hurts terribly, but it must be done. You, Jack, Guy, I mean Guido and Thomas Wintour have seen men undergoing such violent surgery after a battle. You know it pained them cruelly, but you also knew that there was no alternative. You also knew that perhaps the patient would succumb and die. But at least he had a chance to live. And by acting thus as I have described, we too, we Catholics in England will have a chance. For, if not, then all we can do is to condemn ourselves to a truly miserable future and hang our heads and cry at our sorrows."

He stopped, looked round and leaned back in his chair. In truth, he had expected some opposition from Thomas Wintour and even more from Thomas Percy, but he had not expected Wintour's vigour and vociferousness.

For the third time that evening there was a terrible silence in that room as each of the five men reflected between the uselessness of inaction and the possibility of failure. The silence was real and palpable. It could be touched and felt. At last Guido spoke up. "Listen, you fellows. Shall we not go for a walk by the riverside to clear our heads? I for one am in sore need of some fresh air and I'm sure a walk by the Thames will do us all some good."

Catesby was the first to agree. He wanted to break up the heavy atmosphere. "You fellows go downstairs and I will pay the innkeeper. I will also ask him to keep this room for us for when we return, so that we may talk more here later."

The next hour was taken up by the five conspirators walking along the Thamesside path, talking about everything except what they had talked about earlier. As befits old soldiers, Guido and Jack exchanged stories of their experiences in Flanders and Spain. Guido then turned to all of them to tell them in detail of how, while fighting with the Spanish, he had used gunpowder in the successful attack on Calais in 1596. He also told them, with a certain pride in his voice, of how he had used gunpowder to undermine the enemy's defences at the Battle of Nieuport in 1600.

"The explosion that night was really one to start a new century," he recalled with a grin. "There weren't many buildings left standing after that," he said. "This gunpowder stuff is really cunning and lethal. Just put a few barrels of it in certain places and you can change history forever."

"And buildings too," added Jack with a smile. He then told the others of the pedantic rules of protocol that governed the Spanish court and of how he had tried to get round them. The others grinned as Jack mimicked the styles of the various Spanish grandees he had met; how they had bowed to each other and the ladies, and how they had carried their swords.

By the time an unseen clock struck eight o'clock, the now refreshed men had resumed their former places in the upstairs room in the *"Duck and Drake."* To appease the owner, Catesby had ordered five meals and a quantity of mild ale and candles to be brought up for him and his "business companions," but much of this remained untouched as the men returned to discussing the details of Catesby's idea.

As expected, Catesby reopened the proceedings.

"Gentleman, now we are in agreement about what must be done, we will have to discuss the execution of this idea."

"Yes, and I hope it doesn't lead to our own executions," added Percy dryly.

Catesby deliberately ignored him. "I have given much thought to this matter. First of all, we must rent one of the houses as near as possible as we can to Westminster Hall, for that is where the king will open the new session of Parliament."

"And how easy will that be?" asked Jack picking at a lump of cheese.

"Very easy," replied Catesby with a grin. "In fact, I have already done so."

"What? Rented a house near Westminster Hall?" asked Guido.

"Yes, well no. I mean, I have spoken to a Mr. John Whynniard, a man who owns one there, and I casually mentioned that I might want to rent a house there for a while and he agreed. Of course he said that a contract would have to be drawn up, and be signed and sealed as well."

"Have you seen this house?" asked Percy. "Is there anything special about it? Can you see Westminster Hall from it? How many...?"

"And what's this house to be used for? For storage? For meetings? As a hideaway?" asked the ever-practical Guido.

"Whoa! Slowly there!" replied Catesby. "No. The special aspect to this house is that it has a short underground passageway which leads directly underneath to Westminster Hall. My plan calls for storing the gunpowder in Mr. Whynniard's cellar and then transfer it at a later time to a more suitable position, to somewhere under Westminster Hall."

"Wait a minute," Guido interrupted. He was feeling in his element, having had experience with gunpowder, underground mining and storage. "If we store the gunpowder for too long, it is likely to go bad or damp and then it will be completely useless."

"So what you are saying is, is that the timing of our action will be important."

"Very important," said Guido. "I can tell you stories of how we tried to use bad powder in Flanders and..."

"Another time perhaps," Percy broke in. "But not now. It's late enough and we wish to finish this business this evening."

Guido nodded agreement and Catesby was about to continue when Thomas Wintour asked, "Where and how are we going to obtain this gunpowder?"

"Yes, and who is going to pay for it?" added Jack.

Catesby tapped the side of an ale-flagon for silence and then continued. "Listen, you impatient fellows. When I asked you to meet me here, it was not just to talk about ideas, but rather to talk about how to carry them out. So, as I said, to this end I have discussed the renting of a house with Mr. Whynniard. I have also spoken to some military fellows about obtaining some gunpowder and I have agreed to pay for the first payment for it."

"And if we'll need more?" asked Percy.

"Then surely we'll be able to persuade some of our richer brethren to come to our financial aid," said Catesby.

"Yes, but then that will mean that more people will know what we're planning to do," Percy pointed out.

"That's true," replied Catesby. "But they will have to know eventually, especially as we are planning a Catholic rising to follow."

The others nodded their heads in agreement. Now that they thought of this, it was obvious that their plan would have to be known by more people than just themselves, and that some of these people would be useful both in terms of money and influence.

Then Guido asked the next question.

"Robin, please tell us something about this Whynniard house. Does it have a big cellar? Is it dry or not? Did you notice any signs of damp? And does the cellar have a door that opens directly onto the underground passage you mentioned?"

"Well, the house is like most of the houses in the City. It has a fair-sized cellar for storing firewood and coal, while upstairs there are three or four rooms, I think. From one of these rooms, the smallest one I believe, there is a door which leads directly into the House of Lords and..."

"So it really does lie right next to Westminster Hall!" cried out Jack.

"Hush man! Keep your voice down!" hissed Percy sharply before turning to Catesby.

"Carry on Robin," he said. "What else do you know?"

"Well, Whynniard told me that the Lords use such rooms in houses they rent like this, to put on their robes before each session of Parliament."

"How does he know all this? Has he seen them do it? I mean with his own eyes?" Percy asked disbelievingly.

"Of course he has, man," Robin replied. "He should have done. For after all, he is the Keeper of the King's Wardrobe and this is one of his official functions, to help the Lords get ready for Parliament."

"But is not there anyone to examine who enters Westminster Hall, when Parliament is sitting?" asked Guido.

"I think not," said Catesby. "I think this is something we will have to ascertain for ourselves. And now, have we anything else to talk about? The candles are burning low and it's getting dark."

Nobody raised any new topic or problem for discussion.

"Then let us leave here individually and go our separate ways. I suggest that the next time we meet be next Monday afternoon at the small tavern on Ludgate Hill. You know, near the place where Essex was stopped. I have forgotten its name, but you all know where I mean, no?"

Guido shook his head. "You forget Robin. I was in Flanders then."

Catesby pointed to Thomas Wintour. "Thomas, you show Guido. You see," he said smiling, "I remembered your new name this time. You show him where it is on your way home, but then break up and go your own ways. However, before we leave, I think that it is proper that we swear an oath of secrecy between ourselves which I have already prepared. Is that all right with you?"

He looked around at each one of them, full in the face and they in turn nodded their heads in agreement. So taking a slightly crumpled piece of paper out of his pocket, Robert Catesby, in a firm voice, read the oath out aloud.

"You shall swear by the Blessed Trinity and by the Sacrament you now prepare to receive, never to disclose directly or indirectly by word or circumstances the matter that shall be proposed to you, to keep secret nor desist from the execution thereof until the rest shall give you leave."

After a brief swearing ceremony and a quick handshake all round, Guido left with Thomas Wintour. A few minutes later Thomas Percy left on his own and was then followed by Jack Wright. Catesby looked around the room and snuffed out what was remaining of the tallow candles. He descended into the dark and deserted streets of London and after looking behind him, set off in the direction of his home at Lambeth.

Chapter Five
The Ripples Widen

Monday afternoon, a grey day over Ludgate Hill.

As each of the five conspirators entered the small room in the tavern over-looking Ludgate Hill, they shook their damp cloaks and removed their wide-brimmed hats, sending a fine shower over the others as they hung up their outdoor clothes before sitting down. The scene here was in fact very similar to that of the *"Duck and Drake"*. The only differences were that instead of using candles, the room was lit by the weak sunlight and that the owner of the Ludgate Hill tavern, *"The Red Lion"* was a massive fellow with large hairy arms as opposed to his more lightweight counterpart at the *"Duck and Drake."*

Now that they were all settled down around the table, Catesby was about to say something when Percy interrupted him. "I apologize Robin for interrupting you, but gentlemen, I have been thinking very seriously about this matter and in truth, I have not slept well since we last met. And what has been disturbing me since is that, even though I was for your plan at our last meeting, and that I somewhat noisily advocated the use of action, I fear that may not be the case now."

"How so?" asked Robin sharply, perhaps even sharper than he intended.

"Well, the truth is that even if we do believe in such a harsh remedy being applied, to cure our pains, our Catholic pains, then to quote one of the plays that that Shakespeare fellow has written recently, I am not sure that all's well will end well."

"How so?" repeated Catesby.

"On the one hand, if we succeed, then indeed all will end well. And to do so, we will need many supporters and not just promises from the King of Spain. However," and here he looked carefully at each of the four others, "on the other hand, if we fail, the end of this plan, which our enemies will readily call a treasonous plot, will mean our own ends - that is, at the end of the hangman's rope. And - pray do not interrupt me for a minute Robin - and, if we are to succeed, we must make sure that no-one discovers our plans and runs off to inform Cecil or some other member of the Council or any other minister. For remember my friends, our numbers here will have to grow well beyond the five of us who are sitting cosily around this table today."

Wintour was just about to say something but Percy stayed him with his hand. "Just let me finish Thomas. Remember, the price of failure won't just be our own problem, but that of every Catholic in this country - man, woman and child. And not just for now, but from now and for evermore. How do we know if Cecil and the others won't use us, in the event we fail, as a whip to beat all the other Catholics in England? And that gentlemen, is why my enthusiasm of last week has cooled and so I feel I must ask you to consider what I have just said very carefully."

Saying that, he sat back in his chair and waited for the others.

He did not have to wait long, as Jack Wright took up the issue immediately.

"My brother-in-law is correct in many ways," he said. "But for how much longer will we have to suffer in this country? How long can we go one seeing priests banished and others fined and imprisoned for their beliefs while...?"

"And how long will we have to hear about priests being put to death just because they are Catholics?" added Guido.

"But if we fail," replied Thomas Percy, but this time less passionately than before, "even our friends and fellow Catholics will condemn us."

"But think not of failure, think of the glory," Catesby said doing his best to oppose Thomas Percy. "It's not *if* we succeed, but *when* we succeed," and he brought his hand down on the table with a crash to emphasize his words.

"Jack and Guido are right," Catesby continued. "For how much longer are we destined to suffer? See how the ancient Israelites threw off the bonds of slavery. See how the early Christians were persecuted by the Romans. And where are the Romans now? Gone. Thomas Percy, gone," Catesby said looking at the man seated opposite him straight in the eyes, "You must believe in the justness of our cause. You must have faith. Remember what St. Paul said. 'The just shall live by faith.' You are right Thomas to think about our fellow Catholics, but this cause is even greater than that. Just remember this. We are right, Thomas. Just bear with us and be strong. Have courage and all will go well."

After this there was silence. And after what seemed several minutes, Thomas Percy spoke up quietly. "Friends and kinsmen, I am with you. Your conviction in the righteousness of our cause has persuaded me that all will be well. Please forgive me for my momentary weakness. I would like to assure you that I feel stronger now and that I will do everything I can do to further our cause."

He leaned back in his chair and finished off his beaker of ale as the others breathed a sigh of relief.

The rest of the meeting concerned itself with further details, such as the renting of Whynniard's rooms and about the obtaining of the necessary quantities of gunpowder. As before, on leaving, the five men split up into small groups before melting into the evening crowds on Ludgate Hill.

* * * * * * *

Despite his earlier bout of pessimism and lack of faith, it was Thomas Percy who brought the conspirators their next stroke of luck. About two weeks later Percy, as a blood relation to the Earl of Northumberland was appointed as a Gentleman Pensioner and as such, was now able to circulate and mix with those who were considered to be at the centre of the governing establishment. It also meant that he now had a genuine reason to use Whynniard's rooms, especially as his new position meant that he had to live near the court. If this stroke of luck weren't enough, the plotters soon realized that Percy's new venue was situated just over the river and opposite Catesby's house in Lambeth.

The summer of 1604 boded both well and ill for the five men. All went well in that they were able to buy a sufficient quantity of gunpowder and store it in Catesby's riverside residence, but the situation worsened in that the government began to intensify the pressure on England's Catholic population. News of executions around the country travelled like bushfire, as recusant families spread the word about the torturing and deaths of their loved ones. Hurried and whispered conversations like the one below were often repeated.

"Did you hear about Father John Sugar?"

"No. What happened to him? Nothing bad I hope."

"He was executed in Lancaster."

"No! And was he the only one?"

"No. His servant Robert Grissold died with him."

The hearer lowered his eyes in sorrow and just as he was about to cross himself, the speaker continued.

"But comfort thyself brother. He died like a true martyr. Just as they were cutting up his live body, he looked up at the sun and cried out, 'I shall shortly be above yon fellow...'"

"And then he died?"

"No. Not before this holy man called out yet again, 'I shall have a sharp dinner, yet I trust in Jesus Christ I shall have a most holy supper."

"He was indeed holy. It is men like that who will return us to the glory and the greatness we had before these Protestant heretics ruled the land. Praise be the Lord."

While such grim events were unfolding all over the country, all of the conspirators except Guido Fawkes left London and travelled North. This distance from the capital though did not prevent them from hearing of the passing of fresh anti-Catholic legislation. In September 1604, King James commissioned Lord Ellesmere to preside over a committee whose Privy Councillors were charged with getting rid of Jesuits and priests and "divers other corrupt persons employed under the colour of religion." However, the Catholic priests were not the only ones to suffer. Fines were reimposed on the Catholic laymen and recusants, the money being a welcome addition to the royal and the court treasuries. Finally, the Anglo-Spanish treaty, the international commercial and political link between Protestant England and Catholic Spain did not bring the expected relief for England's Catholics. They still remained the persecuted minority.

It was in this oppressive atmosphere that the conspirators felt they had to move forward with their plans, or allow them to wither on the branch and dry up there.

In October 1604, six months after their first meeting at the *"Duck and Drake,"* all the conspirators returned to London, but this time in slightly expanded numbers. The sixth man was Robert Keyes.

One evening Catesby introduced him to the others.

"He should fit in well with us," Percy said after he had fully convinced himself that Robert Catesby's way was the only way to ultimately improve the lot of England's Catholics. "He is tall and ginger, just like Guido."

"Yes, and like Guido, his father was a Protestant but his mother was a Catholic," added Catesby. "And like you Guido, his family also comes from the North."

"From where?"

"We're from North Derbyshire, from Stavely," Keyes said. "That's where I was brought up. But my mother came from Lincolnshire. Her maiden name was Tyrrwhitt and she is related to Lady Urusla Babthorpe."

"Tyrrwhitt. Thyrrwhitt," said Thomas Wintour, half to himself." Isn't there someone in your family named Elizabeth?"

"Certainly," answered Keyes with pride. "She is my very pretty, nay, very beautiful cousin."

"And is she not married to a very rich Catholic called Ambrose Crowood?" continued Wintour.

"You are half right there," answered Keyes smiling. "Except that you have got your bird wrong."

"My bird wrong?"

"Yes. He is certainly a rich Catholic, and has a large stable of fine horses, but his name is Rookwood, not Crowood."

"Ah, so Ambrose Rookwood is related to you. I didn't know that, but I've certainly heard him spoken about with great respect in recusant circles," Catesby said. "You know Robert, you have given me an idea. It might be worth our while bringing him into our little circle, especially since he is related to you and is also known to be a good Catholic too. What say you all to this?"

The others nodded their heads in agreement and then Jack Wright spoke up.

"Robert Keyes, what else can you tell us about yourself? Have you fought in the Spanish Netherlands like Guido here or Thomas Wintour? Have you ever been to Spain or...?"

"Whoa! Wait a minute. Hold your horses," Keyes cut him off and held up his hand. "To answer your questions. No I have never been abroad. In fact I have led a very quiet domestic life. Most of my life over these past few years has been spent in the service of Lord Mordaunt of Drayton."

"Not Lord Mordaunt, the Catholic Lord who sits in Parliament?" asked Percy who had been very quiet up to this point.

"Yes. The same one. I looked after his property in Northamptonshire while my wife Christiana acted as governess to his children."

"Did he pay you well?" asked Catesby. "I have heard he is a good and generous man."

"Oh certainly. He paid me well, both in money and in horses."

"In horses? Well, that is good news. For we are surely going to need horses for our initial escape," Catesby said, thinking ahead.

"For escape? Escaping from whom?" Percy asked.

"From the authorities, of course. We won't be able to get rid of all of them in one blow," Catesby replied warming up to his future plans. "And in any case, we will need fast horses to act as a link between us, no?"

There was a moment's silence around the room as the others thought about the plot and the future.

"So it seems as if you will be bringing us money and horses as well as your own good self," remarked Guido, practical as always.

"Horses yes, money no," replied Keyes.

"What do you mean?"

"Well, although it is true that I do own a few horses, I am certainly not rich. I have had to pay some heavy fines for recusancy in the past, but you may consider me as one of your truest supporters from now on. You will not regret having me amongst you. I will be honest and trusting with you all."

And so it was settled. Robert Keyes joined the group and soon after they took possession of Whynniard's house. A point even more important than this, which they had not realized at first, was that by having unlimited access to the house, they also had unlimited access to the cellar below. They could not have chosen a better place, for the cellar extended to just below the House of Lords. All that the plotters had to do now was, to clear out the years of accumulated rubbish that had gathered there and then breach the wall which would give them a way into the passage underneath Westminster Hall. In order to mask their activities with an air of respectability, Guido moved into the rented house using the name of John Johnson. It was put about that he was the servant of Thomas Percy, the newly appointed Gentleman Pensioner.

Their plans seemed to be proceeding smoothly until one evening when Percy asked the others to meet him at the *"Mermaid Inn"* by the river. He looked nervous as the other five sat down, huddled round a table in the corner.

"My friends," he said in a low voice. "We have problems. Whynniard's wife, a particularly ugly lady, if I may say so, told me yesterday that she wants to use the cellar."

"The cellar and the house, you mean?"

"No. Just the cellar. But you know what that means. The house without the cellar is useless."

"Yes. Like a carriage without a horse," muttered Guido.

"True," said Percy.

"But why does she want it? And why just now?" asked Catesby. "I thought that we had agreed, we had even signed that we were to have them both. At least, that is what was written in the contract we drew up."

"Maybe," Percy said. "But it seems that the tenant before us, a Mr. Skinner wishes to use the cellar for storing wood there for winter fuel and Mrs. Whynniard is amenable to the idea. That's the reason of course I told her that's why I need the cellar. To store winter fuel."

The six men sat around the table thinking of ways of solving this problem. At last Catesby spoke up. "How insistent is she on allowing this Skinner fellow to use the cellar?"

"I'm not sure. But I think that if we cross her palm with more silver than is written in the contract, we will be able to continue using it. She seems to be as grasping as she is ugly a hag to me. The question is, if she'll agree and how much will it cost us if she does?"

The answer came soon enough. Four pounds. In silver. Catesby could afford that. After solving that problem, the plotters continued removing the accumulated rubbish below their property while Guido continued acting out his role as John Johnson, Thomas Percy's faithful servant. Although the work was hard, especially for men who were not used to dirty physical labour in cramped and dark conditions, the cellar was soon cleared out in preparation for breaking through to the subterranean passage below Westminster Hall.

One evening as Guido was sitting in his room reading a religious tract, there was a knocking at his door. Hoping it wasn't that annoying Mrs. Whynniard woman again Guy got up to open the door. It wasn't Mrs. Whynniard but another lady who Guido did not recognize.

"Good evening. Are you Mr. Guy Fawkes?" she asked.

Guido did not say anything but ushered her into the room quickly. He looked around the room and saw that he had not left any incriminating evidence around.

Giving her a slight bow, he said, "Good evening," and pulled up a chair for the young lady.

Before sitting down, she took off her travelled-stained wrap and Guido hung it behind the door.

"Good evening." Guido repeated. "And who might I have the pleasure of addressing?"

"Mistress Ilkely, Elizabeth Ilkely," she replied with a slight smile.

"And no doubt you are from Yorkshire?"

"How do you know that?" she asked, blushing slightly, her blue eyes widening.

"Your name and your accent give you away. Especially the latter."

"Oh, I see," she said and removed her dark brown cap and shook her blonde curls free from its restraint.

"And does Mistress Ilkely from Yorkshire wish to eat and drink anything before she tells me why she is here?" asked Guido deliberately being formal. He was not used to being alone with young ladies, especially pretty ones like this creature and so he preferred this formal stance, even if it did sound a little pompous, even to himself.

"No thank you. Well, on second thoughts, I will have a little ale please. To wash the dust out of my mouth," she added as an excuse. "After all, I have come a long way, you know."

"From Yorkshire?"

"From Knaresborough."

"Ah, that's where I know you from," Guido said suddenly realizing that her name and face were vaguely familiar from the past.

"Yes, of course. Don't you remember, we used to meet with other recusant families near Knaresborough before you left for...Where was it?"

"Flanders and the Low countries. I served in the army there. But tell me Mistress Ilkely, what are you doing here in London? Surely you didn't come here on your own?"

"Oh no. Certainly not."

"And you're not fleeing from trouble?"

"No, no. I came here with my father."

"John Ilkely, the wool-merchant?"

"Yes. That's right. I see you have a good memory."

Guido blushed. He was not used to accepting compliments from young ladies. In fact he was not used to having anything to do with young ladies at all.

Elizabeth Ilkely continued. "My father came to London on some sort of business and decided to bring me with him this time. I haven't been out of Yorkshire for such a long time and I also wanted to bring you a message, a warning in fact."

Guido sat up sharply. "A warning? From whom?"

"That I can't tell you. But all I can say is that someone has heard that you and some others have plans to help the Catholics in England and..."

"But that is nonsense," interrupted Guido, perhaps a little too quickly. "Who am I, but an old soldier. Who am I to do things for the Catholic cause in this country? I hardly know what's happening here in England these days. I'm just a servant, living in this old house in London. Believe me, Mistress Ilkely, I am far removed from politics," replied Guido and turned away from her under the pretext of rearranging some pewter pots on the sideboard. He didn't want her to see his face as he lied to her.

"Guy Fawkes," continued Elizabeth. "I am just telling you what I was instructed to do. I still care for you, as I care for all of us Catholics, and we must all stay together. So do not lie to me about this. And while we are on this, who is this John Johnson? I was told that he lived in this house, not Guy Fawkes."

"Oh he used to rent this place before me," Guido lied, looking away again in the direction of the sideboard. "The person who told you must have made a mistake."

"Are you sure?" she asked coming up behind him quietly and placing her hands on his shoulders.

"Yes, I am sure," Guido replied quickly, keeping his back to her. This conversation and her friendly manner were beginning to get out of control, at least as far as he was concerned. "And now I think you had better return to your father. I'm sure he will be worried about you, being alone in the big city. And where is he anyway?" he asked turning around to face her. He felt safer now that he was asking the questions.

"Oh, he's two streets away talking to another wool-merchant. They are busy brokering a deal about supplying raw wool to some London tailors."

The unwilling host then handed his guest her cap and wrap and watched her as she pushed her curls back into her cap before wrapping herself up to walk over to her father's meeting. Then just as Guido was opening the door, she turned to look at him.

"Remember Guy Fawkes. I don't know what you are doing, but if you are doing something and I, a simple country-lass from Yorkshire can find you, then it will be no problem for the authorities to do the same. So good luck, good night and God be with you."

And she was gone.

It was a very concerned "servant and old soldier" who met with his "master" Thomas Percy the following morning.

"Thomas, I'm worried," Guido began as soon as Percy was settled down in the only comfortable chair in the rather spartan room. He told him of the previous night's meeting with Mistress Ilkely, leaving out none of the details, except that he had thought she was very pretty indeed and that her blonde curls certainly looked very fetching.

"But how does she know about us?" they both kept asking. In the end, Percy attempted to answer this nagging question.

"I'm not sure I know, Guido, but we must be on our guard. Perhaps even more so in the future. But yet, at the same time, as Robin said, we will have to expand our numbers, for six of us are certainly not enough." He scratched his head, deep in thought. At last he said, "Surely none of us has told anyone else. Therefore the only thing that I can think of is that someone, and I don't know who that can be, has seen several of us entering or leaving this house. Or perhaps someone like a government spy has been watching one or other of the taverns where we have met in the past, and has come to some sort of conclusion. We must report this to Robin of course and be even more circumspect in the future."

Guido nodded fervently in agreement. Of course Percy was right, but that did little to allay his fears and suspicions.

"Are you sure one of Robin's servants hasn't seen nor heard anything?" Guido asked after a while. "After all, he has several servants, and as we know, servants will usually work for the person who pays them best."

"Do you mean that one of Robin's servants could be a government informer?"

"It's possible," Guido said. "It won't be the first time. I remember the time when the Spaniards wanted to know something when I was in Brussels and they planted this young girl in a house, promising her a lot of money and..."

"Yes, yes" interrupted Percy impatiently. "We must tell Robin today. If there is a spy, then we must find out who it is immediately. You know," he said, getting up for his hat and cloak, "let us go to Robin's house now and make our report. We have some time at the present."

Two minutes later, Percy left the house and was followed several minutes later by his "servant" John Johnson. Arranging to meet near the south end of London Bridge, they arrived together at Robin's house in Lambeth. Strategically, the house was well situated for the plotters' purpose as it was situated almost on the opposite bank of river facing the Palace of Westminster. This would later mean that the ferrying of the gunpowder over the Thames would be an easy task, but at this moment, neither Guido Fawkes nor Thomas Percy were thinking so far ahead.

After brief and hushed greetings, Catesby ushered them in. They then went into a small room at the back of the house.

"What is the problem with you fellows. You look like you've seen a ghost, or at least one of Cecil's spies."

"You may laugh, but you may not be too far from the truth, Robin," replied Percy dryly and told Guido to describe his previous night's encounter with Mistress Ilkely. Catesby interrupted him just a few times to ask for details. When Guido had finished they all sat silently for a few moments.

"But we cannot remain such a small group," Catesby said. "We have to grow. And it's about that that I wished to speak to you fellows today. I want to bring in one of my own men, one of my servants to join us."

"Who?"

"Thomas Bates."

"After what we have just told you, are you sure he's completely trustworthy?" Percy asked suspiciously. "I'm still thinking of how this Mistress Ilkely found Guido here, and how she'd heard of John Johnson. We still don't know the real truth behind that."

"How much does your Thomas Bates know about us already?" Guido asked before Catesby could answer Percy's question. "What kind of servant is he anyway?"

"Gentlemen," Catesby said trying to calm his fellow plotters, handing them a goblet of red wine apiece. "I know this Ilkely girl has caused you to be worried, but panic won't help us. Now let me set your minds at rest and answer your questions. First of all, he isn't a servant as you usually think of servants, but rather someone whom I trust and carries out business deals for me."

"Such as?"

"As when I have deals concerning the buying and selling of cattle, you know, near my country home at Ashby. And I must tell you fellows, I have always found him to be extremely honest and trustworthy and anyone in my family would vouch for him on that. Remember, he has served the Catesby family well, that is, he and his wife Martha." Catesby looked closely at Guido and Percy before continuing. "It is true that he was not born of gentlemanly stock and that his father was some sort of peasant, but that does not mean that he is not trustworthy, does it? I ask you, does everyone who is born a gentleman always behave like a gentleman? Have there not been those who were born gentlemen but then acted like real villains?"

Guido and Percy smiled in agreement and then Catesby smiled his usual wide smile at them.

"Good. Then if we are in accord, I suggest we call him into this room, say under the pretext of preparing a business contract, just in case any of the other servants sees him and wonder why he is coming into my room. After all, after Guido's meeting last night with the attractive Mistress Ilkely..."

"How do you know she was attractive?" Guido asked blushing.

"That was written all over your face," smiled Catesby. "But let's be serious. If she could find you, anyone could. This means that we will have to be even more careful in the future. So wait here, and I will call on Thomas Bates to join us."

Half an hour later, as the clock struck midday on that grey autumn day, it was agreed that Thomas Bates, longtime and faithful retainer to the Catesby family would join that small circle of plotters, now numbering seven.

Chapter Six
Wider Still and Wider

"'Tis odd, isn't it?" Guido asked Percy one evening after they had been discussing for the hundredth time how King James had disappointed the Catholic population of England, that some people liked the winter and yet others preferred the summer. "Myself, I prefer the summer."

"Why?"

"Well, perhaps it's because of the cold winters we used to suffer when I was growing up in York and then in Scotton."

"True, but you never suffered the effects of the plague that we used to, down in the south of the country, especially before the turn of the century. And they usually happened during the summer months."

"What do you mean?" asked Guido.

"Well, there were outbreaks of the plague in, let me see, ah yes, in 1592, the year after that and then the year after that too. And then there was another in 1596 as well as one last year. That last one was one some people blamed on the new king and maybe they were right," added Percy with a wry smile."

"Well, I was in Flanders and Spain then if you remember. So I missed all that. But tell me, how did these plagues affect life? I know that hundreds, even thousands of people died, but what else happened?"

"Oh the authorities closed all the places where many people gather together, like..."

"...theatres?"

"Yes, and places for bowling and other sports, and of course, the bear-bating pits. And then the queen and the court and the Parliament would leave London for more healthy parts."

"Well," said Guido twirling his moustache, "if that happened now, it would really spoil our plans, wouldn't it? I mean there would not be a Parliament here for us to get rid of and besides that, the king and his court wouldn't be here. And apart from that, all our work in collecting gunpowder and those wooden faggots would all have been in vain. So let's hope that for the near future, we won't have any visitations of the plague."

But Guido was wrong. The following week Catesby arrived at Percy's house in a hurried state and told them the latest news.

"Friends," he began breathlessly, even before sitting down. "I have just heard that Parliament has decided to postpone its official opening from February until October."

"Why?"

"The plague. There are fears of another outbreak and so Parliament and the court are moving out of London."

"Well, we were just talking about that the other day," said Percy.

"But in truth that is good news," Guido said.

"How so?"

"Because it gives us another half year to plan and to recruit more supporters and also to get some help from Flanders and Spain," Guido replied, looking on the bright side.

"Yes," added Percy, but then shook his head. "This knife can cut both ways. It also means that we must keep our plans secret for yet another six months and that we must be on our guard for another six months as well. We must make sure that Cecil and the like don't get to hear of us. For I am still mindful of Guido's recent meeting with Mistress Elizabeth Ilkely."

Guido blushed slightly when Percy mentioned the Yorkshire lass's name again but fortunately for him, the others did not notice.

Following further discussion, the three men decided to tell the others about the delay in opening Parliament, and that they had to make sure their plans would remain a secret. No other person was to know about them. Not even their wives.

In the meantime, they continued clearing out the cellar and the underground tunnel until Christmas, when they took a break from this physical and unfamiliar labour. To men unused to working in dark and cramped spaces, working below Whynniard's house and beyond was exhausting. Certainly to men who were not used to carrying anything heavier than a quill pen or light sword, shifting rough lumps of rock and masonry as well as pieces of splintery wood must have been gruelling labour, leaving them with aching backs and cut and blistered hands. It was one thing for Robert Catesby Esquire to plot and plan, but it was another to actually execute these plans. Actually, to be fair, Catesby usually did join in with

Guido, Percy, Jack Wright and Thomas Wintour as part of the subterranean working party. Generally, while some of them worked and strained below ground, they always made sure that one or two of them were above keeping an eye out for any suspicious looking people or possible spies.

"You know, my friends," Guido said one evening as they were cleaning themselves after a particularly dirty and gruelling session below ground, "this reminds me of the Bible."

"What? We're the Hebrew slaves in Egypt?" asked Catesby with a grin.

"No," replied Guido looking at his blistered hands. "No, it reminds me of the story of Ezra and Nehemiah."

"Who?"

"Ezra and Nehemiah, you know, the two men who led the Children of Israel back to Jerusalem and..."

"...and rebuilt the city walls," Percy finished off Guido's sentence triumphantly.

"That's right," said Guy. "And if you read your Bible, you will see that it says that they both rebuilt the city walls and stood on guard at the same time."

"And if you read further on in the good book," said Percy, washing his hands in a pail of water, "it says that none of the men took off their clothes, even for washing themselves."

"Well, we are not as unfortunate as that," Catesby said, shaking the dust out of his hair. "But we do have another problem, and that is somehow we will have to breach the cellar wall below."

The others looked up from their various acts of washing and cleaning the dust out of their clothes.

"According to the plans I have, we will reach the wall which separates our cellar from the one that lies under Westminster Hall very soon. I believe that we only have a day or two's more work left before we get ready to breach it."

Feeling encouraged by Catesby's words, Guido went below the next day and set to work with even greater enthusiasm. Suddenly he found it easier to work down there, probably because he had more room. He had not been working for more than an hour or so when he heard strange noises coming from underground. They seemed to come from the same level that he was and sounded like the pushing and dragging of heavy objects. Quietly abandoning his work, Guido climbed back up into Whynniard's house and entered through a small door at the back. He sought out Catesby and described what he had heard.

As a result, they stopped their subterranean activities for the day as Percy, as the official tenant, set out to find if his landlord knew anything which would cause such noises.

That night Percy reported to the others that they were in luck. Adjoining their cellar was another underground vault, and its owner, a widow named Mrs. Ellen Bright was busy removing her sacks of coal.

"But why?" asked Guido. "It's winter now. Surely she needs her coal."

"Yes," replied Catesby. "I thought so too. But I heard she's in desperate need of money and is selling it off. So I suggest that we bide our time for a few days and then see if we can purchase the use of her cellar."

And that is what they did. The following week Guido descended once again to the foundations of the house and returned half an hour later, his eyes sparkling above a sooty moustache and beard. He was grinning widely.

"Fellows," he said washing some, but not all of the grime from his face. "We are in luck. The widow's vault is perfectly suitable for us."

"Why is that?"

"It's huge, well, very big," said Guido. " I measured it to be twenty-five paces by ten large paces. And you know the size of my paces. My feet are like those of a bear."

"How high is it?" asked Jack Wright.

"I was coming to that. I estimate it to be nearly twice my height."

"And could we store the gunpowder and faggots there safely?"

"Easily, and with room to spare," replied Guido, washing his face again. "We could even..."

"Wait a minute," interrupted Thomas Wintour. "Let us not be so hasty. Will not the good widow want to rent out her vault again, especially if she is in such desperate need for money?"

"No," replied Percy. "I have learnt that she intends to vacate the premises completely."

"So if that is the situation, we had better start removing the gunpowder from Lambeth and storing it underground here." Catesby said decisively. Then he turned to Guido. "That will be safe, no? It won't suffer from damp here, will it?"

"Is it regular gunpowder or corned gunpowder?"

"Corned gunpowder."

"Good. That is the best. It is less sensitive to movement and damp."

"But what is gunpowder?" asked Wintour. "I would like to know what I am working with."

"Yes, and how I'm going to meet my Maker if I'm not careful," added Jack Wright with a laugh.

"There are two main types of gunpowder," explained Guido. "There is ordinary gunpowder, which used to be called 'Greek Fire.' This was a mixture of half a measure of saltpetre with two quarter measures each of charcoal and sulphur."

"Ah, that's why it smells so horribly," said Keyes.

"Yes," said Guy. "But Robin here says that he has corned gunpowder at Lambeth and that is much better."

"Why?"

"Because it is less sensitive," repeated Guido, happily demonstrating the knowledge he had picked up in Flanders. "And also because if you have the same weight of both ordinary gunpowder and corned gunpowder, the latter will cause a far greater explosion."

There was a short period of silence in the room as the men paused to consider the results of their labours. Pictures of buildings and people exploding into the air flashed through their imaginations.

"Well now you fellows are experts in gunpowder, corned or not," Catesby said, rubbing his hands briskly, "we will see about removing the stuff from my house in Lambeth and bringing it here. And if I must admit, I wasn't truly happy living and sleeping over a whole lot of that stuff, even if Guido here says it's perfectly safe. So I won't object if we remove it from my house to here, and the quicker the better."

"How is it stored?" Guido asked.

"In barrels. There are over thirty of them."

"So we could transfer it by boat, a few barrels at a time," suggested Keyes. "Does that sound possible, Guido?"

The gunpowder expert said yes and that once the barrels were stored, he added, they should be covered with faggots and firewood.

A few nights later, after Widow Bright had vacated the vault, the plotters were kept busy ferrying the gunpowder over the Thames. As soon as it was all in position, under the guise of being a prudent householder, Percy ordered a large amount of winter firewood to cover up the barrels.

"Just be careful with that gunpowder," Catesby said when they had finished. "Don't you let any harm befall that stuff. I paid two hundred pounds for it and we haven't yet finished."

"What do you mean?" Thomas Wintour asked.

"Well, we are going to need horses and will probably have to cross a few people's palms with silver. And I haven't yet paid the boatman who helped us ferry the gunpowder over from Lambeth."

"So we are short of money then?" Guido asked.

"No, not at the moment, but we may be soon," Catesby said. "So I have asked a young man, the man from whom I bought the gunpowder to join us. No do not worry you fellows. I have told him very little about us. I just told him that we wish to talk to him tomorrow evening and that we meet at the *"Mermaid"* again. Is that agreed?"

It was, except that Thomas Wintour said he wouldn't be able to join them as he had arranged some domestic matter with his mother which he didn't wish to postpone again.

They all left that evening, as usual in twos and threes, except Thomas Percy and his servant John Johnson. Catesby returned home via the *"Mermaid,"* where he reserved a room for a "convivial meeting with some old friends" for the following night.

* * * * * * *

The meeting at the *"Mermaid"* was similar in many ways to their earlier meetings. The plotters met in a small room, and after ordering some cakes and ale, asked the innkeeper not to disturb them. About a quarter of an hour after the last plotter had joined them, there was a triple knock on the door followed by a double knock.

"Ah, that must be him," said Catesby getting up to open the door. He ushered in a short young man, who stood in the doorway nervously, fingering the brim of a large hat.

"Why, 'tis my cousin Ambrose!" Keyes said in surprise. "You are surely the last person I expected to see here this night."

"I pray you, why?" asked the cousin with a smile.

"I don't know," replied Keyes slightly embarrassed. "Maybe because we are all older than you and that I've known you since you were an infant all wrapped up in swaddling clothes."

"Well I've grown up since. I am now twenty-five, or thereabouts and Robin here has told me a little of your plans."

"And?" asked Guido.

"I want to know more. As cousin Robert will tell you, I am as staunch a Catholic as all of you, and I have at least more than one reason to have revenge on the authorities," Ambrose said, his smile hardening into a thin line.

"What is that?" Thomas Bates asked.

"Well, my good friends and cousin, I have just been made to pay a huge fine for recusancy by the Middlesex County sessions and..."

"And you couldn't afford it?" asked Bates again.

"No, no. That is not the question. I can afford it, I can afford it easily enough, and for that I thank God. No, I am feeling vengeful for I think it is a crime that we should be fined just because we are Catholics. Do they fine the French and Dutch workers who come into this country? No, of course not. But come, don't let us talk about me and my problems, for I have come here to listen to you and see how I can play my part in all this."

"So before you do so," Catesby said, "please tell the others something about yourself. If I am correct, you were in Flanders like Guido here, no?"

"Yes, but not as soldiers. We went there, or more correctly, we were smuggled there by Father John Gerard when we were young."

"We?"

"Yes. My brothers and my sisters. My sisters became nuns and my younger brother became a priest. My older brother died in Spain."

His listeners cast their eyes down at this news, but Ambrose continued. "After I left the seminary school of St. Omer's, I returned to England in time to inherit my father's estates at Coldham."

"And they are large, if I remember," interrupted Keyes.

"True. And then I married my beautiful Elizabeth, and with that gentlemen," Ambrose said with a slight bow, "you know all about me."

"Not true," said Jack Wright.

"What do you mean?"

"You have forgotten to mention that you own a stable of fine horses."

"Ah yes. That is true. In fact gentlemen, I even prefer my horses to my clothes, for which I have a passion, as cousin Robert will vouch for, no?"

Robert Keyes smiled in assent.

"So now, here I am with you," Ambrose said. "How can I be of any help. I know my horses will be useful, but at the moment they are far away in my stable at Stanningfield in Suffolk."

"That is exactly what I wanted to talk about with you," Catesby said. "I think it would be a good idea if you rented some property nearer London. I mean, not in the city of London, but a place which would serve as a half-way house for our possible escape from the hue and cry that will surely follow the explosion."

"And where were you thinking Robin?"

"I know of a place at Clopton. It's called Clopton House and it's for rent."

"And where is this Clopton House?"

"It's near Stratford-upon-Avon."

"But that's in Warwickshire. That's not near London."

"I know," said Robin. "It's about a hundred miles away."

"But safe in Catholic country," added Ambrose with his infectious smile. "That sounds rather a good idea to me."

"So now we are all agreed on that," Catesby said. "I suggest we drink a toast to our success and to our expanded numbers. As that Shakespeare fellow would say, 'We band of brothers. We happy few.' Thomas Bates, will you please go and ask the landlord to bring us a flagon of wine, for we cannot raise a toast on buttermilk, can we?"

As they were drinking their toast soon after, Robert Catesby stood up and tapped on the table for attention.

"Gentlemen. I have been giving the following much deep thought and I have come up with two conclusions. The first is that since we now have the use of the widow's vault, we should stop any further tunnelling activities. It is dirty and noisy and it may attract unwanted attention in the future. Secondly, the wall that we intended to breach is far too thick for us, that is, to do it quietly."

"We could use some of the gunpowder," Percy said dryly.

"Thank you for your suggestion, Thomas," Catesby said, and smiled.

"You mean that we have finished with blistered hands and aching backs?" Guido asked.

"Aye."

"Then that really is worth a toast," said Jack Wright, and poured himself another measure of wine. He finished it off with one noisy swallow. Wiping his mouth with the back of his hand he laughed, "Such news is well worth two toasts. I was beginning to think that it was such hard work to rid ourselves of these Protestants, but now, with the widow's unwitting help, it seems as if we have Divine Providence on our side. I would drink again to that, if there were any wine left, but the good Lord will just have to do with the spirit of the toast, if not the toast itself."

"Oh, very spiritual," laughed Ambrose.

"Well I have something to add that is less spiritual," said Catesby looking around. "And that is that I think we should dispatch Guido back to Flanders in order to acquaint our friends there about our activities here. I also think that..."

But he was not able to continue with his next point. Immediately on hearing about Guido's possible journey abroad, a noisy discussion broke out around the table.

"But is that wise?"

"Won't too many people know?"

"Who is he going to inform?"

"What about spies?"

"Should he go alone? Who will go with him?"

"But two men will attract more attention."

"True, but they can look out for each other."

"But what if someone suspects Guido?"

"But why Guido? Isn't he needed here to keep an eye on the cellar?"

"Gentlemen, gentlemen" called out Catesby clapping his hands to get attention. "I am calling for order." As he spoke, the hubbub died down. "Listen you fellows. I told the landlord that we were here to have a convivial meeting of old friends. If you don't keep quiet, he will call out the Watch, and then where will we be?" He stopped for a moment and then continued. "Let me explain myself. I suggest that Guido goes only for a short time, and certainly not for such a long time that the gunpowder will spoil. He will be there just long enough to inform certain persons over there, and perhaps, if we're lucky, he will be able to return with some money as well."

"Who will he speak to?"

"Well, as I said, I have given this matter much thought. I think he should speak to Sir William Stanley and also to Hugh Owen."

"Sir William I have heard of," Bates said. "But who is this Hugh Owen?"

"Hugh Owen, my friend, is a past-master of hating the Protestant authorities. He is Welsh and has served various men of nobility and also the King of Spain before the Anglo-Spanish treaty was signed. In addition, he is one of the keenest men I know who wishes to cause problems for Lord Cecil. In fact, he more than annoyed Cecil's father, Lord Burghley in the past, and, excuse the expression, but he created hell on earth for Walsingham's spies. So I would say that our friend Hugh Owen, is the ideal person to be informed of our activities here. Does anyone object?"

No one did. And so it was decided that night that Guido was to sail to Flanders as soon as possible and at the same time, the circle of plotters would have to be widened, both in England and in the Low Countries.

That night the conspirators tied up a few loose ends. Apart from Thomas Percy who would remain at his post as a Gentleman Pensioner, the others would return to their various homes in the North and the Midlands. They would only come together again when they received a clear signal from Robert Catesby to do so.

Chapter Seven
Bath, Lambeth, and Final Details

August 1605. The *"Lion Inn,"* Westgate Street, Bath, Somerset.

The *"Lion Inn,"* Westgate Street, Bath could have been an inn in any city in England. Outside, the afternoon sun shone in an almost cloudless sky as the carriages and carts drew up in the busy yard to load and unload their passengers, trunks or barrels of wine and ale. Travellers and their servants descended from the carriages into the hustle and bustle, shaking the dust off their hats and cloaks. Ostlers and the innkeeper's men rushed to serve both man and beast hoping for a fat tip in return for their troubles. The traditional questions asked by travellers over the years echoed once again across the yard.

"Have you got a room for the night?"

"How is the food here?"

"Are the beds clean?"

"Is there a carriage leaving here for Bristol tomorrow morning?"

"Well, hello Master Charlecombe. And how is your good lady wife?"

The noise was somewhat more subdued as one moved into the main room of the inn itself. There, seated around the scattered tables sat farmers and landlords as well as the few moneyed people who had come to take the famous waters of this old Roman town. Here and there sat a few single men drinking ale, with or without a meal. One such man was Robert Catesby.

He had positioned himself near the main door so that he could keep an eye on all who entered. As usual in such places, he wore his black and conical wide-brimmed hat low over his forehead. His jacket was dark blue, as were his breeches. Being dressed in such colours he felt he did not look conspicuous. He had told the others to wear dark and dull colours when they met in public places, and they had all readily agreed. All of them that is, except Ambrose Rookwood who loved to wear bright colours. However, once the seriousness of the plot had been explained to him, he became as externally dull and unattractive as the others.

Catesby was just about to order some more bread when he felt a friendly pat on the shoulder.

"Robin, I've arrived."

"Guido, I'm pleased to see you. Sit down," he said pointing to a well-worn wooden chair. "You're looking well."

"Well, I should, even though I'm not the bearer of glad tidings."

"So just keep them to yourself for a little longer as Percy and Wintour are due to arrive soon. Then you can tell us all."

"What about Ambrose and Thomas Bates and the others?" asked Guido easing himself out of his jacket.

"They won't be coming this time, but order yourself something to eat and drink. We might be here for some time."

Guy signalled a round-faced serving-wench to bring him a drink. "I hear the cider is good down here in the West Country."

"It is, but just be careful it doesn't make you too merry or loosen your tongue Mister Fawkes," laughed Catesby. "Especially as you don't seem to be ordering any food to go with it."

"Robin, you should know me by now. I know how to keep a secret. Wild horses or the rack would never make me divulge anything I know."

"I know that, my friend. Just let's hope you never have to prove your words. Now," he continued in a business-like tone, "tell me about your new house."

"Mrs. Herbert's? Near St. Clement's church?"

"Aye."

"Well, I am no longer there."

"Why not?" Catesby asked in surprise.

"I had a strong feeling that the lady began to suspect that I was a Catholic and I felt that I was being watched."

"And were you?"

"I'm not sure. But I think that on at least one occasion I was followed as I was walking down the Strand, in the direction of Westminster, that is."

"But you couldn't prove this?"

"No."

"So where are you living now?"

"In a small house in a lane north of Smithfield market," Guido replied quietly. "By the way, Robin, what were you reading when I came in here just before? You looked as if you could not put it down."

"Oh, 'tis a short list of what I wish to talk about when the others arrive. Here, take a look."

He handed the small notebook over to Guido who scanned the list. It read:

-GF Fl S O

- New RW JG KW

  - gp

  - Tes

  - warn OS

He handed it back to Catesby. "What is this? A secret code? The only words I can understand are 'new' and 'warn.' What else does it say? Is 'GF' me?"

"You guessed right, Guido. Maybe you should work for Cecil's spy organization."

Guido pretended to look shocked and hurt and just as he was about to say something, a large shape in the doorway blocked out the afternoon light. They looked up to see Thomas Percy and Thomas Wintour looking down on them.

"Well, it's good to see you fellows at last," Catesby said with a smile of welcome. "Now we can get started."

A few minutes later after food and drink had been ordered, Percy motioned that he wanted to ask something.

"First of all, Robin, why are we meeting here in Bath and not in London. Surely we're not here for the waters?"

"Yes," Wintour added." You know, Robin, there are other inns and taverns in London apart from the "*Duck and Drake*" and the "*Mermaid?* If you don't like them, or feel that we've been seen there too often, we can always meet somewhere else."

"No, my good friends," Catesby replied. "We are here in Bath for two reasons. The first is, that despite Thomas Percy's jibes, I have indeed been taking the waters here for two months."

"And the second reason is...?" interrupted Wintour.

"The second reason is that I think that it will be prudent if the fewer the meetings we have in London the better. As it is, just before you arrived, Guido was telling me about how he thought he was being followed in London. And not only that, but he has also moved his address because of his suspicions."

And Guido repeated to the others what he had just told Catesby, with a few additional details. The others sat silently for a minute. They were all aware of the importance of secrecy.

"Come on, my merry men. Don't you look so gloomy." Catesby said, "Let us hear what Guido has to tell us about his journey to Flanders."

"Well, before I do that, I would just like to tell you fellows that before I went abroad, I discovered that some of the gunpowder in London had gone bad, that is, had gone damp. So I spoke to several soldiers I know in Flanders and I managed to obtain some more."

"Didn't they ask you what you wanted it for?" Percy asked.

"Yes. I told them it was for demolishing an old wall, and that seemed to have satisfied them."

"You couldn't have dried it out instead of buying more?" Percy persisted.

"Well, sometimes that has been known to work on occasion, but at other times it has led to terrible accidents, with people getting blown up as a stray spark has set it off. But anyway, that problem has been taken care of. So, let me give you a report about my journey to Flanders. Ah, that's what the first line of your code means," Guido said suddenly to Catesby pointing to his list which was lying on the table in front of him. "GF Fl S O. Guido Fawkes, Flanders, Stanley and Owen."

"Very good," Catesby said patting his friend on the shoulder. "Now tell us what happened in Flanders."

"Nothing. Nothing much," replied Guido shrugging his shoulders. He turned to Catesby. "I told you that I was not the bearer of glad tidings."

"Please continue," urged Percy.

"Well, I met Sir William Stanley and Hugh Owen near Amsterdam, and I tried to impress upon them the seriousness of our plans and said that we are in need of more money. But I must say their support if any, seemed rather lukewarm."

"What do you mean?"

"I tried to impress upon them how the king had hardened his heart against the Catholics in England, rather like Pharaoh hardening his heart towards the Children of Israel in Egypt, but they didn't really seem to understand me."

"How so?"

Guido stopped and thought for a moment before continuing with his report. "They kept talking about this new Anglo-Spanish treaty, and that if the king was dealing with Catholic Spain, then surely I must be mistaken. I kept telling them that it was they who were mistaken, but I fear I did not convince them."

"So are they going to help us in any way?" asked Wintour.

"Well, in the end they did give me some money, which I have buried in the garden in London, but I fear we will not be able to count on them in the future and…"

"So anything we plan to do we'll have to do ourselves, without the Spanish," Percy said bitterly, concluding Guido's report.

"Aye, you are right there," Guido said. "I'm sorry, but that's how I see it too."

For a moment there was silence. All that could be heard was the hum of voices in the inn, while the sounds of horse brasses and hoofs could be heard in the yard from outside.

"Come on, cheer up you fellows," Catesby said pointing to the second row of initials on his page. "I have some better news."

Three pairs of eyes looked up at him expectantly.

"Has the king been stabbed at last?" asked Percy, dry as ever.

"Are the laws against recusants about to be changed?" Wintour asked.

"No," Catesby said with a smile. "This news isn't as good as that, but what I want to say is that I've bought in three more men into our secret."

"Who?"

Catesby looked at Thomas Wintour. "The first is your brother Robert."

"Robert? My brother? Sweet Jesus!" Wintour swore. "I was thinking of telling him all the time, but I never did. And now you have. Well that is good news indeed."

"Who else?" Guido asked as Wintour sat there digesting the latest piece of news.

"Kit Wright."

"Jack's brother?"

"Aye. He's a useful man to have around. I've heard that he's a good a swordsman as Jack, and God knows, we may have need of such men one day."

Guido smiled as he thought back on his happy schooldays with the Wright brothers.

"And the third man is?" asked Wintour, having apparently recovered from hearing about his brother joining them.

"John Grant."

"John Grant?" Wintour asked. "My brother-in-law?"

"Aye, and my kinsman" Catesby replied. "Come, Thomas Wintour. You don't look pleased at the news."

"Well, I'm not sure he's a suitable addition," Wintour said carefully.

"Why?"

"First of all, I think he is rather a scholarly and withdrawn person. And as far as I know, he prefers reading serious treatises to while away the time, and sometimes I think that when the time comes to take action, he seems rather slow."

"You maybe right there, but you cannot deny that he does show spirit when he has to," Catesby said in Grant's defence.

"How? When?" Guido asked. "Remember, I'm not one of your cousins or in-laws and I've never heard of this John Grant before."

"Oh well, you should have. His name is so feared by those prosecutors and government agents who have come to his house at Norbrook, near Stratford looking for hidden priests that they have given up looking there entirely," Catesby said with a grin. "In fact, according to Father John Gerard, my kinsman prefers to pay his tormentors not with crowns of gold, but with cracked heads instead. Thomas Wintour, your scholarly brother-in-law, as you describe him, is sometimes less than scholarly in his behaviour, preferring to berate these people soundly rather than letting them step foot in Norbrook."

"So it seems," Guido summarized, "that John Grant may be a scholar and not a swordsman or soldier, but he is certainly able to take care of himself."

"That's true enough," Catesby agreed. "You should have seen him at the Essex Rebellion."

"He was there too? It seems that half the Catholic men of England were there."

"Aye, he was there too. Together with me, Jack Wright and Francis Tresham."

"Who's Francis Tresham?"

Catesby smiled. "Oh, he's another in the Catesby, Wintour and Tresham family. No doubt we'll meet him sometime. But now let us return to what we have to do here in Bath."

"Wait a moment Robin," Guido said and started counting something off on his fingers. "That means," he said, "that there are eleven of us now in our secret."

"No," Catesby said quietly. "There are twelve of us."

"How so?" Percy asked.

"Because I confessed all of our plans to..."

"Father Gerard?" Percy continued.

"No, Thomas. To Father Tesimond."

"Father Tesimond?" Guido asked, his mouth open in surprise. "Father Oswald Tesimond from York?"

"Yes. Why?"

"Because he was at school with me. At St. Peter's. I was there with him and Jack and Kit Wright."

"I know," Catesby said. "Except that for today, for obvious reasons, he sometimes uses the name of Father Greenway."

"And you confessed everything to him?"

"Aye."

"Including our names?"

"No. Fear not. I just told him our plans." He looked around at the three men. "I told him all this within the confessional, so our secret is safe with him. Forever."

"I hope so," Percy said fervently. "If Father Tesimond, or Greenway as he calls himself is ever interrogated, yon Cecil's men have ways of making the bravest of men tell all they know. Few men can withstand the rack." And he drew his forefinger across his neck and grimaced horribly. They all stopped and thought of this ever-present threat to their plans. Racking bodies and leaking secrets.

"When did you confess all this to Father Tesimond?" Guido asked after a while.

"A couple of months ago. And it has been on my conscience since then, that I did not confess it to you all at the time. But our secret was just too much for me to bear alone."

"Robin, where did all this take place?" Percy asked.

"In a room in Thames Street."

"By the Tower?"

"Aye. Naturally we were the only people there."

"Naturally," added Percy dryly. "Well let us hope and pray that Father Tesimond's conscience is stronger than yours, Robin. For if not, we will not live out our threescore years and ten."

Fortunately perhaps for Percy and the others, that they did not realize how close he was to the truth. Catesby's confession to Tesimond proved too much for his friend and confessor to bear, and soon after, while kneeling in confession,

Father Tesimond confessed all that he knew to Father Henry Garnet. Tesimond was able to quieten his conscience by saying that he had told everything informally to Garnet in a garden and not in a confessional. Garnet understood the spirit of Tesimond's words but saw them as a confession nevertheless. This meant that he could not divulge any of this information to the authorities if the situation ever arose, even though he was completely shocked by what he had heard.

Perhaps, in an effort to alleviate his own spiritual torment, Father Garnet wrote to his own mentor in Rome. He asked him for two things. First of all he wanted advice on how to handle this matter, both physically and metaphysically, and he also requested some form of injunction that he could use to prevent the conspirators from carrying out their terrible deed. He also contacted Sir Edmund Baynham, the English Catholic missionary to Rome to see if he could help him.

In fact, Father Garnet went even further than this and wrote to Pope Paul V urging him to make a public statement against the use of violence as a means to achieving ones ends, however noble they may seem. After informing the authorities in Rome, Garnet sat back and waited. Since he was bound by an oath of secrecy to Father Tesimond, he felt that for the time being he had done all he could in order to prevent the plotters from carrying out their conspiracy.

Of course, none of the plotters had any idea of these behind-the-scenes activities, as Catesby ordered another pitcher of ale and some more bread and cheese, before outlining further details.

"The last thing gentlemen, that we must talk about this evening is are we to warn anybody about what we are about to do?"

He looked around at each of them in turn.

"What do you mean?" Wintour asked.

"Well," Catesby said slowly. "Since we last met, I have been giving this matter some serious thought. And even though I said the cruel situation we Catholics find ourselves in this country needs a sharp remedy, I have been wondering if our proposed remedy may not be a little too sharp."

"What? Not kill the king?" Guido asked.

"No, not that Guido. That we must do. But should we try and warn some of the Catholic gentlemen who will be sitting there in Parliament with the king that night?"

"Who are you thinking about?" Wintour asked.

"Well, I am thinking of at least four such gentlemen." And Catesby counted them off on his fingers. "First, the Earl of Northumberland."

"My patron," said Percy.

"Aye. And then there is Sir Edward Harewell."

"From Worcestershire?"

"Aye. And then there is Baron Stourton."

"And who else?"

"Baron Monteagle."

"You mean William Parker?"

"Aye. The same."

"Isn't that the man who fought with Essex in Ireland and was even knighted for it?"

"Aye."

"So," continued Wintour. "He is not likely to prattle to the authorities then. After all, if I recall, after Essex's Rebellion, he even tried to stop Cecil's men from proclaiming Essex as a traitor."

"True," Percy added. "And didn't he surrender after that and then spend some six months in the Tower?"

"Aye."

"And then he was forced to pay a huge fine, no?" Percy continued.

"That's right Thomas," Catesby said. "I heard that it was about eight thousand pounds."

"Then it doesn't sound as if this Monteagle is going to rush off to Cecil's men and blab his mouth off about us then, does it?"

"So now," Catesby said tapping on the table. "We have to decide. Shall we warn a few select gentlemen about our plans or not? Or will they have to pay the same price as the king and his ministers?"

However, this question was not to be answered. For just then the landlord came over and told them that as his wife was ill, he would have to close earlier than usual that night. And if the good gentlemen wished to continue their conversation, "their business meeting," he said looking at Catesby, then they could do so at the "*Three Castles*" in nearby York Street. "They serve good wine there, but not so good as here, of course."

And with that unexpected announcement, the Bath meeting came to an abrupt end. It was resumed a few days later, at a small out-of-the-way tavern in

Lambeth, not too far from Catesby's London address. This time all the plotters except Thomas Bates were present.

As the men were settling down around the long table, Catesby asked Jack Wright to bring in two more chairs.

"We are going to have some company soon, gentlemen," he announced.

"Who? Monteagle or Stourton?" Guido asked.

"Neither. I have asked my cousin Francis Tresham to join us together with Sir Everard Digby."

"Is that wise?" Percy asked.

"Why do you ask?"

"Robin, if you haven't noticed, unlike you, I tend to be a trifle more suspicious of my fellow man than you. And I think that the more people who know about us, the more dangerous it is. Our secret will soon be leaking out like a pail of water full of holes."

"My friend," Catesby said, laying a leader's hand on Percy's shoulder. "Think about it like this. A dozen of us are not enough, even if we are all devoted to the cause. Listen, I have learnt that Parliament is finally going to open in a couple of weeks' time, on November the fifth to be exact. If we are hoping to lead a successful rising after the explosion, then we must expand our numbers, no?"

Percy nodded his head in agreement, but it was clear that he was not fully convinced by Catesby's pragmatism

"So tell us something about your cousin before he arrives," Guido said. "For after all, it behoves all of us to know as much as we can about each other."

"True," said Ambrose. " *Nam et ipsa scienta potest as est.* "

"Pardon me, my good Latin scholar," said Jack Wright standing up to make a mock bow. "But could you translate that for such an unlettered Yorkshireman as my humble self?"

"Of course, you Northern clodpoll," Ambrose replied smiling. "It means 'Knowledge itself is power.'"

"And where did you find that one in the Bible?"

"It's not from the Bible. Sir Francis Bacon said it while..."

"Gentlemen," interrupted Catesby. "We are not here to discuss Latin philosophy. Come, let us return to our own matters. Now, as I was telling you about Francis Tresham, he is of our age and like us he has sorely suffered for his Catholic beliefs. His father, Sir Thomas Tresham was tried in the Star Chamber for harbouring Father Edmund Campion. As a result, he was imprisoned or kept under close house-arrest for seven years. Then, if that wasn't enough, he was fined very heavily at least twice for recusancy."

"So young Francis cannot have loved Cecil and his government much if that's what they did to his father," Kit Wright reflected aloud.

"True Kit. And then he himself was also arrested and imprisoned."

"When?"

"About ten years ago, when he was accused of being involved in the 'Poisoned Pommel' conspiracy and..."

"Ah, that's where I've heard of him," Jack Wright broke in. "Don't you remember him brother?" he said turning to Kit.

"Aye, I do now. And wasn't he involved in the Essex Rebellion as well?"

"Yes," Catesby said. "But he managed to get out of that by bribing someone. I think he paid him over one thousand pounds. And then after that, he still had to pay another two thousand in fines."

"Well it's a good thing he has that sort of money, for we will be needing some more shortly," Percy noted.

"And who is this Digby fellow?" Guido asked. He was feeling a little out of his depth, for it seemed whenever Catesby mentioned someone's name, he was either related to them, or that they had taken part in some common action in the past such as the abortive Essex Rebellion.

"Everard Digby," Catesby said. "Nobleman, bon-vivant and gallant courtier. In a way he is much like you Ambrose, and like you two, Jack and Kit. He's an excellent swordsman and he has some fine horses too."

"But are you sure he's a Catholic, Robin?" Ambrose asked. "For I have heard that he has been accepted in the highest levels of society and has even been called 'the goodliest man in the whole court'."

"Well, lay your doubts at rest Master Rookwood," Catesby replied authoritatively. "He converted to Catholicism several years ago. Father Gerard was responsible for that, and since then, you will find no stauncher Catholic than he. So now my friends," he concluded looking around the crowded table, "we now number thirteen."

"Hmm," muttered Thomas Percy. "The same number as Jesus Christ's disciples. Well let's hope that no-one here is called Judas Iscariot."

They all looked at him. He held up his hands in an act of surrender.

"'Tis true my friends. That was a tasteless jest and I withdraw it. I beg your forgiveness."

The tension was relieved just then as the assembled men heard a triple knock on the door. Catesby rose to unlock the door and then ushered in Francis Tresham and Sir Everard Digby. Both men were well, even fashionably well-dressed in doublets and jerkins of rich material. They both wore slashed and padded breeches and looked as affluent as any up-and-coming courtier could hope to look. They had each crowned their whole appearance by wearing fashionable hats, Tresham's being made of dark velvet, while Sir Everard's velvet hat was of a lighter hue, but trimmed with a dark brown slinky fur. The whole effect was to remind the seated men that Catesby had said that the two newcomers had money, and that the picture of these two framed in the open doorway certainly confirmed it.

They looked around at the men at the table, and taking their cue from Catesby, they removed their hats and cloaks before sitting down. After a few minutes spent in exchanging news and gossip with the new arrivals, Catesby knocked on the table with a small beaker and called the meeting back to order.

"Gentlemen, I would like to remind you we are here for a purpose, and not just to gossip here like a crowd of fishwives."

This had the desired effect. To be compared to a crowd of gossiping fishwives was no great honour and all attention was now concentrated on Robert Catesby.

"Thank you gentlemen. So now I would like to remind you that we have a definite date on which to execute our plans."

"I don't like the word 'execute,'" said Percy.

"Listen, Percy old fellow. Will you please give your imagination and vocabulary a rest?" Jack Wright said, sliding a pitcher of wine over the table to him. "Take a drink of this. That should help your sense of humour."

Percy took a good swallow, wiped his mouth with the back of his hand and smiled. "You were right, Jack. I needed that."

"So now we're all together, that is apart from Thomas Bates, let's talk about our final plans." Catesby took out a piece of paper full of strange looking marks and squiggles.

Something about the words 'final plans' seemed to cut through any feelings of joviality. All twelve men pulled their chairs nearer the dark oval table in a collective act of concentration and leaned in as one towards its centre.

"This is how I see it," Catesby started in a very matter-of-fact tone. "Guido here, as our most experienced man with gunpowder will be responsible for lighting the fuses. He will fire a slow fuse, as he explained it to me once, and as soon as he has done so, he will flee the scene and take a boat across to the south bank. For obvious reasons, he will not land near my house in Lambeth. Is that understood, Guido?"

The experienced man of gunpowder nodded his head solemnly and Catesby continued in the same factual manner. "At the same time, there will be a rising in the Midlands amongst our own people. Later on we will see who of us here will be responsible for organizing that. I think it should be carried out by those of us who live in the area. After all, they know the people better and that they are also more familiar with the roads there. But don't you look so worried Jack and Kit. Your knowledge of the North will also come in useful, but at a later stage. In the meantime, I am sure your swordsmanship will be in demand. Have no fear about that," he added, as the two Yorkshire brothers were looking downcast and disappointed about apparently being left out of all the action, at least at the beginning.

"Now, while all this is taking place, a number of us with some other supporters will take over Princess Elizabeth from her country home near Coventry..."

"Coombe Abbey?" Ambrose asked.

"Aye, and then she will be held until such time that we can proclaim her as the future queen and..."

"Sorry for interrupting you, Robin, but what do I do after I have escaped?" Guido asked suddenly.

"I was just coming to that. You will make your way back to Flanders and raise support for us there. You are to inform King Philip, either yourself, or someone you can trust completely, and tell him that the coast is clear for him to come and help us with both men and money. Of course, you will have to explain to him, that killing King James was a necessary step and that he, King Philip should not think that just because he signed a treaty with England last year, that he will be next. You will tell him that this blow is against Protestants, not against kings. I am sure, that once he understands why we had to remove the king, he will forget his compromise with Protestantism." Catesby stopped and looked around at the assembled men. "Does anyone have any questions?"

There were none. It all seemed to make sense. Catesby's plan and planning seemed perfectly logical. For most of them, they had talked and thought of little else since Robert Catesby had first broached the matter to them months ago.

Now all that was needed was to carry out this bold plan. As far as they could see, the planning stages were over. Only a few more minor details needed to be arranged and put into place. Then England would revert to the Old Faith of Mary Tudor and England's Catholics would be able to hold their heads up high again, as proud and God-fearing Catholics living as their brothers in Spain and the Spanish Netherlands.

Thomas Percy's cynical remarks about execution and Judas Iscariot were forgotten entirely as the meeting broke up and they all quietly melted into the evening crowds walking along the Thames at Lambeth. Now all they had to do was cause the divine light, the Catholic light to shine once again in the new England of Queen Elizabeth II, Queen Elizabeth Stuart.

Chapter Eight
Lord Robert Cecil Takes a Hand

Queen Elizabeth! Queen Elizabeth Stuart! What a lot of villainous nonsense! What a lot of arrant stupidity! The arrogance of it all! I, Robert Cecil, the First Earl of Salisbury, the man who has served two monarchs, first, Queen Elizabeth until her death two years ago, and now King James, should be deceived by this bunch of traitorous Catholic upstarts? Who do they think they are fooling? I've been following their petty games ever since James VI came down from Scotland to become King James I here in London. And they're not the first band of Catholic traitors that I have known about. Or dealt with. Oh no!

What about the Main and the Bye plots? And the Des Trappes plot, with its forged documents and the French ambassador? Trying to put a bag of gunpowder under the queen's bed. Of course I knew about these plots. Oh, these Catholics never learn. Still, one has to be aware of such devious conspiracies if one is to serve His Majesty well, no? And we all know how sensitive he is with regards to plots and plotters. Well, he would be, wouldn't he? After all, his own father Henry Darnley was blown sky high while lying abed in Kirk o' Field near Edinburgh castle one night. And if that weren't bad enough, the king himself was nearly assassinated in the Gowrie conspiracy at the turn of the century. So I'm not really surprised that His Majesty insists on wearing thickly padded clothes. After all, they should keep the murderer's dagger out. In fact, I'd also wear such padding if I were in his position.

But these conspirators, you know what they remind me of? Of a nest of ants, that's what. They're all busy running around, scurrying about hither and thither, to and fro, leaving trails and messages and all feeling full of their own self-importance. And they're so busy, so preoccupied with all this, that they do not notice the outside world looking on. And oh, how we've been looking on! After all, we've had enough practice at it, no?

"Who's 'we?'" you may ask. Oh my father and myself of course, to say nothing of Walsingham, Sir Francis Walsingham that is. But more about him later. But first let me tell you a little about my father, William Cecil, Lord

Burghley, or Burley, if you prefer.

Now here was a man who went through many ups and downs during his life, and remember, he lived a long life too. When he died, some seven years ago in 1598, he was 78 years old. He started in public life as a Secretary to the powerful Duke of Somerset, you know, the duke who acted as Protector for the young King Edward VI. But as luck would have it, Somerset fell and my father was sent to the Tower. Fortunately for him, he was only there for two months, and a year later he was the Secretary of State again and was even knighted for his troubles. So much for the wheel of fate, if you believe in that sort of thing. I don't. But I am convinced that we are what we make of ourselves. Anyway, I have to admit it though, but I think my father must have been a somewhat devious character, for when Mary Tudor became queen, he became a Catholic and was even sent on a mission to see the Pope in Rome. Someone even compared him to a cat, which, when thrown, always lands on its feet. Not very flattering perhaps, but true nevertheless.

Anyway, he then became involved in some dangerous politics again when he signed a document which nominated that poor girl, Lady Jane Grey as Edward's successor. And again my pater was lucky. For he was able to convince the authorities that he had only signed the paper as a passive witness and that saved him from being tried for treason. So during Mary Tudor's reign he laid low most of the time, but remained in secret communication with her sister, Princess Elizabeth. Then when Mary died in 1558 and Elizabeth became queen, my father's career really began to flourish. Even though she used to argue with him and threaten to box his ears and send him back to the Tower, she really appreciated him and employed him as her Principal Secretary of State for the next forty years until he died seven years ago. In fact, his last position was Lord Treasurer. Like me, he worked hard to rid this country of its Catholics and nothing kept him happier than when he heard of the failure of such Catholic or Spanish actions, such as the destruction of the Spanish Armada in 1588.

So where my father controlled foreign policy, that is, as far as Elizabeth allowed him to do so, Sir Francis Walsingham built up his network of spies, and out of his own pocket too, in order to control and intimidate the Catholic population here in England. He was another ingenious fellow, that Sir Francis Walsingham, forever setting up spy networks, such as the one that Gilbert Gifford fellow was in, allowing us to learn about Babington's plot to free Mary Queen of Scots. But that wasn't the only plot that Walsingham uncovered. Oh no, not he. For that spider, as the Catholics called him, also had spies planted in Flanders and the Low Countries as well. Sometimes he would catch someone, say, a Catholic, and just before he was about to be tortured, Walsingham would promise him his life, if he agreed to work for him instead. Oh you would be surprised to see how many of these staunch Papists would break, even before they were tortured. All you had to do was just take them down to the dungeons in the Tower, really slimy holes they are, and show them some hot irons, thumb screws or the rack itself, and these Catholics would become your best friends for life. As both my father and Walsingham would ask: What can you do with a dead Catholic? They would only become martyrs and besides, turning them into spies was much more profitable.

You see, I said my father was devious, no? Well, although he was determined to rid the country of the Catholics and limit the Spanish influence at court and elsewhere, he didn't want to rub their noses in the dirt too much, for he wished to keep the Franco-Spanish pot boiling happily. As he reckoned, while they were busy battling each other in Europe and on the high seas, they would leave us well alone here in England. And I must say, for the most part, the old man was right. And that is where he and the queen always saw eye to eye. They both considered that war and fighting was a stupid waste of money, especially if you could get what you wanted by cheaper and more peaceful ways.

And that is what these Catholic extremists have not yet comprehended. I have, with the king, King James that is, made peace with Spain. This is not because I love or respect King Philip III, who in my opinion is really a weak ruler who is only interested in court amusements and his wife Margaret of Austria, but because a state of peace will allow us to grow and prosper here in England.

Oh yes. There's one more chapter in my father's story I feel that I should tell you about. That is the one concerning his main political enemy, Robert Devereux, the Earl of Essex. Now that was something. He was known as the queen's favourite courtier, and as such he felt he could get away with murder. Well, he and my father fought like cats to obtain more influence and favours at court. Sometimes it was my father's turn to be on top, sometimes it was Essex's. In a way it was easier for Essex. After all, he had been knighted for gallantry while fighting in the Netherlands and had returned to court as a hero. This had helped him gain the upper hand with the queen, but then he threw this advantage away because he loved to quarrel. And if that wasn't enough, he went and angered the queen by going and marrying the widow of Sir Philip Sidney. Then, for a while he was no longer the queen's 'dearest Robin,' especially when he turned his back on her in front of the whole court and she then boxed his ears in return!

Well it was about this time that my father died and I took over the helm. I wasn't completely new or inexperienced for this position, as my father had been an excellent teacher and I had been a more than a willing pupil. In any case, I had undergone my own practical training as well. I had thrice been an M.P. in 1584, 1586 and again in 1589. The first two times I represented Westminster and the last time I represented Hertfordshire.

I had also served Her Majesty by going abroad with the Earl of Derby in order to negotiate a peace treaty with Spain in 1588. We failed, but the mission taught me more about people's minds as well as the art of conducting negotiations. It was also about this time that I married Elizabeth Brooke and then we had two children. Our daughter was named Elizabeth, in honour of the queen and my son William was named after my father. The queen must have been pleased with me, for soon after she knighted me, and then at the age of 28 I was sworn in as the youngest member of her Privy Council.

But none of this of course prevented Essex from trying out his old tricks on me just as he had tried with my father. Soon we were arguing over all the different spheres of influence at court, and especially vicious were our fights about the post of Master of the Court of Wards and Liveries. This was a powerful position and after a long, and may I say, a dirty fight, I won.

After the dust had settled over this affair I managed to persuade Essex to go to Ireland and bring some law and order into that outlandish place. I made this offer sound like his earlier Flanders success and he jumped at the opportunity. But don't misunderstand me. I wasn't being generous for nothing, and I certainly wasn't giving him the chance to regain his position as the royal favourite again. Oh no. All I wanted was for him to be out of court. But things didn't go according to plan for either of us. Within six months he had failed to make any headway against the Irish Catholics and to make matters worse, he abandoned his men in Ireland and rushed back to London without the queen's permission.

And if all that weren't bad enough, as soon as he reached the court, he burst into the queen's private apartments unannounced, and if what the gossips reported is true, the queen wasn't dressed, how shall I put it? - completely royally. She was furious with him and cast him out of court in disgrace for some time, and in public too! For a man of his status, that was a terrible punishment. He was also forced to cool his heels in the Tower for nearly a year, but then the queen in her own unpredictable way brought him back to court again. Women! I'll never understand them.

It was also during this time that my father put forward the idea of King James VI of Scotland succeeding the queen, but I preferred the Spanish Archduchess Isabella for this role. This would have bought peace to England but then Essex got up to his old tricks again. He decided to incite the City of London against the queen with that fiasco of a Rebellion of his. Fortunately he lost, the Rebellion fizzled out and he was condemned for treason. This time his charm failed him and anyway, Elizabeth had had enough of him by now. He was beheaded at the Tower in February 1601.

For reasons best kept to myself, I decided that in the end it would be better if King James VI became the next king of England instead of Isabella. And so when Elizabeth died at the beginning of 1603, I was one of those who were instrumental in making sure that the throne passed quickly and smoothly over to the new king. For most people, this was the first time that they had seen a change in the monarchy. Elizabeth had reigned for 45 years, glorious years, and as far as I was especially concerned, they were 45 glorious Protestant years.

Soon after King James was crowned, I put down two potential insurrections-the Bye Plot and the Main plot. Fortunately they didn't amount to much, and I was able to spare one of the chief plotters, my brother-in-law, Lord Cobham as well as Sir Walter Raleigh. I was also able to save Sir Griffin Markham from the axe and then exiled the thankful man to the Continent. There, taking a leaf out of Walsingham's book, I had Sir Griffin act as one of my spies and keep a weather eye on such notorious Catholics as Sir William Stanley and Hugh Owen. However, the Catholic priests, Clarke and Watson, who were involved in this shambles weren't so lucky

They were hanged, drawn and quartered, a punishment they both richly deserved. However, I must admit it, the English Catholics were quite shocked by this treatment of their Holy Fathers, but I believe in justice being seen to be done. Still, as Sir Francis Bacon would phrase it, I suppose that this was a kind of 'wild justice,' all in all.

Of course none of this made me popular with the Catholic community in England and because of my hunched back, more than one comparison was made between King Richard III and me. You've heard of him surely? The last of the

Plantagenet kings who was supposed to have murdered the two little princes in the Tower.

Anyway, after those two plots had been put down, quite a number of Catholic gentry approached me and stated quite clearly that all they wanted was peace and quiet. I know that many others continued living their recusant existence, especially those living in the Midlands and in Northamptonshire, but as long as they kept their beliefs and practices secret, or at least not spread their dubious ideas about, I was not going to be troubled by this. After all is said and done, it is impossible to run a kingdom if everyone lives their lives in permanent fear, no? Then nothing is achieved. Pragmatism often needs to be stronger than principles. Just remember how my father became a Catholic, albeit temporarily, over fifty years ago. Of course some of the Catholics decided to give up the fight simply because they were tired of it, but others, like Baron Monteagle decided to do so, so that his family honours and estates would be returned to him. The king also approved of this pragmatic policy of live and let live, and I even have before me here Monteagle's letter to the king. Just listen to this excerpt:

> *I was bred up in the Romish religion and walked in that because I knew no better...I had come to discern the ignorance I was formerly wrapped in, as I now wonder that either myself, or any other of common understanding, should be so blinded.*

Anyway, after reading such noble and pious sentiments, I decided that this Baron Monteagle was a good man to cultivate. In the same way that I made sure that no harm was to befall Lord Cobham or Sir Griffin Markham, I decided it was my duty to look after Monteagle. Therefore I was not surprised when yesterday evening, that is October the twenty-sixth, Monteagle himself, looking very flustered, suddenly appeared at my Whitehall home. I was just about to take a light supper with the Earls of Suffolk, Worcester and Northampton when my servant ushered him into the room. He seemed quite flustered and immediately requested a private word with me. After offering him a goblet of good French wine to calm himself down, I took him to a small room at the back of the house and asked him what was the cause of his present state of agitation. Without saying a word, he put his hand into his jacket and pulled out a neatly folded page on which was written the following letter:

> *my lord, out of the love i bear to some of your friends i have a care of your preservation therefore i would advise you, as you tender your life to devise some excuse to shift of your attendance at this parliament for god*

and man have concurred to punish the wickedness of this time and think not slightly of this advertisement but retire yourself into your country where you may expect the event in safety for though there be no appearance of stir yet I say they shall receive a terrible blow this parliament and yet they shall not see who hurts them this counsel is not to be condemned because it may do you good and can do you no harm for the danger is passed as soon as you have burnt the letter and i hope god will give you the grace to make good use of it to whose holy protection commend you
To the right honourable
The Lord Monteagle.

After re-reading it, I asked Monteagle if I could keep the letter for a while. He agreed and I then put it in a locked strongbox. By now, he was in a much calmer state of mind. I suppose the passing of time and the sharing of his knowledge with me, as well as a draught of good red wine also helped. We then had a conversation which went something like this:

"So tell me my good Lord, how did you come by this letter?"

"Well my Lord Secretary, it was like this. It all happened yesterday evening. I was at home, at my place in Hoxton, you know, just a few miles north of London and I was about to sit down for my evening meal. Just then..."

"Excuse me, but when did you sit down to eat?"

"Oh, about seven o'clock, sire."

"Please continue."

"So, as I was saying, I was about to sit down to partake of my evening meal when one of my servants approached me. Naturally I thought he was about to bring me the sauce that I had requested, but instead, he gave me the letter you have just read and locked away."

"Did you question him on how he obtained this letter?"

"Of course. He said that someone had given it to him just a little while earlier, while he was busy running an errand for me."

"But did he say who actually gave it to him?"

"No, sire. That he did not say. He just said that the person was completely unknown to him."

"Well did he say what this unknown messenger looked like?"

"Yes, sire."

"Well, that's good. So what did he look like?"

"My servant said that he was reasonably tall and that he charged him, my servant that is, to make sure he placed this letter in my hand personally."

"And that's all the description of have of your messenger? 'A reasonably tall man.' I'm afraid that is not very helpful, my lord. Now tell me this. Was this letter sealed when your servant gave it to you? Do you know if your servant had read the letter at all, that is before you?"

"Oh no, sire. I can assure you that apart from your good self, no one else has read this letter. I haven't even shown it to Mistress Elizabeth."

"Mistress Elizabeth?"

"My wife sire."

"Ah yes, of course. I had forgotten her name. It was Elizabeth Tresham, no?"

"Yes, sire. She is the younger sister of Francis Tresham."

"Hmm. One of those noisome Catholics."

"Pardon me, sire?"

"No, no, it's nothing. Please continue Monteagle. What you are telling me is most interesting."

"Well as you can guess my Lord, I was somewhat perplexed by this letter, and as a dutiful and loyal subject of His Majesty, I saw that it was my duty to convey this letter to you and inform you of its rather surprising, nay, shocking contents."

"You certainly did the right thing there. But my dear Lord Monteagle, do you not have any idea at all who was the author of this letter, or who sent it?"

"No, sire. However, I could not help but notice that there are some errors in the spelling and that there are no capital letters nor punctuation."

"That's right. But let us examine it again." I took it out of the strongbox and reread it, carefully. Twice, in fact. Monteagle was right. The letter had been badly written in a small and cursive hand and Monteagle's comments were correct.

"How very curious. Tell me Monteagle, what do you make of it?"

"Well, sire. It would seem that it was written by someone who cares sufficiently about the safety of my person but, that that person is barely literate. Or, I think..." Monteagle began.

"Think what?"

"Or, and this sire is only a faint possibility, I must add, but maybe, er...maybe, it was written by someone who is completely literate, but who, for some reason best known to himself, wishes to disguise his writing from me and so conceal his identity, sire."

"Well, can you think of such a person?"

"No, sire. I have been racking my brains ever since I received this letter and I have not been able to come up with the name of a single person."

"Monteagle, are you sure?"

"Yes, sire. I cannot think of any semi-literate person, say a servant who would wish to warn me in this manner. And equally, I cannot think of any literate person I know who could not tell me to my face about the 'terrible blow,' as they put it that will occur at the opening of Parliament in a few days."

"Now think carefully, my dear Monteagle. Are you sure it couldn't be a member of your family who wishes to warn you? Remember, and this is a trifle distasteful for me to say this, but you are related to some well-known recusant Catholics, are you not?"

"Sire?"

"You know, like your wife's family, the Treshams, or her cousins, the Catesbys. And, if I am not mistaken, you yourself are related, that is by marriage, to the Wintour family and the Grants, no?"

I noticed that at this point, he hung his head low and blushed like a chastened schoolboy. He began to squirm uncomfortably in his chair, but that did not bother me.

"Yes, that is true, sire, but I rarely ever see any of the people you have just mentioned. And that is especially true since our present king ascended the throne."

"That is good to hear, Monteagle, but were not you once more deeply involved with that Robert Catesby fellow? You know the one who used to live at Ashby St. Ledgers in Northamptonshire with his mother. Am I correct in thinking thus?"

"Oh sire, that was about four years ago when I made the foolish mistake of joining Essex's Rebellion and..."

"And you fell into the Thames beating a hasty retreat, no?"

"Yes, sire, and very embarrassing it was sire."

"And no doubt the eight thousand pound fine was very embarrassing too, was it not?"

"Yes, sire. But I have learnt my lesson well since then my Lord and I have nothing to do with those Catholics today."

I didn't want to make him feel too uncomfortable about this unfortunate escapade, so I changed the subject.

"Good. So let us return to the present. You have absolutely no idea who sent you this letter?"

"None whatsoever, sire."

"And are you convinced that your servant did not recognize the man who gave him this letter?"

"Yes, sire."

"Well in that case, there is not much we can do about this at this late hour, so I suggest that you return home now. But you must promise me not to mention a word about this to anyone."

"Fear not, sire. I give you my word. *Dictum meum pactum*."

"My word is my bond. Nothing like Latin to add a certain solemnity to the occasion, is there? So I will bid you good night Lord Monteagle and sleep well. You may rest assured that your letter is in safe hands with me. No doubt we will get to the heart of this matter very shortly."

I then shook hands with him. My handshake was firm. His was loose and clammy. "All that remains for me to do," I said bringing this conversation to a close, "is to thank you once again for fulfilling your duty as a loyal subject to the crown and for bringing this note over to me as soon as possible. Good night, sir."

He nodded his head emphatically in agreement, obviously relieved that the knowledge and the responsibility of this letter had passed from his shoulders to mine, hunch-backed as they were. I then escorted him out of the room to where one of my servants gave him his hat and cloak. A few minutes later he was gone. I returned to the supper room to find Suffolk, Worcester and Northampton having an animated conversation about the new play '*The Honest Whore*' by Dekker and Middleton.

As soon as I entered the room, they stopped and immediately asked me the reason for Monteagle's surprise visit. Without showing them the actual letter, I told them of its contents and we then discussed this missive for nearly an hour. Worcester seemed to be quite knowledgeable about the present Catholic situation in England.

"Well, I for one have heard something about Catholic plots recently."

"Where? When?"

"Oh both here in England and also on the Continent."

"Can you be more specific?"

"Yes I can. There is, or there certainly was talk about some Catholic priests in France."

"And, my dear Worcester, what did these priests plan to do?"

"Well, sire, I'm not acquainted with all the details of course, but a William Turner..."

"One of our informers in Brussels?"

"Yes, well he told me that Hugh Owen and several other Jesuits had been overheard plotting some kind of invasion."

"Of England?"

"Yes."

"Who? Just them? Just this gang of Jesuits?"

"Oh no, my Lord Salisbury. They were to be supported by a number of French and Spanish Catholics. Something like fifteen hundred of them."

I told Worcester that I had already heard of such a plan, but I was glad that others had got wind of it too. This meant that too many people on both sides of the English Channel had loose tongues and that the chances of it succeeding would come to nought.

"Well, gentlemen," I said at last. "I think we have done a good night's work here. All that remains for us to do is to work on this information that Monteagle has brought us."

We discussed a few more details and soon after, the three earls left, well wrapped up in their cloaks to keep out the chilly late night air. I then sat back in my favourite leather armchair by the fire and began to take stock of this new situation.

Monteagle's information was certainly not new. Of course I knew that, through my informers, that certain Catholics were planning some mischief, but the question was, which plans were merely empty-headed ones and which ones could cause real murder and mayhem. I know that some people will hastily compare me with my father and Sir Francis Walsingham and say that I was really behind all this, just as a way to scourge these Catholics. Like I've heard it said on more than one occasion, that it was really Walsingham who was behind Babington's plot. Not that there wasn't a Catholic hot-head called Babington of course, but that that Gifford fellow kept urging him on, when all the time Gifford was being encouraged by Walsingham. This deviousness killed two sparrows with the same stone. It enabled Walsingham and my father to persuade

Elizabeth, after many delays, to sign the death warrant for Mary Queen of Scots and it also gave the authorities the opportunity to tighten the screws on the Catholics even more so.

Of course, now that Monteagle had brought me this letter, it put me in a bit of a sticky situation. On the one hand, could I admit that I already knew something about such plots, and that I was merely exploiting the very pliable and by now very nervous Lord Monteagle? However, on the other hand, should I hide behind its anonymity and claim that I had known absolutely nothing about the letter until it had been shown to me tonight? I had deliberately not shown it to the three earls. Certainly its scrawly writing and badly written style would not be able to be traced back to me, if at some later date I would be accused of causing Monteagle to fall into a trap. At this stage of course, I am not going to admit to any man if I did write this letter or not, or caused it to be written. But I may say something later if it proves beneficial.

All I know is, is that at this point I am going to show it to His Majesty when he returns from what he calls his 'hunting exercise' near Cambridge, but that won't be until the end of this month, October, that is, in a few days' time. If in the future I am asked why I didn't take it to the king immediately, I will say that he forbade me to disturb him on matters of state while he was away. And anyway, I will say that I was trying to deal with this matter in my own quiet way. If that isn't convincing enough, I will always be able to say that I postponed telling him so that the plotters would have more time to supply me with even more proof of their seditious plot. How will I phrase it? Probably something like, 'Give a man enough rope, and he will hang himself.' What an apt saying! These Catholic plotters will certainly do that. Of that I am sure.

Meanwhile I will inform the Master of the Guard, casually of course, to be more thorough. It would surely be very sad to let these miserable plotters succeed with their 'terrible blow' when we have most, if not all of the aces up our sleeve, no?

Chapter Nine
The Plot Begins to Unravel

Friday, November 1st 1605 was a typical November day in London; grey, miserable and threatening. The citizens of the nation's capital were going about their business unaware of the conspiracy that was beginning to unravel at the edges. As the many passenger-boats, ferries and ships of trade were sailing up and down the River Thames; as the many craftsmen, artisans and traders were trying to earn an honest living and as Messers. Richard Burbage and William Shakespeare were making their final preparations to present 'The Merry Wives of Windsor' at court in a day or so, King James was reading the Monteagle letter very closely.

Cecil had brought it to the king at Whitehall Palace as soon as His Majesty had returned from his hunting trip. The king looked as fit and as healthy as his ungainly and unathletic body would allow. He greeted his Principal Secretary as an old friend, which in fact he was, that is, as friendly as one could be with this somewhat distant-minded ruler who preferred writing academic treatises such as 'Basilikon Doron' or hunting.

"And so, Mr. Secretary, what make you of this letter?" the king asked while indicating that Cecil should approach him and sit down.

"Your Majesty, I think it was written by an idiot."

The king's eyebrows shot up for a second as he received this straight answer. "That is correct, my good Cecil, he is certainly illiterate. Just note the style and the lack of punctuation." And he pointed at various mistakes on the page as a schoolmaster might show an errant pupil where he had gone wrong.

"True sire. But what do you think lies behind this note? Why should anyone wish to warn Lord Monteagle? And what do you think they are warning him about?"

"Ah, Mr. Secretary. Let us read it again, but more carefully this time, and see if we can discover any secret or hidden messages concealed between the lines."

After having read the badly written warning yet again, Cecil looked up. "Your Majesty, I am sure that this letter is connected in some way to the Catholics in your kingdom."

"Yes?"

"In fact I would go as far as to say, Your Majesty, that it concerns not only your kingdom, but even you yourself and your Parliament."

"That makes sense," the king said as he too reread the letter for perhaps the tenth time that morning.

"But what I do not know, Sire is, what these plotters, and I assume there are several or even many of them, mean when they say 'to punish the wickedness of the time.' All I can say is that it certainly sounds like a religious phrase, or even one that has been taken from the Bible, say one that has been taken from the Book of Elijah or from the story of Job."

"I certainly agree with you there. Or perhaps it was taken from the book of Isaiah, you know, when he says, 'To loose the bands of wickedness, to undo the heavy burdens, and to let the oppressed go free.' That sounds like the language of a fanatical Catholic, don't you agree?"

"Yes, Your Majesty."

"But what I would dearly like to know," the king said knitting his brow as if he was attempting to solve some perplexing problem in Latin, "is what form this 'terrible blow' will take?"

"Your Majesty, I hate to say this and I hope that I am not over-reaching myself, but I think it could refer to an attempt to murder your royal self," Cecil said carefully.

"That may be the case, but I think that there is more to it than that. Look," he said, moving the royal finger over the unfolded and somewhat crumpled page. "First of all it says 'they shall receive a royal blow.' In other words, these plotters, these Catholics as you think they may be, are planning not just to harm me, but also to others who attend Parliament. And in addition to that," the king continued in his scholarly manner moving his ringed finger yet again across the page, "this letter says that whoever deals this 'terrible blow' will remain unseen."

"Yes sire. 'Yet they shall not see who hurts them.'"

"Aye," the king said in his thick Scottish accent. "And we think the only way they can do that is with gunpowder or poison, but we don't really think it is the latter, since that is normally used against individuals and not against a group of people such a gathering in Parliament. So my dear Cecil, we think the answer here is gunpowder."

"Your Majesty, are you sure?"

"Aye, my dear Cecil. You must remember, that for someone whose father was blown up in the middle of the night, we are more than a wee bit suspicious of invisible murderers. And this all but smacks of that, do you not agree?"

"Yes sire. I certainly do think that it is entirely within the realms of possibility. Especially sire, when one considers past plotters who had hoped to use similar means in order to achieve their murderous ends."

"Well Mr. Secretary, now that we agree that these plotters intend to blow us to kingdom come, though for the moment we prefer this present earthly kingdom, we must take preventative action. Today is the first of November, is it not?"

"Yes, sire."

"And Parliament is due to open next Tuesday..."

"On the fifth, sire."

"Aye, on the fifth. So therefore we must inform the Earl of Suffolk, in his capacity as Lord Chamberlain and the man who is responsible for the safety and orderly conduct of this Parliament, to be especially rigorous in his search for villains and their confounded gunpowder."

"Yes, sire. That is if they are to use gunpowder, sire. But anyway, I'll see to it that he is informed immediately."

"Good. But now Mr. Secretary, do you have any ideas who sent this warning letter to Lord Monteagle? He must be a Catholic, no? Well, at least to your way of thinking."

"Yes, sire. But one who has decided to shun the extremist Jesuits and their like." Cecil then smiled a half-smile and showed a few yellowing teeth. "Perhaps it is one who was forced to pay a heavy fine for recusancy and or who sat in prison for several months and has come to see the light as it were, sire."

"Are you implying Mr. Secretary, that he is one of your, how shall we describe him? one of your bearers of information?"

"Oh Your Majesty. I would not quite phrase it like that. But I am sure we will not find him consorting with such as those who wish to, as you said earlier, blow us to kingdom come."

"Well we are progressing, are we not? Now, who amongst Lord Monteagle's family and friends do you know to be fervent and active Catholic?" the king asked, draining off a goblet of wine.

"Active, Your Majesty?"

"Yes, actively involved in recusant politics and the like."

"I know his brother-in-law Francis Tresham could be such a character, sire."

"Why ? What do you know about him?"

"Sire, he is a very bitter and dubious person."

"Bitter and dubious? Why?"

"Well, this is partly something that he inherited from his father sire, that is Sir Thomas Tresham. He was rather a militant Catholic and spent about seven years, if I remember correctly, in the Fleet prison for his activities. And then when he was released sire, he started spending fortunes on building up his estates at Rushdon in Northamptonshire and at Lyvedon."

"Mr. Secretary. Permit us to say this, but you constantly amaze us at the amount of trifling yet obviously important information you always seem to have at your fingertips. How do you do it?"

"Thank you sire." And for once the Secretary blushed in embarrassment. "I think that it must be due to my father's training."

"Yes, possibly so. So, to return to young Francis Tresham. It seems that he came into property if not money then?"

"Yes and no, Your Majesty."

"Please explain yourself, sir."

"Francis Tresham certainly inherited property, but he also inherited his father's debts sire."

"How so?"

"Well, Your Majesty, his father it seems was very generous with his daughters' dowries, too generous in fact, and this meant..."

"...that young Francis had good reason to feel bitter."

"Yes, sire. And we know, that since then, he was involved in the Essex Rebellion."

"What, he too was involved in that great fiasco? It seems to me that many dissatisfied Catholics were involved in it as well, no?"

"Yes, sire. And as I was saying, my informers tell me that for the past four to five years, this Francis Tresham has been meeting with other Catholic recusants."

"Such as?"

"Robert Catesby sire, and Thomas Wintour for a start. And also one of their priests, a Father Henry Garnet. In addition, Tresham has been seen recently in the company of a certain Guy Fawkes."

"Oh I see, Mr. Secretary. Well we must say that you have certainly earned your position in our government. Your detailed knowledge about my subjects, especially my, let us say, potentially troublesome ones never ceases to amaze me. Tell me. Is there anyone you don't know anything about, or whom they see or meet with?"

Cecil lowered his head modestly. "Thank you, Your Majesty. Of course there are several other Catholics we are investigating and no doubt I will be able to inform you of their whereabouts and activities soon."

"No doubt. And who else are you investigating?"

"Thomas Habington sire. Lord Monteagle's brother-in-law."

"Ah yes. We have heard of this man."

"How so, Your Majesty?"

"We remember that he was involved in one of those Catholic plots to rescue our mother."

"Is that true, sire? Please do tell me more."

"Well Mr. Secretary, you mean you don't know? Well, this time it seems that we have a dirty little story to tell you. We don't recall all the details but we do remember that this all happened over fifteen years ago. However, what we do recall is that young Habington spent some six years in the Tower as a result of his nefarious activities."

"And since then, sire?"

"All we know is that after he was released, he retired to his house at Hindlip in Worcestershire. Therefore we might be right in guessing that he may well be one of those accursed recusants. And if that is the situation then, he is surely going to be lying very low."

"That is true, Your Majesty. But if he is involved with this Monteagle letter, you may rest assured that we will definitely catch him. That's at least one good thing with these Catholics. They are not united of purpose. Some, like Monteagle have seen on which side their bread is buttered and they certainly do not approve of any extreme Papist activity. You know sire," Cecil added, "I could give you a list of Catholic informers who..."

"Not now, Mr. Secretary," the king said, getting up in readiness to leave the small chamber. "But we think the time has come for us to discuss this matter with some of the other members of the Council. We also think that we should not act too hastily at this moment. Instead, we will be alert and see if we can catch these plotters red-handed. You see my dear Secretary, if we catch a few small fry and so nip this thing in the bud, we may allow the bigger fish to escape. Do you not agree with me?"

With that, the king turned to walk off in the direction of the larger chamber where the Council would be waiting for him.

"I certainly do sire," replied Cecil smiling, and feeling glad that his king was being as devious and as circumspect as himself. "No need to rush these matters, Your Majesty. I am sure all the parts will fall into place presently."

"Do not be too smug, Mr. Secretary. "The falling into place as you so colourfully put it may be the falling of our parts as well as the parts of an exploding Parliament building. Please do not forget that."

* * * * * * * *

Less than forty-eight hours later and a mile away, another meeting was taking place. The atmosphere of this one was just as intimate as the royal one, even if the number of those participating was just a little larger. This time the meeting was attended by Robert Catesby, Thomas Wintour and Guido Fawkes.

In the middle of their preliminary discussion about their various return journeys to the capital from the Midlands, Catesby suddenly stopped in mid-sentence.

"Thomas Wintour. You look very nervous. What is the matter? Are you not well?"

"Robin, you know you mean much to me, as a friend and as a kinsman. Well, I have been thinking. I want us to stop all this. To put an end to our plans."

"Stop? Why?"

"Because our plans are no longer secret."

"What do you mean?" Catesby and Guido asked together.

"Thomas Ward..."

"Lord Monteagle's servant?"

"Aye. The same. Well he knows something is up."

"But how does he know?" Catesby asked.

"Well, you know that in addition to his being Monteagle's servant, he is also related by marriage to Jack and Kit Wright."

"How?"

"I don't know exactly, but I do know that there is a family connection somehow, that is, through the women in the family. Through Jack and Kit's sister, Ursula I think."

"But this is impossible," half-shouted Catesby, banging his fist on the table. "We cannot stop now. Not after all this planning. And just because a servant may have guessed at something, that is not a reason to cancel all this. No my friends, it is too late to call this off."

"Well," Wintour said quietly. "It looks as if someone amongst us is a traitor. After all, how else could Ward know anything?"

"I am afraid but I agree with you Tom," Catesby said equally quietly. "But the question is, who?"

"Tresham," Wintour replied immediately.

"I fear you may be right there," Catesby said. "What say you, Guido?"

"I fear that I have to agree with you, Robin, even though he is your cousin. But tell me. Why would he have done this?"

"Either he has been bribed," Wintour said. "I know he is in urgent need of money. And if it's not that, maybe he is really worried about his kinsman, Monteagle."

"But we have discussed all that, and we came to a final decision," Catesby said. "No one was to tell anyone of our plans, even if they were family."

"True," agreed Wintour. "But don't you remember how much Francis wanted to warn Monteagle and Lord Stourton?"

"I do," Catesby replied. "But now it seems that we had better talk to him as soon as possible and hear what he has to say for himself. Thomas, I have an idea. Tell him that we are going to hold a supper party later this evening at the 'Red Lion.' That way we will be able to find out all about this Monteagle business."

"True. If he comes, we'll learn the truth," Guido said. "And if he doesn't come, then it looks as if Tresham has played us false."

Later that evening at the 'Red Lion' a tight and tense band of plotters met in an upstairs room. Those present included Catesby, Tom Wintour Guido Fawkes and Francis Tresham. This time there were none of the usual opening pleasantries. It was obvious that Tresham guessed that something was amiss when he saw his associates' grim and unsmiling faces.

"Where are the others? Jack and Kit? Thomas Percy, Ambrose and Robert Keyes?" Tresham asked. "And the others too?"

"They're not here and they're not coming tonight," Catesby answered him tersely.

"Now tell us what you know about Lord Monteagle."

"He's my brother-in-law."

"Yes, we know that. But what is this about a letter we have learned about?"

"A letter that Monteagle has received?"

"Aye, that one. Did you write it?" Catesby asked, looking Tresham straight in the eye. If there had previously been any cousinly spirit between the two plotters, it certainly was not present now.

"No. No, of course not."

"But," interrupted Wintour. "You were the one who wanted to warn Monteagle and Stourton."

"I-I-I know," Tresham stammered. B-But I never did. I'll swear my oath on it that I n-never did. E-even though I t-talked about doing so earlier."

Catesby did not look impressed. He looked at Guido and Wintour to see if their faces gave away their feelings. They both looked as though they agreed with him.

Catesby continued. "Francis Tresham. If you informed Lord Monteagle, I will personally hang thee from the nearest tree, if thou be family or no. Do you understand?"

"But I didn't," repeated Tresham, beads of sweat and fear glistening on his forehead. He had never seen his cousin Robin like this. He had known him as a fun-loving, kind and generous man. Now he was seeing another side and it frightened him.

"Robin, you must believe me. All I know is that Monteagle received a letter, but I assure you, I don't know who wrote it. All I know is that a messenger delivered it to his Lordship on the evening of the twenty-sixth, last."

Guido still looked unconvinced. "For a man who swears on his oath that he doesn't know anything about this Monteagle letter, you seem to very well acquainted with it."

"What can I tell you gentlemen that will persuade you of my innocence?" Tresham looked desperate and was sweating profusely. "As a Catholic, haven't I suffered as much as you? Haven't I been fined and imprisoned like many of you? Hasn't my father suffered for his beliefs? Wasn't he tried in the Star Chamber because of the help he rendered unto Edmund Campion? Isn't this all true?"

The other three sat around the table looking at him impassively. None of them said a word.

"Didn't I become seriously ill while I was in the Fleet prison? Don't my guts still pain me from the time I spent there? Hasn't my family suffered so much because of my recusancy? Answer me this."

Like dripping water on a stone, Francis Tresham's questions began to have their desired effect. Catesby, Guido and Wintour hanged their heads and began to admit to themselves that there was much truth in Tresham's barrage of questions. The truth was, that they did want to believe him. It was just that their nerves were naturally feeling taut and the thought that someone had betrayed them was just too much.

"And surely gentlemen," continued an exhausted Tresham at last. "If I had written that letter, would I have come here tonight to meet you? Surely I would have known that Monteagle would have told other Catholics, and probably Cecil too who were due to attend the opening ceremony of Parliament, no?"

He paused, to let the logic of his question sink in. "Remember, fellows. I have known my brother-in-law Monteagle for many years now and I know he would not suffer any other Catholics coming to harm. So for me to have written this letter just does not make sense, does it?"

By the end of this meeting, Tresham had convinced his fellow conspirators of his innocence and in a much lighter spirit than the meeting had opened, they agreed to meet the following day at Lincoln's Inn Walks.

This meeting began in a much calmer atmosphere than the night before. This time the four men were joined by Jack and Kit Wright.

"Where's Thomas Percy, Bates, Keyes, Ambrose and the others?" Kit asked.

"They'll be here tomorrow. They cannot come tonight." Catesby said. "But now let us proceed. We don't have much time left. So let us go over the final details. On those we will either sink or swim."

"Or be blown up," Jack said with a half-grin.

Final plans were arranged regarding the location of men and getaway horses. Maps and sketches were drawn and a feeling of calm satisfaction worked to dispel any nervousness that had been present earlier.

Then, just as the meeting was drawing to a close, Francis Tresham stood up

"You may have noticed tonight gentlemen, that unlike last night, I have been very quiet.

"Aye, I did notice," Thomas Wintour said. "And I was wondering why. Could it be about anything that was mentioned yesterday? The Monteagle letter perhaps?"

"No, no. It's not that. Well that's not completely true. The truth is that since I first heard about that letter last week, I haven't slept well."

"Why? What do you know that we don't?" Percy asked suspiciously.

"Please, gentlemen," Guido said, holding up his hands. "We talked about that last night. It's water under the bridge. What is the problem Tresham?"

"The problem as you call it, is that I've been thinking, that even at this late date, if we shouldn't abandon the whole plan. I mean if Monteagle..."

He was not able to expound upon his speculation for Catesby had jumped up and banged his clenched fist down on the table just as he had done the previous night.

"What!" he shouted. "Are we to go through all that again? Last night we decided with clear and cool reason to proceed with this matter. We cannot stop now. Our situation, the situation of the Catholics in this country is so bad, so desperate, that we must do something to change it." And here he seemed to be spewing out the words into the air. "We cannot just sit here like cows in a field and not to do anything any more. How much longer will we have to be fined, persecuted and exiled before we do anything about it? Do you hear me Francis? Do you hear me?"

"But what if...?" Francis Tresham pleaded, trying to stand his ground against Catesby's pounding questions. "What if...?"

"But what if we are caught, you ask? Then we will die knowing that we died trying to change something. We will die knowing that we tried to improve our lot. That's what if." And mopping the sweat off his forehead he slumped down in his chair, momentarily drained of all energy.

Tresham also sat down. He knew that he had been defeated. He had hoped that pure logic; the knowledge that the authorities knew that something was afoot although he didn't know what, would somehow manage to persuade his fellow conspirators to abandon, change or at least delay their plans. Now, when he looked around at the others seated around the table, he could tell from their faces that he had lost. One by one, they shook their heads at him as he searched their eyes for support. Defeated, he leaned forward in his chair, supporting his head in his hands. Tomorrow he thought, some of the men, like Guido would remain in London, while the others would flee the capital in order to organize their supporters in the Midlands. Everything had been arranged. All I can do now, thought Tresham, is to be carried along by the momentum of the plot.

For one fleeting moment a past vision of the Essex Rebellion and the Fleet prison filled his mind, but this mental picture was shattered as Guido slapped him on the back.

"In two days' time my friend, you and the country will know if you are a live Catholic hero or a dead Catholic martyr. So be strong and of good courage." And Guido thumped him on the back again in an act of physical support.

Tresham smiled back weakly at first, and then feeling the warmth and fellowship of his comrades, he stood up and shook hands firmly with each and every one of them. He sat down feeling strengthened, marvelling to himself where his fellow plotters found their faith. Then Catesby rose and shook his hand again. By now any doubts that Tresham may have held as to their ultimate success were dispelled.

Of the thirteen conspirators who met on that fateful evening, it could be noticed that the two who were the calmest were Guido Fawkes and Robert Catesby. Guido was calm as he knew exactly what he had to do and also because his soldierly instincts and training had keyed him up for the final stage. Catesby felt equally calm in the sense that he felt that he was approaching the final lap in a long race, when everything, or almost everything had gone as planned. There had been many hurdles on the way but they had all been surmounted. Friends and supporters were waiting in readiness in Flanders and the Midlands, while he had been assured that King Philip III would add his strength to the enterprise. The important and immediate questions of escape routes, safehouses and fast horses had all been dealt with. All that remained, Catesby noted to himself, was for Guido, our Guy, to carry out his part successfully. And for that, he would be aided by Robert Keyes.

Much later that evening, the few plotters who had not left London for their pre-arranged destinations in the Midlands in the meanwhile had their final meeting. As usual Catesby took the lead.

"Guido, is the gunpowder ready?"

Guido nodded.

"Are you sure?"

"Aye, 'tis under the firewood and coal. It hasn't been disturbed at all."

"Good. That's a good sign. If it had been, I might have thought that there had been something in that Monteagle letter business, but now I know that everything is in order." He smiled at the seated men and then continued. "Then tonight, Guido, after we disperse, you go to Robert Keyes' lodgings and collect the timepiece that Thomas Percy has left there for you. Is that clear?"

"Aye."

"You did leave it there, didn't you Thomas?"

"A couple of days ago," Percy assured Catesby. "By the way, Robin, where are you going to be when Guido sets off the gunpowder?"

"I'll be off on my way North with Jack Wright and Thomas Bates. We'll travel first to Dunstable in Bedfordshire and then meet up with the others at Dunchurch."

"Using Ambrose's and Digby's horses?"

"Yes, and then we..."

The flow of his words was suddenly cut off by two sharp knocks on the door. The plotters looked at each other quickly. Who could it be? Maybe there was something after all that Tresham had said about the Monteagle letter? While Catesby went to open the door, Guido rolled up the large map of the Midlands and hid it behind a curtain. The second round of knocking was cut short as Catesby half-opened the door to reveal a dark heavy-set man holding a long parcel. Catesby did not recognize the man who was standing there alone and neither did any of the others. Catesby was about to ask the man who he was when the man stuck his head around the doorway.

"Is Mr. Rookwood here? Mr. Ambrose Rookwood?"

"No, he isn't," answered Thomas Percy. "And who might you be?"

"Me? I am Master Craftsman John Craddock. Of the Strand, if you please," the man said proudly, swelling out his chest.

Catesby, assured that the man was who he claimed to be, opened the door and ushered in the Master Craftsman.

"I have a sword here for Mr. Rookwood. Now gentlemen, if he isn't here, would you be so kind as to tell me where I might find him? He told me to deliver it to him here, but I see that will be impossible."

"You may leave it here with us Master Craddock," Catesby said, hoping the man would not try and insist on waiting for Ambrose. "He is away at the moment, but fear not, I will make sure that he will receive it."

To everyone's relief, the Master Craftsman handed over the sword to Catesby. "Well, thank you, sir. You have indeed spared me from making another journey. But just tell him to use it carefully, though I hope he never has to, of course. As it says in the Gospel of St. John, and this I tell all my worthy customers, 'Put up thy sword into the sheath.' So, good sirs, I will wish you good night and God bless." And making a small salute, he turned and was gone.

Catesby put the sword aside in the corner as Guido retrieved the map and unrolled it on the table.

"Now, where were we?"

"You were telling us of your route, Robin."

"True. And as I was saying, the others and myself will ride to Dunstable and Dunchurch, and you others, that is Robert Keyes and you Thomas Percy will catch up with us later. Guido will travel south as planned. Are there any more questions?"

There were none and soon after a hurried round of handshakes and fervent 'Good lucks,' the remaining conspirators broke up. Taking their hats and cloaks, they disappeared into the night in pairs as they had become accustomed to over the past year. Little did they know that when they were to meet up again, it would be under completely different circumstances to the ones that they had imagined.

Chapter Ten
Discovery!

Lord Monteagle was just about to sit himself down in order to enjoy a tasty meal of roast pig, delicately spiced of course, when he was disturbed by three sharp knocks on the door. Dispatching his servant to enquire what the unseemly noise was all about, Monteagle settled himself down at the table yet again, when his servant reappeared accompanied by another man, wearing a dark blue and gold aristocratic- looking livery.

"Sir," the servant began. "I apologize for the disturbance, but this man, a messenger from the Earl of Suffolk insists on speaking with you now." Monteagle did not say a word and although the servant shifted uncomfortably in front of his lordship, he continued. "I tried to persuade him to wait until you had eaten, sir, but he wouldn't do so. He insists that he must speak with you now, sir."

"Oh, he did, did he?" Monteagle was feeling a bit put out by all this. He was feeling rather hungry, and the smells of the freshly roasted and spiced pig, which had wafted up to his lordship's nostrils, had tended to increase his pangs of hunger even more.

"Well, my good man. What is it that is so urgent that you must tell me just as I am about to sit down and dine on that pig, eh?"

"It's just this, sir," Suffolk's messenger began, nervously fiddling with the brim of his hat. "It's just that my master wishes for you to meet him at the Palace of Westminster as soon as possible, sir."

"As soon as possible, you say?"

"Yes, sir. Those were his exact words, sir."

"Even before I have dined?"

"He didn't say anything about dining, sir. He just said that you were to come immediately. As soon as I told you, sir."

"So be it," Monteagle said resignedly, and called for his servant to bring him his hat, cloak and cane. "And make sure my coach is ready, too."

"Yes, sir."

Soon after this, his lordship's coach rumbled into the Palace courtyard where it was met by another of Suffolk's servants.

"Please follow me, sir," he said and escorted Monteagle over to the Earl of Suffolk who was standing there waiting impatiently by a pillar.

"Good evening, Monteagle. Glad you could come immediately. I hope you weren't put out by this sudden call. But anyway, come with me. Cecil, I mean Salisbury has asked me to check out the lower levels of the Palace tonight. It seems that some of our Catholic friends are determined to cause some noisy mischief in the near future and the Secretary wishes to see if there is any truth in some of the rumours that have reached his ears. And you know, of course, that Salisbury has a very fine set of ears for hearing all manner of things, no?"

"There are always rumours about these Catholics," replied Monteagle, deliberately being vague.

"True, but please accompany me and these men sir, and let us see if there is any truth behind all this. By the way, are you armed, sir?"

"I have this," and Monteagle held up his stout walking cane with its golden knob bearing the family crest.

"Well, that should be enough, although I doubt if we will be needing it. I have my sword and we have a few pikemen who will be accompanying us. Ah yes, I almost forgot. Allow me to introduce this gentleman to you. His name is John Whynniard, Esquire." And John Whynniard, Esquire, the proud but now worried homeowner, stepped out of the shadows. "These cellars belong to him. He hasn't been using them of late, but he knows his way around these underground passages and he'll be coming with us as a guide. So come. Let us get to work."

Minutes later, aided by swinging lanterns, the short procession consisting of the two aristocrats and a small group of soldiers, all led by John Whynniard were walking, slowly and half-bent over, along the unfamiliar and stuffy passages beneath the Parliament building. There the king and the nation's leaders were due to meet on the morrow, November the fifth. Their lordships would be there of course in order to attend the much-delayed opening session of Parliament. As Suffolk and his men moved along, the light of the swinging lanterns caused their shadows to lurch and dance about blackly and wildly around the walls of the underground passage.

"Not good for the nerves, eh, Monteagle?" Suffolk murmured.

"No, sir. And certainly not on my empty stomach too."

Suffolk grimaced and they continued picking their subterranean way carefully.

Suddenly, the silence, save that of their footsteps, was broken as a soldier tripped, dropped his lantern and cursed steadily as he rubbed his injured leg. As he picked himself up and started to dust himself off, he found himself looking up at the tense face of the Earl of Suffolk.

"Well, what was it man? Too much ale?"

"N-No sir. I-I-I f-fell over a bundle of f-faggots, s-sir."

"Faggots, man?"

"Y-Yes sir. Like firewood, sir. There," he pointed. "There, in the corner. Oh, I'm sorry for dropping the lantern, sir."

"Well just be more careful, man. Your lantern nearly went out."

"Yes sir." And the small procession continued on its way.

Just as they were rounding a corner, the swinging lanterns casting their weird and ghost-like dancing shapes in advance of the guard, the leading pikeman stopped, and placed a finger to his lips. Ssssh! He pointed with his lantern to where a shadowy silhouette of a figure was moving darkly in the jumping shapes, just a few yards ahead of them.

Suffolk immediately caught up with the soldier. "What is it?" he whispered. "Is it a person?"

"I don't know, sir. But I'll go and have a look. Please wait here sir. I'll just take a couple of the men with me to see what's up."

The soldier moved off to where the dark figure was crouched, half-hidden behind a column. A few minutes later the soldier returned to face the impatient Suffolk.

"Well, what was it man? Was it a man after all?"

"Yes, sir."

"Well then, what's he doing here?"

"Says he's a servant, sir."

"A servant? Whose servant? And what's he doing down here in the dark? And at this time of night, too. Doesn't even have a light with him, heh?"

"Yes, sir. Says he works for Thomas Percy sir."

"Thomas Percy? Who's that?"

"Says he's a Gentleman Pensioner, sir. You know, works for the king's bodyguard..."

"Yes, yes, I know what these Pensioner fellows are," Suffolk replied brusquely. "But did you ask him what he was doing here, down here in the dark?"

"Yes, sir. He said he was just checking the winter firewood, sir."

"Winter firewood? Checking it at this time of the night? And did you ask him why he was doing his checking at night?"

The soldier shuffled his feet uncomfortably in front of the earl. "No, sir," he muttered. "I'm sorry sir, but I didn't know to ask him that, sir."

"Well, never mind man," Suffolk said grudgingly. "You did your best. Now wait here while I discuss this with Lord Monteagle. Be so good and ask him to catch up with me. And be quick about it. And in the meanwhile, send two of your men to make sure this servant fellow doesn't go and disappear in the dark. But don't do anything else 'til I tell you."

As the soldier turned to do the earl's bidding, Suffolk called after him, "Make sure the men you send have a light with them."

A few minutes later Suffolk spoke his mind to the other lord.

"Monteagle, damned strange business this. Tell me, what do you think Percy's servant is doing down here at this time of night checking his winter firewood as he says? And in the dark, too."

"I also think it's strange, Suffolk. Tell me, what did this fellow look like?"

"I don't know. I didn't get a close look at him. Only one of the soldiers did. He said he couldn't see his face very clearly since he only had a lantern with him and that this servant-fellow was wearing a wide-brimmed hat."

"Wait a moment, Suffolk," Monteagle said, scratching the side of his head in thought. "The man said his name was Percy?"

"No. The man said he was Percy's servant. Why?"

"Because there is a well-known Catholic fellow called Percy. Thomas Percy. Now I wonder if he's got anything to do with this?"

"He may well have, Monteagle. Let's report this to Salisbury immediately. I'm sure he would like to know all about this. We'll leave the soldiers here under the sergeant's command. They'll keep an eye on this servant-fellow, if that's indeed who he is. But I still think it's a strange business though. Checking firewood in the middle of the night. And in the dark, too, and without a lantern. Come, let's get moving. I'm getting cold just standing here. The dampness down here isn't too good for my old bones."

Within half-an-hour, not only was Robert Cecil, the Earl of Salisbury, informed, but so was his master, the master of them all, King James I of England and VI of Scotland.

Making excuses for their dusty appearance, Suffolk wasted no time in reporting their underground meeting with the tall servant in the shadows who claimed that he was looking after his master's firewood.

"Very commendable. Very faithful," the king commented in his dry Scottish accent. "Now return to the vaults and see what more you can learn from this devoted servant. But be cautious and take Sir Thomas Knyvett here with you. He is a magistrate as you know, and if anyone is to be arrested, it will be prudent if he is present."

"Yes, Your Majesty."

"And don't forget to take another dozen men with you. And make sure that they are well-armed. If there is something afoot, a wee bit of help from a few soldiers will be useful. If there is something up with this dark and desperate fellow as you described him, you may find that he is not alone skulking around down there in the dark. Thomas Percy's servant? Hmm. Now, get you hence, and quickly."

Even quicker than it took Suffolk and Monteagle to reach the king, they were back underground, but this time accompanied by Sir Thomas Knyvett and a dozen soldiers.

Suddenly the two leading soldiers stopped, and as before, signalled the others to stop as they, together with the magistrate moved cautiously ahead. And as before, they came across Thomas Percy's servant half-hidden in the dark shadows, but now guarded by two pikemen. This time, the soldiers did not hesitate.

"You there! Come here!" the leading soldier called out.

The shadowy figure froze and then tried to slip away from his guards into the darkness.

"Put down that wood and come out here! Now!" the soldier shouted out again.

Thomas Percy's devoted servant moved out of the swaying shadows into the yellow light of the lanterns.

"Who are you? And make sure it's the truth." the magistrate demanded, taking over from the soldiers who had now surrounded the lone figure.

"Master John Johnson, sir. Servant to Thomas Percy, Gentleman Pensioner, sir," replied Guido keeping his face low.

"And what are you doing down here at this time of night, Johnson?" Sir Thomas asked sharply.

"Seeing my master's firewood and faggots are ready for the winter, sir."

"Ready? At this time of night man?"

"Yes, sir. That they are not damp sir. I've just seen that the damp hasn't got through and spoiled them. You see sir..."

"And do you always perform this task in the dark while you are booted and spurred, eh my man? I would have thought that such accoutrements would not be necessary for such a mundane task," Sir Thomas remarked somewhat sarcastically.

"Yes sir. I mean no sir. I mean that I am so dressed so that I may return home immediately I have finished my task, sir."

"I see," Suffolk said, having joined them. "You must be a very valuable servant if your master, this Thomas Percy you said? Provides you with a horse to travel from his cellar here to his house above ground, eh?"

"Yes sir. I..."

"But if you are a servant," interrupted Sir Thomas, "you have no need to be dressed thus. Surely you live here, that is upstairs or thereabouts, no?"

"Yes sir. But..."

"Silence man!" and Sir Thomas called John Whynniard over to him. "Tell me sir. Isn't your place near here? The one that this Percy fellow has rented?"

"Yes sir. 'Tis just above us," Whynniard replied. "Or near enough, that is. It's hard to know exactly in the dark sir. But if you come back here tomorrow sir, in daylight, that is when some light does manage to get through..."

"Yes, yes, I'm sure. I'm also sure that this John Johnson fellow doesn't need his master's horse to return home either," the magistrate said turning his attention back to the servant who was looking around anxiously. "Now remove your hat and cloak," Sir Thomas commanded. "Let me see if I recognize you."

The servant dutifully removed his hat and cloak.

"No. I don't. But that's a heavy cloak. You wouldn't be thinking of travelling far, would you? Especially at this time of the night."

"No, sir. Just home to bed. That is after checking the firewood sir."

"Pray tell me, Johnson," Suffolk said. "How were you going to examine the state of the firewood in the dark?"

"I had a lantern with me sir, but I dropped it and I was left in the dark."

Suffolk did not look convinced.

"Firewood, eh? You," and he pointed to a couple of soldiers who had been listening intently all the while. "Go and check this servant's firewood. See if he doesn't have anything else hidden there. Like some barrels."

"Barrels sir? Barrels of what?"

"Barrels of wine, of course."

"Yes, sir." And within a minute the sound of wooden barrels being pushed around and heavier noises soon filled the underground vault. Then one of the soldiers came running over to where Suffolk and the magistrate were standing.

"Sir. You were right. There are some barrels under the firewood, and...."

"Ha! I told you there was some mischief afoot here tonight," Suffolk said triumphantly to Sir Thomas. "Now, how many barrels of wine are there?"

"They're not barrels of wine, sir. They're barrels of gunpowder sir!"

"Gunpowder? Are you sure?"

"Yes, sir. I'm sure, sir."

"...and there's over thirty of them sir," panted another soldier who had just joined them. "I counted them myself, sir."

"Well, just go and check them again," ordered Suffolk. "And take another man with you. And for sweet Jesus' sake, don't leave any lights near those barrels!"

"And you," Sir Thomas said, using his magisterial powers, and placing his hand on Johnson's shoulder. "You are under arrest!"

He then turned to two soldiers. "You two! Search his man and see if he is hiding any arms or anything in connection with this confounded gunpowder. Now!"

A moment later, the stouter soldier had Thomas Percy's servant's arms pinned behind him while the other held up in the light of the lanterns, a timepiece, some matches and some touchwood.

"Sir, we have found these things hidden on the prisoner. They can be used for..."

"Yes, yes, I know what they can be used for," Sir Thomas said curtly. "I've also been a soldier in my time. Now bind up this man's hands, and very securely and let us leave this place. I think we still have a lot of work ahead of us this night."

So pushing the bound servant in front of them, the small procession left the underground vaults and proceeded in the direction of their royal master who was waiting impatiently for their return, above ground in the palace.

Despite the apparent urgency of the situation, very little was done immediately. John Johnson was interrogated three times in the early hours of the morning, but would only repeat that his name was John Johnson and that he worked for The Honourable Thomas Percy, Gentleman Pensioner. He said nothing about his fellow conspirators, but only muttered something about the king and his Scottish ancestry. Seeing that the interrogation was not producing any satisfactory results, the king ordered that the prisoner be sent to the Tower, "and under heavy guard, too."

In the meanwhile, the following Royal Proclamation was issued with reference to Johnson's employer:

> The said Percy is a tall man, with a great broad beard, a good face, the colour of his beard and head mingled with white hairs, but the head more white than the beard. He is somewhat bent-shouldered, well-coloured in the face, is long-footed and small-legged.

At about the same time that this proclamation was being issued, the king's Principal Secretary, the first Earl of Salisbury, was conducting an emergency meeting of the Council.

"First of all, gentlemen, there are two measures that we have to carry out immediately. The first is to order the closure of all ports, especially those on the south and east coasts. And the second, is to provide some military protection for the ambassador from Spain."

"Only for the Spanish Ambassador?"

"Yes. For the time being. I fear that the London mob will associate him with Catholicism and try to carry out its own form of justice, er, religious correction on that man. Are there any questions? Yes, Suffolk?"

"Mr. Secretary. What is to happen with respect to this Thomas Percy?"

"Fear not, Suffolk, and the rest of you. Sir John Popham, the Lord Chief Justice has already instigated a search for this man. He has also ordered that his property be thoroughly searched. As you know, Sir John has many connections with the Catholic world and no doubt, he will produce some interesting results soon."

Salisbury looked around to see if anyone disagreed with him, but no-one did.

"I have also recommended to His Majesty, that he delay, once again, the opening of Parliament until this coming Saturday. That is, after we have held a very brief meeting of explanation this afternoon. Are we agreed gentlemen?"

They were.

"And that leaves just one more matter to be dealt with. And that is the question of this cousin of Thomas Percy, that is, his patron Henry Percy, who is better known to you as the Earl of Northumberland."

"Is he mixed up in this too?" Suffolk asked incredulously.

"We are not sure of that yet," replied Salisbury. "But I know that the earl, one of His Majesty's greatest subjects and councillors, is well-connected to his less illustrious kinsman, and it really behoves us to get to the bottom of this matter. I therefore suggest, as before, that we adjoin this meeting for the present and meet again here this afternoon. Then I hope I will have some more information for you all. So good day gentlemen and I thank you all for your patience for meeting me here at this ungodly hour. Godspeed to you."

But it was not a good day for several of the plotters who were not too far from the Royal Council chamber. For, not too far away, chaos and confusion were breaking out in the Strand where several of the nation's leading aristocrats had their London homes.

This turmoil also affected members of the lower classes too. Among the latter, a certain Kit Wright was being rudely and noisily awakened from a deep sleep. As soon as he was dressed, he rushed over to the "*Duck and Drake*" where his fellow conspirator Tom Wintour was staying.

"Tom! Tom!" Kit hissed to the half-sleeping man. "The game is up!" And he looked out of the window to see if he had been followed.

"What do you mean man 'The game is up?'" asked Wintour, wiping the sleep out of his eyes.

"The gunpowder, man. Wake up! Guido has been arrested and I overheard someone say just over half-an-hour ago that Lord Worcester was going to see Monteagle in order to call on the Earl of Northumberland."

"Northumberland? Percy's cousin?" asked Wintour, now showing signs of understanding what was happening.

"Aye man. The same. Come, come. We must fly or we are lost."

"No, no. Wait," Wintour said now fully awake and taking command. "Get you back to Essex House and as discreetly as possible, confirm your story and then come back to me. I will be waiting for you here. Knock three times and then I'll know it is you. If I am not in the house, go round to the back and I'll be waiting for you there. But go now and don't forget to be discreet."

Kit, feeling relieved that he was no longer in charge, raced back to the Strand only to learn that his previous suspicions had been confirmed. Returning to the 'Duck and Drake,' he knocked three times quickly on Wintour's door and the flustered man was let in immediately.

"Tom, I was right. The king's men are looking for Thomas Percy and they are also asking questions about Northumberland. We must flee for our lives. Do you have a good horse?"

"Aye, I do that, but I want to stay for a while and see what is happening. There is no point in jumping from the frying pan into the fire. So listen to me man, and listen carefully. Get you over to Percy's lodgings and tell him to leave London and head for the Midlands, post-haste. Tell him to make sure that he is not followed and you do the same. Now go, and may the Lord be with us."

"Amen to that," Kit said fervently. "But what about taking some supplies for the journey?"

"Do you have any money?"

"Aye," and he patted the leather pouch hanging from his belt.

"Then just go man, and purchase any supplies on the way. But for God's sake, be careful and take care of whom you speak to or who speaks to you. Remember, Cecil's got spies everywhere. Now go!"

Kit Wright's luck was in. No-one seemed to pay attention to the tall horseman and soon he and Thomas Percy had reached the northern outskirts of the capital without attracting any attention. As soon as they were in the open country, they set off in the direction of Bedfordshire as fast as their galloping and sweating horses could take them.

An hour or so later, Robert Keyes decided it was time to flee London for the North, word having reached him through his neighbour's noisy gossiping below his window. Now only Francis Tresham, Ambrose Rookwood and Thomas Wintour remained in London. But not for long. Some time that morning, the morning of November the fifth, both Rookwood and Wintour came to the conclusion that to delay their departure was dangerously foolish and so they also set off in a northerly direction as planned. Rookwood made the best progress as he had the better horse and was soon separated from Wintour. In fact, soon after he left the capital, he overtook Robert Keyes at Highgate and then raced on towards their rendezvous at Dunsmore Heath. Near Dunstable he met Kit Wright and Thomas Percy.

"Ambrose Rookwood. Are we glad it's you who caught up with us," Kit said. "When we saw the cloud of dust you kicked up behind you, we were sure that it was the king's men who were after us. Are you alone? Have you seen any of the others? What news do you have?"

"Yes, I'm alone, but I passed Robert Keyes as I was leaving London. I don't expect him to catch up with us for some time, and I don't know what happened to Tom Wintour and Francis Tresham."

"Tresham! I had completely forgotten about him," Percy suddenly said. "Did anyone tell him we are undone?"

"I don't know," called out Ambrose, preparing to mount his horse and race off again. "But I'll go ahead and inform Catesby what has happened. I'm sure he is in the dark about it all."

And before the other two could say anything, Ambrose had urged his chestnut stallion into a full gallop and soon was seen no more. Only a column of dust told the other plotters of his general direction. After several miles of hard riding Ambrose caught sight of Catesby, Jack Wright and Thomas Bates.

"Catesby! Catesby!" he shouted out clattering to a halt. "We are lost! We are undone!"

"What do you mean, man? Who is lost? Who is undone?" Catesby shouted back among the dust and smell of sweating horses. "What's happened?"

"Guido has been arrested. Someone must have betrayed us. Guido's been taken to the Tower and Parliament isn't meeting until next Saturday."

"Tell me this isn't true!" Catesby cried out looking at Ambrose. "It's not true, is it?"

"Yes, man. It's true. Every word of it. They have raised the hue and cry for Thomas Percy and the Earl of Northumberland. They..."

"Where is Percy?" Jack Wright called out "And where is my brother? Have you seen him? What's happened to him?"

"Fear not, Jack," Ambrose said reassuringly. "Your brother and Thomas Percy are making their way North. I passed them some time back. They'll catch up with us soon. But Robin, we must flee, and now! All of us and get to Dunchurch as quickly as possible. Come. What are we wasting time here for?"

"True," said Catesby trying to come to grips with the fact that his plans were unravelling about his ears. "Let's ride to Dunchurch as fast as possible. Digby has fresh horses waiting for us there."

"I'm not going with you!"

"Who said that?" Catesby asked sharply.

"Me," answered Robert Keyes. "I'm leaving you here for Drayton."

"Drayton? Why?"

"I'll hide out at Lord Mordaunt's house. He has many places where a man can hide and I'll try my luck there. Besides, if we split up, we stand a better chance."

"Yes, but Robert," Catesby began. But before he could complete his sentence, Keyes had viciously dug his spurs into his horse's flanks and had charged off in a north-easterly direction. None of the men there could guess, that the next time they would meet, at least, those who were still alive, would be in the Tower of London at the end of the month.

Apart from the forgotten Francis Tresham and the imprisoned Guido, only John Wintour remained in London. Pulling down his wide-brimmed hat over his forehead and pulling his collar high, ostensibly to keep out the early November winds, he made his way on foot over to Westminster. Trying not to sound too interested, he approached a couple of housewives on their way to the fishmarket.

"Excuse me ladies. But why are there so many guards and soldiers about the streets? Is there to be a parade today?"

"Oh no, sir," the taller one replied. "They have uncovered a plot."

"A plot?"

"Why yes, young man. A plot to kill the king."

"And his Parliament," the second woman added, anxious not to be left out of this latest news.

"Who would want to kill the king?" Wintour asked as innocently as possible.

"It's those Catholics, sir. They wanted to blow him up," the taller one said, taking the lead again.

"But how would they do that? Blow him up?"

"With gunpowder, sir."

"Yes. Barrels and barrels of it. They found them under where Parliament was to sit at Westminster Palace, sir."

"Yes, over a hundred barrels," the second housewife added happily, embellishing the few details she had heard in the time-honoured nature of improving on gossip.

"And what happened?" Wintour asked, trying to look and sound as nonchalant and as casual as possible.

"The king's soldiers came and arrested them, sir."

"Yes. All of them," the taller one added, again with relish.

"And no doubt they'll hang 'em too."

"Yes. For treason. That's what they usually do."

"Probably draw and quarter them as well no doubt."

"And how many of these traitors were there?" Wintour continued, still trying to sound nonchalant, even as he inwardly shuddered at the thought of the grim punishments he had just heard described.

"Oh, he don't know much, does he, Alice?" said the one nudging the other in the ribs. "They caught about twenty of them, sir, didn't they?"

"I heard that it was even more, Jane. Someone told me there was about fifty of them Catholics."

"Well, I don't know how many there were exactly. But all I know is that you can't trust 'em. So you be on guard young man and look after yourself carefully. Come on, Jane Rawlings. We can't stand here gossiping all day like common fishwives. We've got some shopping to do."

"Well, thank you kindly ladies. I'll certainly stay away from those Catholics. They sound most dangerous."

And pulling his collar up even higher he started off, but they called out to him. "Sir! Sir! You can't go that way. The soldiers won't let you. You'll have to go in the direction of the city."

Wintour nodded his head in thanks and set off in the direction of his stable, trying not to hurry too much or to attract any attention. One hour later, mounted on his horse, he made his way north-west to Norbrook where he planned to spend the night with his sister Dorothy and her husband, fellow-plotter John Grant. The next day he would continue on to Huddington where he would link up with Robert, his brother and fellow-plotter.

Parallel with the plotters' movements across the southern half of England, the government's forces were also moving in London. On the evening of 6 November, a flushed but self-satisfied looking Chief Justice was being ushered into Salisbury's chambers.

"Come in, Sir John. You look like the proverbial cat who not only has caught the mouse, but which has devoured a whole family of them."

"And so I have, your Lordship," bowed Sir John. "At least a good number of them. For I have here a list of many of our possible conspirators."

"So quickly. You have done well. Now, please tell me who is, or who might be involved in this evil plot."

"Here sir. I will read out the relevant parts of my report. I think it be better that I read it rather than you, as my writing is so illegible." The Chief Justice cleared his throat and began. "By examinations supervised by me this afternoon, I am sure that the following persons are responsible or partly so for the attempt to blow up our beloved king and his Parliament whilst they were sitting in the Palace at..."

"Names, sir. Give me names," Salisbury said impatiently.

"Yes, sir. I was coming to that," and he unrolled a long piece of paper. "Ah yes, here we are. The names sir. Robert Catesby, Robert or James Keyes, I'm not sure yet, Thomas Wintour, sometimes spelt Winter, Jack Wright and his brother Kit, also known as Christopher, Ambrose Rookwood and we also suspect a certain recusant called John Grant."

"What about Thomas Percy and the Earl of Northumberland?"

"True, sir. But you knew about them already."

"Yes," Salisbury nodded. "But I'm not sure about Northumberland, Sir John."

"We're busy examining him, sir, and..."

"And what about this John Johnson fellow? The one we arrested the other night. The one who claims he is Percy's servant. How is he involved with all this?"

"Well, we are not sure yet, sir. But we don't think his name is really John Johnson, and so far we haven't been able to ascertain how much he knows or how much he is involved in this thing."

Salisbury didn't say anything. He knew Sir John would get to the truth. He always did.

"But rest assured sir," the Chief Justice continued. "We will find out everything there is to know. I'm sure it won't take us more than a day or two. As you know, we do have our ways of obtaining information, sir."

"Yes, Sir John. I was coming to that. For today I received a letter from His Majesty and it says," and here the Secretary reached across the large desk for the necessary document. "Ah here it is. His Majesty writes, 'the gentler tortures are to be first used unto him and..." Salisbury looked up. "How is your Latin, Sir John?"

"Test me and we shall see."

"As I was saying, first used unto him and *et sic per gradus ad ima tenditur.*"

"And so by degrees proceeding to the worst," Sir John said, translating the phrase with a smile.

"I see you were a good Latin scholar. So there you are. In the king's own hand too. Signed and sealed."

Salisbury beamed and then turned the document over to Sir John who examined it carefully before replacing it on the desk.

"Now I wonder how far those fellows have got to?"

"The other plotters, your Lordship?"

"Yes. Probably skulking around London or the Midlands, if my informers have the latest information. Hiding, and hoping this thing will blow over like a squall at sea. But you note my words Sir John. I won't let this thing go until I've got to the bottom of it. I have a feeling that this thing is much greater than either the Bye or the Main plots and you know of course how sensitive His Majesty is when it comes to such activities."

"Yes," Sir John said. "Especially after the Gowrie plot."

"That's right. Now this time these Catholics have gone too far. You'll see."

Chapter Eleven
More Unravelling

Salisbury was right. Apart from Francis Tresham, the other twelve plotters, in the Secretary's own words, were skulking around in the Midlands. Actually, skulking around is not the best way to describe their movements, but rather, meandering, as they criss-crossed Warwickshire and Worcestershire and the southern Midlands looking for arms and support.

East of the Midlands, at Ashby St. Ledgers in Northamptonshire, was a modest country house which was owned by Lady Catesby. This building, with its stone-finished lower storey topped by a Tudor style upper storey was one of the first stops that Robert Catesby, Thomas Bates, Thomas Percy, Ambrose Rookwood and the Wright brothers and a few of their supporters arrived at on their way to their rendezvous at Dunchurch.

"Come Robin," Percy urged on his leader. "Let us continue on to the house instead of waiting out here in the fields. I am hungry, and I'm sure the same can be said for the others as well and I'm sure our horses need a rest as well."

"No, Thomas, we can't rest here. My mother does not know about our plans at all and we cannot involve her in any of this. We will just sleep here tonight in one of the barns and then leave at daybreak."

Percy was just about to mutter something when he caught sight of a lone horseman approaching them. Pulling out their swords in readiness, Catesby and Percy pointed their horses' heads in the direction of the newcomer.

"Robin, Tom. How I am glad to see you here. I have just ridden over from Huddington."

The two plotters visibly relaxed, as did the others, when they saw that the heavily cloaked horseman was none other than Robert Wintour.

"Have you seen my brother Tom?' he asked, even before he had dismounted.

"No," Catesby said. "We thought he was with you. We haven't seen him since we left London."

"Well, why are you waiting here?" Wintour asked. "Didn't you say that we were all to meet at Dunchurch?"

"Haven't you heard?" Catesby asked in reply. "Guido has been arrested and..."

"...What! The plot's been discovered?" Wintour asked, hoping he was wrong.

"Aye," said Robert Keyes. "I think yon Tresham betrayed us. We haven't seen him for a couple of days and no-one seems to know where he is or what's become of him."

He spat bitterly into the grass.

"But Robert, we're not sure he's a turncoat," said Ambrose. "Maybe one of our servants gave us away. You know how Salisbury likes to use servants as spies."

"Aye," Jack Wright said bitterly. "As we used to say at home in Yorkshire, 'Money will buy owt.'"

"Come gentlemen. This isn't going to help us now. Let us bed down in the barn over there," Catesby said trying to sooth the fugitives shattered nerves. "We'll sleep here tonight and then tomorrow we'll head for Dunchurch and then north-west for Warwickshire."

"I just hope they remember that they are Catholics there," added Percy cynically. "For we're going to need all the help we can get."

At sunrise the following morning, the seven plotters, together with about two dozen supporters set out for Dunchurch. None of the band was in a good mood as the lack of food and good bedding was a particularly new and unpleasant experience for them. It was only Robert Catesby's optimism and leadership that seemed to bind them together.

"Come on you fellows. Just wait till we get further west. And tonight we'll dine in Warwick."

One or two of them tried to smile, but the rest just sat damp, spiritless and hunched over in the saddle as the heavy early morning dew dampened their spirits even further. Some good news or something urgent was needed to boost their morale as they set off. This occurred half-way through the morning when Sir Everard Digby mounted on a fine aristocratic looking horse suddenly loomed out of the mist.

"Ho, Sir Everard! How long have you been here?" called out Catesby. The tall and handsome courtier guided his horse over to Catesby's.

"About two hours I believe. I had breakfast in that tavern about half a mile back. It was very good, but now I'm hungry again."

"Pray do not talk about food," Kit said rubbing his stomach, "For we have hardly eaten anything since we left London."

"By the way," the second Wright asked before everyone could start complaining about their empty and rumbling stomachs. "Have you seen any signs of the king's men in the area?"

"Of soldiers, you mean?"

"Aye, soldiers."

"No, but I heard some people in the tavern talking about a gunpowder plot while I was having breakfast in the tavern."

"What were they saying?"

"Not much," Digby said flatly. "Just that some Catholics had tried to blow up the king but his life had been spared and that those responsible had been caught."

"Did you catch any names or any other details?"

"Yes. Someone said a man called Johnson had been caught, but I didn't dare ask any questions."

"Hmm. News certainly travels fast, doesn't it?"

"Aye. Especially news like this," Percy said bitterly.

" But what are we going to do now that all is lost?" Sir Everard asked.

"But all is not lost, my friend," Catesby said vehemently. "If we can arouse all the Catholics between here and Wales, and make them join us, then we'll have a good fighting chance."

"But what if...?" the courtly aristocrat began, obviously not convinced.

"There will be no 'What ifs,' Sir Everard. We must win. We have no choice. The Lord must be on our side. Don't you feel that? Look at all the men who have joined us! They surely believe in us and our cause."

Sir Everard looked around. All he saw were the plotters standing around in a small group near their horses, and another group of two dozen men waiting for some kind of sign of command and leadership. Both groups were quiet. Sir Everard could detect no signs of action nor enthusiasm.

"But Robin," he protested again. "Look how few we are. A mere thirty men or so."

"I agree," Catesby conceded. "But after we obtain more supplies at Warwick, then others will see how serious we are and join us."

"Is that where we're bound for next, Warwick?"

"Aye, and after that I assure you that you will see all this in a different light, my friend. So tell the others to mount up and let's be on our way."

Sir Everard shrugged his shoulders and moved apathetically towards the other men. The light and fire seemed to have gone out of him. The well-loved knight and sporting courtier now moved like an automaton. He was no longer thinking of his beautiful wife Mary, or of his horses, dogs and falcons. All he wanted to do was escape from this nightmare; this great dream that had gone wrong. He was born to hunt and chase, not be hunted or chased like a proud stag.

And so it was Warwick Castle, where the tired and dispirited band reached that night. The original Saxon structure had been improved by the construction of a wooden castle surrounded by a ditch in the mid-eleventh century. This in turn had been replaced nearly two hundred years later by a large stone structure and it was to this impressive building that Robert Catesby led his band of disappointed men that cold and damp November night.

"Where's the armoury?" asked Jack Wright, as they approached the castle. "You know, Robin, I'll take Kit and a half-dozen others and see if we can find it and then get some more muskets and gunpowder."

"No," said Catesby. "There's no need for that. I think we have enough already. If we take any more it will slow down our progress. And anyway, we have a supply waiting for us at Norbrook."

"So what do we need?"

"About ten fresh horses. Mine has been in trouble and limping since it threw a shoe near Dunchurch and I know Bates needs a fresh horse as well."

"True," added Bates. "And we also need some fresh horses for the wagon of gunpowder we've got. If we don't replace them soon, we will have to abandon it."

"But we can't take horses from here," Robert Wintour interrupted. "That would be stealing. And that will cause even more uproar. They'll say that we are thieves as well."

"As well as what?" Percy asked curtly.

"Murderers."

"But we haven't killed anyone," Jack Wright said, somewhat naively.

"Well, have it your own way then. But I still think we are going to do ourselves more harm than good," muttered Robert Wintour, and cantered off to speak to a few men who had joined them at Dunchurch.

However, despite Wintour's objections, Catesby and a few men did manage to steal, or 'exchange' a dozen horses from the castle's stables. They salved their consciences by saying that they were leaving their own horses behind instead. From Warwick they set out for Norbrook, the home of plotter John Grant together with about another twenty men who had just joined them. These additional forces seemed to bring hope to the original band and so they all set off in a much more optimistic frame of mind.

As they were leaving the city, Robert Wintour was pleased to recognize his step-brother ride up and meet them accompanied by two of his own men.

"John," Robert called out, sounding happy for the first time that day, "Oh I am glad to see you. But why are you here?"

"I have come to join your cause and I've also brought by close friend Stephen Littleton with me."

Robert shook hands with the newcomer and asked who the third man was.

"Henry Morgan. He's a friend of John Grant."

"So welcome to you too," Wintour said, shaking his hand too. "Let me go and inform Robin about your joining us. We need all the good news we can get at the moment." And before John Wintour could ask why, Robert had cantered off to find their leader.

It did not take long to cover the few miles to Norbrook and after loading up their wagon with another fifty muskets and gunpowder, the men moved into a field behind the house to rest and allow their horses do the same.

While they were resting, Sir Everard called Thomas Bates over to him.

"Thomas, I've just asked Robin if he will let you go and do a favour for me and he has agreed. So take this letter. It's for my wife, Mary. She will be at home at Coughton..."

"Coughton sir?"

"Yes, it's near Alcester. Do you know it?"

"Yes, sir. It's just a few miles north-west of Stratford."

"Good. So here's the letter, and if you meet Father Garnet and Father Greenway there, tell them about our situation and in which direction we are heading, west, that is."

"Yes sir," Bates said, preparing to mount.

"Ah, and Bates. Not a word to my wife about how I look. She is not used to hearing reports about me dressed as a dirty vagrant."

"Excuse me, sir. But you're not a vagrant."

"Well I'm not too sure about that at the moment. But get you gone and keep a sharp look out for any of the king's men."

"Yes, sir," and Catesby's servant galloped off in a westerly direction.

Sometime in the afternoon he returned with another man and the two of them rode over to where Catesby, Sir Everard, Percy and the Wright brothers were considering their next move.

"I gave the letter to your wife sir," Bates said, addressing the knight. "And Father Greenway decided to join me for the return journey."

The Jesuit priest came forward and shook hands with many of the assembled men, having met many of them in the past in his capacity as their confessor. Looking at some of the more despondent faces he said, "Fear not. Put your faith in the Lord. This day is not over yet. Remember my friends, faith and hope are what we need. So let us smile and pray and remember that our Lord died for us. And look over yonder. Isn't that a sign? Look, yet another man has come to join and support us."

And as the men strained their eyes, they could just make out the form of Thomas Wintour who had ridden from London as fast as his horse would allow him. Within minutes his aching body was helped down from the saddle as he was being pressed for the latest news from the capital.

"Have you seen Guido?"

"Did he divulge any names?"

"Do they know his true name?"

"Do they know how many there are of us?"

"Did they find the gunpowder?"

"Slowly friends," Wintour said, holding up a hand. "One question at a time, but first give me something to eat and then I'll have the strength to tell you all that I know."

After a snatched meal of damp bread, cheese and an apple, he told them of all the news and gossip that he had picked up.

"I do not know if what I have just told you be Gospel truth or not," he said at last, "but now I must sleep for at least two hours."

But this was not to be. An hour later, a rider came up to Catesby and said, "I'm not sure how true my report is, but I have heard that there is a band of the king's men not too far away out looking for us."

"Where?"

"East of here. East of Warwick, that is, somewhere in the direction of Ashby and Dunchurch."

"Ashby!" Catesby reacted, aghast at this piece of news. "My mother! I hope they don't question her."

"But Robin, it may not be true," Jack Wright said trying to calm his leader down.

"We cannot risk anything. Wake up Thomas Wintour and let us move on. We must put as great a distance as possible between us and the king's men. If the king's men are indeed east of Warwick, it won't take them long to hear of us or indeed to learn in which direction we are bound. So come everybody, mount up and be prepared to move off now."

"Yes," added Percy. "It's not every day in winter that fifty or sixty horsemen pass through some of these little villages."

All that afternoon, the band of Catholic fugitives rode west in the direction of Huddington, one of the Wintour clan's family homes. That night, for the first time since the plotters had left London, as well as for many of the others, it was the first time they had slept well and eaten a good meal. But when they left the following morning, they had to leave the comfort of the warm and dry country home and set off again, but this time in a driving rainstorm. After a quick conference between Catesby, the Wright brothers, the Wintours, Percy and Stephen Littleton, it was decided to change direction and aim for the latter's country house of Holbeach Hall in Staffordshire.

"By leaving now, and in the rain, and by changing our direction and heading north instead of west, I hope we'll fool anyone who is trying to follow us," Catesby told Percy and the Wright brothers.

"And hopefully, in the meanwhile more of our supporters will join us," Jack added.

But both Catesby and Jack were wrong.

As they set out in the direction of Holbeach, like wax on a rapidly melting candle, their numbers began to melt away in the rain. From over fifty supporters who had left Huddington in the early morning, they now numbered only three dozen. And if Catesby thought that he had thrown the king's men off the scent, he had made a fatal mistake. For at that moment, the authorities under the command of Sir Richard Walsh, the High Sheriff of Worcestershire were beginning to close in on the plotters' trail.

Robert Catesby had been extremely naive to think that a band of over fifty horsemen, together with a wagon load or two of supplies could cross the country during a national hue and cry, without attracting any official attention. Perhaps fortunately for the instigator of the plot, he was not aware of this as the sopping wet band made a short stop at Hewell Grange on their way north. The aim was to obtain more supplies and support from the fourteen-year old Lord Windsor, but he was not at home to greet them. It was only after they had taken more arms, which were not really necessary, more gunpowder and sixty pounds from a large money chest, did the fleeing men continue on their northbound route.

Leaving Hewell Grange, Catesby, as optimistic as ever, tried to persuade the local population who were standing by the roadside that the men were "for God and country." The only reply he received from the sombre and sulky bystanders was, "We are also for God and country - and King James."

Late that night, tired, saddlesore and hungry, the plotters and their remaining supporters arrived at Holbeach House. Although they were all in dire need of sleep, they realized they would have to guard and fortify the house.

"Listen, Robin," Robert Wintour said with a sense of urgency as some of the men were stacking some heavy chairs behind the front door, "I will go to Pepperhill, to my sister-in-law Gertrude's father, to see if I can get some more men to join us. And I will take Stephen Littleton with me."

"How far is that from here?"

"'Tis ten miles. And Stephen says that we'll be able to find our way there, even if the king's men are out there, for he knows this country well. We should be back in a few hours, so farewell and let's hope we return with John Talbot and some of his men."

"Farewell," replied Catesby. "But just one more thing. Leave quietly by the back gate so the others will not see you. If they do, they might think that you are deserting us."

Saluting Catesby, Robert Wintour and Littleton casually led their horses round to the back of the house, and as quietly as possible, mounted them and disappeared into the murky darkness and woods that were close by.

In the meanwhile, Catesby began to organize the defences of Littleton's two-storey red-brick house. As he was assigning the men to different look-out positions, Kit Wright came running up to him, completely out of breath.

"Robin, Robin," he gasped. "My brother and I have just discovered that about half of the gunpowder that we brought over in the first wagon has been ruined in the rain."

"What do you mean, ruined?"

"It's damp. It will be useless."

"So we cannot use it?"

"Not as it is. But if we warm it up in front of the fire, it should dry out."

"But that's dangerous. It could explode."

"Not if it's done carefully. It's been done before. Guido's told me some stories about things like that when he was in the army in Flanders."

"Well, be careful then. And keep the men away from it," Catesby called out after Kit's retreating back."

But the warning came too late. Several of the men had already started to spread the damp gunpowder out on the floor in front of the fireplace. Fifteen minutes Holbeach House was rocked by a tremendous thunderclap of an explosion as an ember landed in the mound of drying gunpowder. John Grant, who was on look-out duty in the room was immediately blinded, while Ambrose and Henry Morgan, who were standing near him with their backs to the fire were both badly burnt. As Jack burst into the room as a result of the noise, he found the three men writhing about and moaning in agony. John Grant was holding his hands to his eyes as blood trickled through his fingers making red rivulets over his blackened cheeks. Jack quickly took command of the situation.

"Quickly! quickly! Bring bandages! Get these wounds bound up!" he yelled as other men set to work to smother the burning embers and pieces of burnt furniture before there was yet another explosion. "And where's Bates and John Wintour? I need them here! Now! Go and find them!" he shouted to his brother.

Outside the building, in the Holbeach grounds, Sir Richard Walsh also heard the explosion followed by the anguished cries of the wounded men.

"What was that?" he asked a captain standing beside him.

"Sounds like exploding gunpowder to me, sir."

"Yes. I think you're right. Maybe they're trying to kill themselves before we get to them, eh?"

"That would save us a lot of trouble, sir."

Sir Richard ignored the cynical remark. "Captain," he commanded. "Take half of your men to the right of the house, near the trees there and wait. When you hear a single pistol shot, attack the northern wing. Sir Thomas Lawley will go with you."

"Yes, sir."

"I will take the left side and we'll both attack at the same time. I think that there's about thirty of them in there, so be careful. And keep an eye open for the top floor windows. Remember, we don't know how well they can see us from up there, even though it's dark."

"Yes, sir."

"And remember too. We don't know what that explosion was about. It might have been a ruse set to fool us, so be careful. And try and make sure your men don't fire on my men. Is all that understood?"

"Yes, sir."

"And by the way, if you can, try and take the men inside alive. I need some prisoners who can talk. At least, that's what the instructions that I received from London say, but if necessary, you may shoot those found inside or anyone trying to escape. Understood?"

"Yes, sir."

"Then off you go, and good luck."

"Thank you, sir."

The captain signalled his men to follow him, and by crouching low and ducking behind the garden shrubbery and walls, they moved into the shadows near the house. A few minutes later, the Wright brothers and Catesby heard a sharp crack from down below in the gardens.

"What was that?" Kit asked his brother.

"What?"

"That noise. Sounded like a firecracker to me."

"Could have been a pistol or a piece of wood breaking," Jack guessed.

"I don't know what it was," Catesby said. "But just be ready to fire back. This might be our last chance" he added and crossed himself fervently.

Kit looked at him and did the same.

"Come, let us pray," Catesby said, and knelt down, pulling out a small wooden cross out of his jerkin as he did so. He held it out high in front of him. A beam of light caught the small carved figure in the centre. "O Lord, and Jesus Christ Our Saviour," Catesby prayed. "If we are to lose our lives this night, please receive our souls knowing that all we have done was to bring honour to thee and the Catholic Church and the True Faith. Grant us this night the courage and steadfastness in the hours to come, so that we may carry out Thy holy work. This we do for Thy sake and for Thy sake alone. Amen."

"Amen."

"Now," Catesby said replacing the crucifix, "take up your places and God be with you all."

Silently the men shook hands with each other in a subdued and final manner before moving off to their assigned positions. It was as if they knew that they would not be seeing each other again. Thomas Percy stood next to Catesby by an open window, while Thomas Wintour slipped out to cross the courtyard to take up a forward position near the gate.

At the same time, Sir Richard gave his men their final orders.

"All right men. Have your muskets primed. Now let's go."

They moved out of the dark shadows and shrubs towards the dimly lit house. Acrid smoke was billowing out of the smashed window where the gunpowder had exploded. From inside, the king's men below could still hear the sounds of the men inside moaning in agony.

"Keep close to the walls unless you see any of them," Sir Thomas Lawley hissed to his men. "And try not to hit any of Sir Richard's men."

Relentlessly, like the pincers on a crab, the attacking forces closed in on the house.

"Quick man! There's one of them!" Sir Richard whispered to two sharpshooters next to him. "Shoot!"

They shot and saw Tom Wintour drop his musket with a crash and grab his shoulder where the musket-ball had torn through his muscles.

"Quick! Again!" Sir Richard shouted to another sharpshooter, but by then it was too late. By the time the soldier had taken aim, Tom Wintour had rushed out of sight into the house, pulling out his sword as he did so.

"Well, that looks like we have one man, or at least half a man less to deal with," the soldier said grimly.

"True. Now, let's get this thing over with," Sir Richard said as he indicated to his men to be prepared to charge the house.

As he said so, Jack Wright suddenly showed up, silhouetted against an upper floor window. Putting his finger to his lips Sir Richard motioned to four men to take up positions and aim up at the window. Two musket shots rang out and the men saw Jack Wright suddenly jump up into the air, as if a naughty girl had thrown her rag-doll about, and then fall, slumped over the window-sill. His musket, now hanging uselessly by his side, had its strap caught by the fallen man's elbow. Still looking up at the window, Sir Richard heard Kit call out to his brother.

"Jack! Jack! Are you all right? Dear God, what...?" And as his half-lit profile came into view by the window, two more shots rang out and Kit Wright fell back, throwing his drawn sword out of the window as he did so. The famous Wright sword clattered to the ground and after that there was silence; an intense silence that could almost be touched as well as felt. Crouching again in the shadows again, both Sir Richard's and Sir Thomas' forces could make out ghost-like shadows flitting about the dimly-lit house, but no more of the defenders were to be seen by the windows.

Suddenly a tall form appeared at one of the ground floor windows. It was holding a sword. "Shoot!" ordered Sir Richard and a moment later, a dazed Ambrose Rookwood was lying on the floor, clutching his torn and bleeding sword arm. The earlier accidental explosion of the gunpowder had left him dizzy and short of breath, and in his dizziness he had not realized that he had walked in front of an open window. Now he knew. The stinging pain in his upper arm had cleared away his dizziness. Keeping low, he crawled upstairs to where Catesby and Percy were standing hidden behind a heavy curtain.

"Robin, Thomas. There's no hope. We've failed. We're completely surrounded."

"Not true, Ambrose," Catesby replied trying to sound optimistic. "Robert Wintour and Stephen Littleton have gone to get help, and we're not completely surrounded yet. Let me see." And he moved out from behind the heavy curtain, calling out to Percy to do the same.

"Come, Tom. Can you see if we're surrounded or not?"

"No, not from here."

Suddenly there was a lull in the shooting.

"Tom, let's go downstairs to the front door and get a better view of our situation."

"But it's dangerous down there."

"Fear not. That thick wooden door will protect us from any musket-ball. Here, don't forget your own musket."

"But it's no use," Percy replied weakly. "I can't use my right arm and I can't use a sword with my left, so..."

But his last words were drowned out by a fresh round of shooting.

"Come, Tom. Let's race for that tree. It will give us shelter and allow us to see where the king's men are. We'll do it one at a time. That will give them a smaller target."

Seconds later, Catesby reached the broad trunk of the tree and signalled Percy to follow him. Percy succeeded in gaining the tree and stood by his leader, his right arm dangling uselessly by his side; his sword still in its scabbard. The sounds of exploding musket-balls grew louder and more menacing.

"Robin, they seem nearer," Percy whispered.

"Fear not, Tom. Stand by me and we will die together."

As he said this, John Streete of the Worcester militia took a careful and unhurried aim at the two figures under the tree and fired. When the cloud of acrid smoke had cleared, he could see Thomas Percy was lying on the ground in a rapidly growing pool of his own blood, while a couple of yards away, Robert Catesby lay writhing on the ground. His final act was to pull out his crucifix, kiss it and then throw out his arms in death, just like his beloved Saviour on the cross.

Following this bout of shooting, silence descended once again. Hidden behind a low stone wall, Sir Richard whispered a message to one of the soldiers next to him.

"Get you over to Sir Thomas Lawley and tell him when he hears another pistol shot from me in a few minutes, then he is to charge the house. Tell him to take anyone remaining in there alive. Remember, London wants some live witnesses. Now go, and..." as the soldier was preparing to dash off on his mission," don't forget to keep your head down."

A few minutes later, Sir Richard was able to make out Sir Thomas' raised white-gloved hand, signalling that he had received the message. As before, a pistol shot rang out, echoing around the courtyard.

"Charge!" yelled the two commanders in unison, as their men rushed the darkened outline of Holbeach House, their boots crunching over the gravel. Those expecting a long and protracted bout of shooting were disappointed. It was all over in a few minutes. The wounded Thomas Wintour, his shoulder now wrapped up in a bloody shirt was quickly overpowered as was Ambrose Rookwood. They found the latter sitting in a corner, nursing his smashed hand;

the sword that he had been so proud of, lying uselessly on the floor several feet away from him. After both men had been forced to stand, their arms were roughly pulled behind them and they were tightly bound. The soldiers were impervious to the plotters' screams of agony as their torn muscles and ligaments were subject to even more wrenching. No-one paid any attention as Tom Wintour's broken shoulder-joint cracked as a result of this rough treatment and started bleeding afresh. The red stain on his beige jacket started spreading out again. In the corner of a ground floor room Ambrose tried to get his captors to be more gentle with his bloody and mangled hand, but they would have none of it.

"Traitor!" they mocked him. "Blow up our king, would you?"

"Catholic scum!"

And one or two of the soldiers kicked the two plotters in the groin for good measure before hauling them outside to where the other prisoners were being gathered together.

"Be thankful we're not hanging you here, off yonder tree," a soldier cried out, pointing to the tree which had momentarily protected Catesby and Percy earlier on.

"Aye. That's a shame," said another. "A real shame."

"But fear not," called out his friend carrying a still smoking musket. "They'll have that pleasure to look forward to in London."

"And 'anging and quartering as well, no doubt," added another, drawing his finger across his throat.

And in the meanwhile, the remaining soldiers rushed through the darkened rooms and passageways of both floors looking for the remaining plotters and their supporters. In one of the upper rooms, they came across the bodies of Jack and Kit Wright lying bloodily across each other.

"See what we have here," gloated a fat sergeant, waving a lantern and ordering two of his men to bring more. "Two more of the traitors. Gone to their Maker, I'll be bound." He scratched his head as if in thought. "Strange how they look alike these two, no?" And he gave the two bodies a gratuitous kick or two.

"Well, better them dead than you, sergeant."

"Aye, true enough. But look at them boots and swords. Shame to leave 'em lying around. Real waste that is. Here, you and you. Help me get them off 'em." And with no respect for the dead brothers, they were stripped on the spot for their fine clothes and boots. A few minutes later, the bodies of the two swordsmen from York were bumped down the stairs and dragged across the gravelly yard leaving a bloody trail to mark their final passage. Outside in the busy courtyard, two more soldiers picked up the bleeding bodies and dumped them like sacks of flour onto a waiting farmcart.

"Shame they was killed in a way," one of the soldiers remarked. "They would have made a pretty pair of witnesses in London."

"Well, they don't look too pretty now, do they?" the fat sergeant added as he whirled Jack Wright's ornately engraved sword around his head. "Come, let's see if there's anyone else in the house. Maybe there's a few more swords like this to be had."

"Or boots like those," added his friend, and they returned in the direction of the house with a few more men looking for bodies and plunder.

"Here, sergeant! Here's two more of them!" called out one of the men as he almost tripped over the bodies of Robert Catesby and Thomas Percy lying under a tree. This time, the men did not rush the bodies for loot. Maybe it was the sight of Catesby's cross held above his head that caused them to stop. Then one of them gingerly prised open Catesby's fingers and took the small crucifix.

"Now, there's a fine piece of carving," he remarked, examining it quickly before stuffing it in his pocket. "My wife will certainly like that."

"Well, just don't tell her how you got it. Women tend to be a bit squeamish about things like that," his friend advised him, and they moved off into the house, following the others.

"Come, let's get these two on the cart with their friends," one of the other soldiers said.

"So, how many's that altogether, dead that is?"

"Four. There's those two what look like brothers and these two."

Suddenly they heard more shouting. "Here's another two traitors. Come here quickly before they try and escape!" But John Grant and Henry Morgan were beyond escaping. For they were found couching in a dark corner, the smell of burnt flesh hanging over them; their clothes charred and blackened.

"Oh, here's another pretty pair," jeered a friend of the sergeant. "But they don't smell too sweet now, do they?" he added, holding his nose in an exaggerated fashion.

"Come on. Get up you two," and he poked them with the point of his sword. Morgan was able to stand, but the shocked and blinded Grant did not understand what was going on around him. All he was aware of was the incessant ringing in his ears and the searing pain from where his eyes had once been.

The soldier prodded him again with his sword point. "Get up, you traitor," and forced the hapless Grant to stand. Like their fellow-plotters, Tom Wintour and Ambrose Rookwood, their arms were forced behind them before being roughly bound.

"Now take them outside with the others," the sergeant ordered, and Morgan and Grant were led away.

"What? Can't you see?" scoffed one of the men as Grant stumbled along the corridor and walked into a wall.

"'Course not," another mocked. "Look where his eyes used to be. Ugh! All that blood and stuff!"

"Well, he's a lucky fellow really," his friend added. "He won't be able to see the 'angman's rope when they put it 'round 'is neck now, will 'e?" And he pushed the unfortunate Grant along the wood panelled corridor towards the front door. As the blinded plotter was being pushed forward round a corner, he was suddenly knocked sideways by another soldier. "Careful man. You don't want to fall down one of your priest's 'oles, now do you?"

Down by the entrance hall, one of the soldiers was trying to prise a couple of musket balls out of the heavy wooden door. "Leave it man," his friend said. "There's plenty more where they came from. And I don't think we'll be needing any more tonight, do you? Now let's go and see what's happening outside."

As the remaining plotters and their few supporters were being rounded up and accounted for, Robert Wintour and Stephen Littleton were making their way back to Holbeach House, using little-used side-roads and bridle-paths.

About a quarter mile from the house, Wintour reined his horse to a halt and signalled to Littleton to do the same.

"Stephen. Can you hear shooting?" Wintour whispered, cupping his hands.

"Aye, I can and I'm sure it's coming from Holbeach."

"What do you think is...?" Wintour started to ask when suddenly he stopped. Standing there in front of him was one of their supporters who had joined them at Huddington.

"Sirs. I didn't mean to alarm you," he said as he saw both men reach for their swords. "But I have a message for you. All is lost and everyone has fled. That is those who could."

"But what happened? What went wrong? What...?"

"I don't know sir. Just that there was an almighty explosion and now the king's soldiers are all over the house. So take my advice and fly while you can."

And before Wintour and Littleton could ask any questions, the man had shot off into the dark and rambling undergrowth like a frightened rabbit and was gone.

"So Tom, what do we do now?" Littleton asked. It was obvious that the messenger, whoever he was, had touched a raw nerve and Littleton was visibly shaking.

"Stephen, I don't know what to think any more. But all I know is that it would serve no purpose in returning to Holbeach now."

"So, where shall we go?" the still shaking Stephen asked.

"I don't know. Wait. Wait a minute. Don't you have an uncle who lives near here?"

"Uncle Humphrey?"

"Aye. That's him."

"Well, doesn't he have a house near here?"

"Aye. Hagley House."

"And it's not too far, is it?"

"No. Just a few miles to the south-east," Littleton replied, thankful that Robert had taken the lead and that they would be heading away from the smoking building which had been his family home.

"So come. Let's get going. We cannot wait around in these woods for long. If that other fellow found us as he did, it won't take that long for the king's soldiers to find us. So let's get moving."

Meanwhile, several miles north of where Wintour and Littleton were now in the process of changing direction, Sir Everard Digby, together with another two men who had succeeded in escaping from Holbeach under the cover of darkness had managed to get to Dudley. However, here they were spotted by a number of the king's troopers who had been instructed to keep a sharp look out for small groups of horsemen travelling along little-used routes.

"Halt! or I fire!" shouted a local militiaman.

Digby looked at the two men with him, and with a slight movement of his head indicated that they should try and flee the posse by going through the nearby woods. Suddenly, shots rang out and Digby galloped into the direction of the woods, closely followed by the other two fugitives.

"Here, we'll hide in this ditch and hope they miss us. It's our only chance," hissed Digby after a few minutes. Dismounting from their horses, they put their hands over the creatures' muzzles and hoped that the blackness and the foliage would swallow them up. It didn't. Suddenly, the rustling of the nearby leaves was shattered by a cry, "Here they are! Here they are!" It was followed by the sound of their pursuers' hooves crashing through the undergrowth towards them.

"Here they are! Here they are!" the militiaman shouted again.

"Here he is indeed!" Digby shouted back. "But what then?" And before the posse could catch up with him, he had bounded into the saddle and leapt out of the ditch in one smooth movement and raced along a track in the wood. Suddenly he brought his horse to a halt. In front of him he could see what looked like a hundred of the king's men. They had fanned out over the track and Digby saw that there was no way of escape. For a moment, he thought of trying to outrace them, but on looking behind, he saw that he was completely surrounded. And not only that, but several of the men were standing near their horses, their muskets ready. To the right of him, Digby noted the two men who had escaped with him were now mounted, but with their arms bound behind them. Digby saw that he had no choice. The game was up. The noble courtier, gallant as ever, removed his hat with an elegant sweep and then gently raised his arms in surrender.

"Throw down your sword!...and slowly!" an officer ordered. Digby slowly leaned over in the saddle and unbuckled his scabbard, as if he had all the time in the world. He gently let it slide to the ground with a clatter.

"Back to Holbeach with you! You traitor." the officer said pompously and ordered one of his men to tie the plotter's arms up behind his back.

"And then?" Digby asked, keeping his voice calm.

"London, and the hangman's rope I expect," came the curt reply. And they all clattered off in the direction of Holbeach where Sir Richard Walsh was standing in the centre of the courtyard trying to make some order out of the noisy and chaotic situation.

"Now, who have you got there?" he asked, as the officer of the militia rode over to him to make his report.

"Three prisoners, sir. One of them is Sir Everard Digby, and the other two include a John Arden and a William something or other. He can't speak too well on account of a wound on his face sir. We found them a few miles back, in a wood near Dudley. You know, where you told us to be on a special look out for such men. They were trying to escape but we caught them in the end."

"Very good. You did a good job there," Sir Richard said, laying a gloved hand on the officer's shoulder. "Now let's see who else we have here. The more the merrier I would say. Salisbury is going to be very pleased with this night's work. So tell me, who have we got here now. It's time to make a list."

"There's Ambrose Rookwood, sir."

"The one whose hand was shot up?"

"Yes, sir. And with him are Henry Morgan and John Grant."

"The one who was blinded in the explosion?"

"Yes, sir."

"Well you might say that that was quite ironic," Sir Richard remarked with a bitter smile. "They got their gunpowder explosion, you might say, but the wrong men got hurt. At least, that is what they would say, no? And so, right, now who else is there?"

"There's a Thomas Wintour, sir, and..."

"And who of them was shot?"

"A Robert Catesby, sir and a Thomas Percy. And you'll never believe it sir, but they were killed by the same musket-ball," the officer said. "I've recommended that the man who did that particular piece of work, Master John Streete, be recommended for a prize, sir."

"Very good. Now weren't two others found shot? In the house?"

"Yes sir. Two brothers. Jack and Kit Wright."

"But there's still a few more of them, no?"

"Yes, sir. Sir Everard Digby is being held with the other captured men upstairs where they can't escape, in one of the small rooms at the back, and I think there are still a few men whom we haven't caught yet, and as such, I don't know their names, sir."

Sir Richard took a piece of paper from his pouch.

"This is the list the Earl of Salisbury sent to us. Now according to this, Thomas Bates, that is, Catesby's servant and Robert Keyes are still missing. And so is a certain Robert Wintour. And while we are here, I would dearly like to get my hands on Mister Stephen Littleton. He's the owner of this house, and I would like to know if he was a willing accomplice to all this, or if he was forced to give over his house to these men."

"Yes, sir. I doubt if the missing men have got very far sir. If we've managed to capture this Sir Everard fellow, no doubt we'll get the others very soon. In fact sir, according to some reports my men have received, the local Catholics don't want anything to do with these men. No-one wants to be tainted with treason sir, if you know what I mean."

"I do," the Sheriff of Worcester said grimly and made the sign of the cross. "But I wonder just where these men are. I would like to be able to send the whole lot of them to London in one package as it were. It would be much easier than to send them in small groups and then have to worry about arranging guards for them. It would also be good for the reputation of our local militia, no?"

But Sir Richard Walsh did not have to wonder for very long, at least as far as Robert Keyes was concerned. He was spotted the next day in Warwickshire and was accused of trying to link up with his fellow recusants in the Midlands. He was interrogated by Sir Fulke Greville for a few days in Warwick, and by the end of the month he was sent to London to join the other plotters in the Tower.

On the same day Keyes was being questioned, Thomas Bates was captured in Staffordshire, not too far away from Holbeach House. Just as he noticed the king's men were closing in on him, he buried a pouch containing a hundred pounds that Kit Wright had thrown to him just before he fled Holbeach House.

Hauled before the local magistrate, it was quickly established that Thomas Bates was of lower birth, and as such he was imprisoned temporarily in the Staffordshire Gatehouse prison, together with such undesirable characters as cut-purses, debtors and vagabonds. He was not to stay in their company for long. For soon after, like his fellow conspirators, he was dispatched to the dungeons in London, where he would be questioned regarding his complicity in the gunpowder plot. Now only Robert Wintour and Stephen Littleton remained on the run and in hiding, doing their desperate best to stay out of Salisbury's clutches.

The night of 7 November found the two fugitives hidden in the woods, about a mile away from Holbeach House. They were dirty, scared and very nervous. Both were lightly armed only with their swords as they had buried their unwieldy muskets in the woods. "We won't be needing these," Wintour said, kicking some fallen greenery over the pile of earth. He told Littleton to do the same. "They take too long to fire, and besides, if people see us carrying muskets for no apparent reason, they will take notice of us and then start asking questions."

They continued walking through the forest, straining to catch sight or sound of any of the king's men whom they guessed would be on the look-out. Several hours later, looking as filthy and unkempt as the prisoners in Bates' Staffordshire cell, they threw their exhausted bodies down at the foot of a huge oak tree. Covering themselves with branches, more for camouflage than for warmth, they immediately fell asleep. They were woken up a few hours later by the sounds of heavy footsteps squashing the leaves and cracking the twigs.

"Oh, what have we here?" sang the drunken poacher. "Two babes in the wood. I wonder if they be alive or not."

"Sssh man," hissed Wintour, already wide awake.

"Why? What's up?" asked the poacher, grinning and slurring his words.

"Nothing man. Now are you alone?" Littleton asked, now standing up and fully awake.

"Can you see anyone with me?" the poacher asked, leaning on the tree trunk to support him. "My wife has cast me out. Have yours done the same? Women, huh!" he added with contempt. "What a world we have come to, if wives can throw their menfolk out of the house! Huh!"

"We're not married," said Littleton, not wanting to talk about women. "But by the way, do you have any food in that bag of yours?"

"Aye," said the poacher, slowly eyeing Wintour and Littleton. "But it'll cost you. I've had a good night and I bagged a rabbit or two."

Half an hour later, crouched around a smouldering fire of charcoal and embers, the three men were eating bits of rabbit with their fingers. The two plotters were too hungry to comment on the quality of their meal or on how they were eating it. It was obvious to them, that the world that they had known had completely changed. As they were finishing off and licking their fingers, Wintour motioned to Littleton to come closer.

"Stephen, we cannot let this fellow wander off and tell everyone that he has seen us."

"So what shall we do with him?" Littleton asked, who had accepted Wintour as his leader.

"Either we kill him or tie him up."

"I cannot kill him," Littleton asserted. "Can you?"

"No. Not really."

Five minutes later, a very surprised, and by now, a very sober poacher found himself trussed up like one of his rabbits, complete with a rag for a gag in his mouth. His attackers were very apologetic.

"Sorry, my good man. But we have no choice," Littleton said. "But take this for your pains." And he laid a few coins on the ground near the squirming poacher.

"Come. Let's move," commanded Wintour.

"But where to? We cannot live in the forest like Robin Hood."

"We'll continue to your Uncle Humphrey's house at Hagley as planned," replied Wintour. "He won't give us away, will he?"

"Who? Red Humphrey? Of course not. He's an ardent Catholic. He even tried to get a Catholic elected as an M.P."

"Well, that sounds safe enough for me. So let's make for your uncle's then."

However, soon after the two men reached Hagley, Uncle Humphrey had to move them out of the house itself. That evening, in one of the out-buildings, their host came out to explain the situation.

"Listen. Government agents have put out handbills describing you. I've got one here. They are not very flattering descriptions and maybe you're lucky that there aren't any pictures, but..."

"Let me see," Littleton said, snatching the page from his uncle's hand.

"You're right," Wintour agreed. "They don't flatter us."

"So what are we going to do?" Littleton asked. "You can't just throw us out into the winter cold. It's raining now and..."

"Yes, yes. I know all that," Humphrey replied quickly. "But fear not. I have already made arrangements what to do with you. I have bribed one of my tenant farmers near Bowley Regis to hide you and there you will stay till this hue and cry blows over. And don't worry, for nobody apart from the three of us knows the truth about this business. I've told him to tell his wife, if she asks any questions about the money, that he made a good deal at the market in Dudley."

"So when are we to move?"

"Tonight. I'll hide you in a cart and take you over to Bowley later. Now eat up and let us get ready."

For the next few weeks, the two runaways remained hidden in different barns and out-buildings in the Bowley Regis area. Every few nights, they moved from one hiding place to another, moving only after sunset and then only for a brief while.

One evening, a drunken stranger, looking for a straw bed and shelter, staggered into their barn. Before he could escape, Wintour and Littleton caught him and handed him over to Humphrey's servant, Parkes. He was held for five days, but then managed to escape. To make sure his nephew and Wintour would not be discovered at Bowley, Humphrey had them brought back to Hagley. This proved to be their undoing.

John Finwood, Humphrey's cook, became suspicious about the extra portions he was told to prepare. He asked around and Humphrey's widowed sister-in-law, Muriel did not give him any convincing answers. Soon, the cat was out of the bag.

As a result, two months after the king and Parliament were supposed to have been blown sky-high, Robert Wintour and Stephen Littleton were captured. Wintour was destined to be executed in London after a short stay in the Tower, while Littleton was executed at Stafford, together with Henry Morgan in April 1606. Uncle Humphrey was sent to Worcester prison where he betrayed several recusants to the authorities in the hope of saving himself from the traditional and grim punishment reserved for traitors. Naturally, the authorities were very pleased with this latest information, but such was the fear and revulsion regarding the Gunpowder Plot and the Catholic network, that Humphrey Littleton was publicly executed at Redhill, Worcestershire some three months later.

With the capture of Robert Wintour and Stephen Littleton, all the plotters were accounted for. For Salisbury it must have been a very pleasing occasion as he sat with the other members of the Council to prepare their trial. Now all he had to do was to arrange the final details. It would be held at the end of January 1606 in Westminster Hall. In the meanwhile, Guido Fawkes had supplied him with more than enough information after Salisbury's men had followed the king's instructions to the letter: '*et sic per gradus ad ima tenditur*' - the gentler tortures proceeding to the worst.

Chapter Twelve
Stamping out the embers

6 November 1605.

Forty pairs of eyes watched Robert Cecil, Earl of Salisbury and Principal Secretary to His Majesty King James pull himself slowly to his feet, adjust his fur-trimmed black velvet hat, and shuffle through the papers he had on the desk in front of him.

"Gentlemen of the Council," he began slowly. "Before I address you and commence with the business of the day, I would like to say that I am truly and sincerely glad to be standing here in front of you this morning, healthy both in wind and limb. For as you will appreciate it, had those evil and wicked Catholic conspirators succeeded in their iniquitous plot, many of us gathered here now, would have been gathered up and this meeting would have had to be held in the heavens above, instead of in here, in these earthly chambers below, in London."

His opening remarks were received with dry laughs and quiet smiles as many of the lords and gentlemen present thought about the Secretary's words. By now they had learnt that they had been a major part of the target for the three dozen barrels of gunpowder which had been concealed below in the cellars at Westminster. A few of those present were beginning to comment on this when Salisbury knocked on the floor for order with his silver-knobbed cane. There was immediate silence.

"Gentlemen," he began again. "I would like to acquaint you with some details pertaining to this plot, that we have, through the grace of God, survived. The first is that I have dispatched a letter to Sir Thomas Parry, our ambassador in France, informing him of the present situation. I will now read to you the opening lines from this copy of the letter:

> *Sir Thomas Parry, I would like to inform you that it has pleased Almighty God, out of His singular goodness, to bring to light the most cruel and detestable practice, against the person of His Majesty and the whole estate of the realm that ever was conceived by the heart of man, at any time, or in any place whatsoever.*

As before, Salisbury's reading was received with thoughtful smiles and nods of the head. After summing up the remainder of the letter, the Secretary placed it on the table in front of him and addressed the Council.

"And if we are to continue with the international ramifications of this plot, then I will now inform you gentlemen that all the ports have been ordered to be closed and all suspicious people found nearby to be taken into custody so that they may be thoroughly questioned.

"However, I must also inform you that in the interests of national and international trade, the ports will not be closed for long. I assume this will be the situation for a week or so at the most. By then, I hope we will have apprehended all the plotters and the scale of their conspiracy will be known. I have also had orders dispatched to our ambassadors in France and Spain, which of course includes the Spanish Netherlands, asking them to inform me if they have learnt anything that might help us with our endeavours to discover the whole truth about this plot."

Disregarding the nods of agreement, the Secretary continued.

"I have also ordered that the Lord Mayors of London and Westminster to double the watch at the gates of the city, and as I said before, all manner of suspicious persons are to be arrested and questioned. In addition, I have also given orders to the civil authorities and the various watches, that mobs must not be allowed to build up and congregate, especially around such properties belonging to foreign Catholic dignitaries and ambassadors serving in this country. This of course applies especially to the Spanish ambassador. Mob rule cannot be allowed, even if it is motivated by patriotism..."

"... or loot," a lord at the back of the room added loudly.

Salisbury acknowledged the truth of this remark with a small smile and continued.

"In fact, I would hasten to add, that several of the ambassadors here in London, including the Catholic ones, have lit their own bonfires of thanksgiving and have also seen fit to distribute alms and other moneys to the poor and the needy.

"But now gentlemen, I wish to inform you, that is, for those of you who do not know all the details, of what has happened since we arrested this Catholic criminal John Johnson two days, or rather, two nights ago."

Salisbury paused, looked around the chamber for effect and proceeded.

"Immediately upon being apprehended underground in the cellars by Sir Thomas Knyvett and his men, this John Johnson was bound up and brought before some of you, the Lords of the Council, who had been especially summoned here for the purpose. By then it was about four o'clock in the morning and His Majesty thought it prudent to be present as well. Having been caught red-handed, complete with the means of setting fire to these barrels of gunpowder, Johnson immediately admitted that indeed it had been his aim to blow up His Majesty together with all the members sitting in Parliament for that opening ceremony. He also admitted to being a Catholic as well."

Some of the Catholic lords present squirmed uncomfortably in their leather chairs, but Salisbury continued unperturbed.

"Immediately after he was arrested, he was questioned and asked if John Johnson was his real name. He replied that it was, and that he came from Yorkshire, his mother and father being called Edith and Thomas Johnson. He was then searched by a soldier and a letter was found on his person. This was addressed to a certain Guido Fawkes. When interrogated about this, he claimed that Guido Fawkes was a name by which some of his friends knew him. Naturally we were very sceptical about this, since when people choose to have other names, or different names thrust upon them, they are usually names given out of love and affection such as Bill for William, Kit for Christopher and so on. And of course, as it seems to be in this case, other names are sometimes given to hide the true identity of the bearer, usually for criminal or other nefarious reasons.

"And gentlemen, this was not the only surprising thing we learnt that night, or early morning, if you wish. For when His Majesty asked the prisoner if he had any regrets for doing, or attempting to do what he planned, he very calmly replied that he had no regrets. He said that not only did he wish to blow up His Majesty for his anti-Catholic actions, but also because he was a Scot and that the planned explosion would have been strong enough to blow him back to Edinburgh. He also said that it was the devil and not God who was responsible for him being caught."

Salisbury stopped and smiled. "Then I must be the devil. For I have known about such plots for a long time, and I must tell you that this bunch of plotters have played into our hands. Is that not so?" And he looked directly at Lord Monteagle and the Earl of Northumberland, Percy's Parliamentary employer. As before, they both squirmed uncomfortably in their seats. To be on the wrong side of Robert Cecil, the Earl of Salisbury in such matters could be dangerous, if not fatal.

The hunchbacked Principal Secretary straightened himself up as much as possible and raised a fistful of papers to show that he had more to report.

"Then gentlemen, His Majesty asked the prisoner, John Johnson or Guido Fawkes, whatever his true name is, how he could have wished to cause the deaths of the king's own innocent children who were to be present in Parliament that night. And what was this criminal's reply, gentlemen? It was an empty cliché, a phrase without meaning. He said that such a dangerous disease, and by that he was referring to His Majesty and us, his servants, required a desperate remedy to be got rid of. Naturally this shocked His Majesty, who then informed the prisoner that not only would he have killed his king, an anointed servant of God, but that he would have killed his family as well as the country's leading lords, some of whom were Catholics like himself."

"And what did he reply to that?" an impatient lord on the front row asked.

"He replied that he would have prayed for their dear departed souls," Salisbury said, trying to keep his face impassive. He repeated his last words slowly, for effect. "Their dear departed souls."

Salisbury looked around the chamber again slowly, his eyes momentarily resting on the Catholic lords present before continuing with his report.

"Finally, the prisoner stated that he refused to recognize His Majesty as his true and legitimate sovereign, and that those present, including myself had no authority to question him. When asked who did have such authority, his reply consisted of a single word - God.

"I must admit to this Council, that His Majesty was much struck by the man's attitude. He immediately compared him to Scaevola, whom you will doubtlessly know from your happy schooldays, was the Etruscan spy who, when captured, held his hand over a sacrificial fire in order to show he did not fear torture. Nevertheless, even though His Majesty may have respected the prisoner's courage and perverse steadfastness of purpose, he has given me this note saying that this John Johnson or Guido Fawkes is to be made to divulge the truth. His Majesty has informed me that torture is to be used if necessary to achieve that end.

"And so gentlemen, I come to the end of my report, and all that remains for me to tell you is that the prisoner is now in the Tower. So far, and I repeat, so far he has refused to tell us the names of the other plotters, or of how many others were involved. But I assure you, that after being looked after by and left to the tender mercies of Sir William Waad, the Lieutenant of the Tower and his worthy assistants, the prisoner will soon be singing like the proverbial nightingale or lark, though probably not as sweetly.

"In the meanwhile, the Chief Justice, Sir John Popham has given me this list and it says:

> There is pregnant suspicion to be had of Robert Catesby, Ambrose Rookwood, Robert Keyes, Thomas Wintour, Jack Wright, Christopher or Kit Wright and a suspicious person of the name of Grant.

"I cannot tell you if this is a true or complete list or not, but no doubt we will know more in a few days. This session is now concluded, and when I have more information I shall recall you. So good day gentlemen, to you all."

If Salisbury were wishing his fellow Privy Councillors a good day, then this was not to be for the man who was the subject of his report, Guido Fawkes. The following day the bound and closely guarded prisoner was led to a poorly lit room at the base of the Bloody Tower and introduced to Sir William Waad, the Lieutenant of the Tower.

"Do you know who I am?" the official began, standing opposite his prisoner, arms akimbo.

"No, sir."

"I am Sir William Waad, the Lieutenant of the Tower, and I have orders here from His Majesty King James to extract the truth from you about this damned Gunpowder Plot. You are Guido or Guy Fawkes, or just plain Fawkes to me, or even John Johnson. My job will be to find out and your job will be to give me this truth. Do you understand me?"

Fawkes looked down and said nothing.

"I see. Now if you tell me everything quickly and easily, all will go well with you. However, if you insist on acting like one of your Catholic heroes, such as Babington or that Father Edmund Campion fellow, then you will find your stay here somewhat painful. Is that understood?"

Fawkes kept looking down at the floor. He did not reply and tried to distract himself from the present situation by thinking about what had happened to his fellow-plotters. Had they got away, or had they been caught? His thoughts were disturbed when Sir William put a long hard finger under his jaw and jerked his head upright in one sharp painful movement.

"That's better. Now look at me. Better still, look at him." And he pointed to a large brawny man standing in the gloom at the back of the cell. "That man is my assistant, and he is very good in persuading silent and stubborn Catholics like yourself to talk. He has a bit of a weird sense of humour and calls it singing instead of talking, but no matter. Whatever it is, it will not be the singing of Psalms or any of your regular Catholic songs. Do you understand me?"

Receiving no reply, Waad continued. "So let us begin. What is your real name? John Johnson or Guido or Guy Fawkes?"

"John Johnson."

"Yes, I've heard that one before. That's what the Earl of Salisbury told me. But he also said that you may be called Guido Fawkes, or Guy Fawkes as well. Now, after listening to me telling you about telling the truth, what is your name, your real name?"

Fawkes remained silent. After two or three minutes of intense silence, when the only sound that could be heard was that of Sir William Waad pacing up and down on the dirty straw. He then stopped, thrust his jaw into his prisoners' face and started again. This time his tone was harder and more insistent.

"Now Mister Fawkes or Johnson, this is the last time. I'm asking you to tell me your real name. Is it Johnson or Fawkes? If you choose not to tell me, I will ask my assistant here to persuade you to do so. He will do so of course, with the help of those manacles and chains you can see on the wall in front of you. Now, have I made myself clear?"

Fawkes did not reply. He was wondering how long he would be able to remain silent while being manacled to the wall. He had heard grisly stories, while he had been in Flanders, of prisoners suffering permanent dislocation in their wrists and other joints after having been manacled. He knew the way they were used. The prisoner would have these iron 'bracelets' locked onto them for an hour or so, and then the wooden box or log would be kicked away. The unfortunate prisoner would then be left to dangle on the wall like a piece of damp washing or loose chain.

He looked up at Sir William defiantly and straightened his back. "My name is John Johnson. I am a Catholic and proud of it, and that is all I am going to tell you."

"Oh is it?" replied the king's chief jailer gleefully. "We'll see about that! Tie him up to the wall and then let him see what I think about him and his fellow Catholic and Papist traitors!"

As Fawkes was having the manacles attached to his wrists, the Lieutenant of the Tower continued his diatribe. "You Catholics are the scourge of this country and I will help His Majesty as best as I can in ridding the country of you all. If you did not know, Mister John Catholic Johnson, or whatever your blessed name is, it was I who was responsible for the racking and interrogations of those who were involved in the Bye and Main plots. I also had a hand in the interrogation of the Babington plotters too. So you can see, my fine fellow, I have had much experience in persuading you miserable Catholics to tell the truth and see the light, that is, before you rot in purgatory. And now," he said turning towards the door, "we'll leave you here for a little while, with your conscience for company, and see if you grow any wiser..."

"...or longer," his assistant added with a leer.

"Or yes indeed longer, by the time we return."

And saying that, he gave a vicious kick to the wooden block under Fawkes' feet and left him hanging there. Sharp needles of pain immediately shot through his unsupported muscles and his head fell forward.

When the Lieutenant, accompanied by some of his men returned a few hours later, they were greeted by a pale and haggard prisoner.

"Well, are you going to tell me your true name, or do you need any more reminding?"

"I will tell you my name," Fawkes managed to say. "But I will tell you nothing more."

"Oh, we are proud, aren't we? So, what is your name?" asked Waad, playfully kicking the wooden block around on the straw and making sure it remained just out of range of the prisoner's dangling feet. "Guy Fawkes or John Johnson? Or is it maybe some other name we haven't yet heard of?"

"No," gasped Fawkes. "It is truly Guy or Guido Fawkes, but that is all that I will tell you."

"So, we'll see about that one. But in the meantime, your manacles will be removed. You will learn that I am not really such a bad man Mister Fawkes, and you will see that it pays to tell the truth here, the whole truth that is. And now I will hasten away to the Earl of Salisbury and inform him that you have begun to talk." And giving orders to his assistant to unlock the manacles, he walked towards the door.

Just as he was about to leave the cell, he stopped and looked back at his prisoner, now lying on the dirty straw, rubbing his raw wrists.

"Think on your sins, Catholic. For tomorrow, unless you start talking, I have been given personal instructions, that is from the Earl of Salisbury himself, to use the rack or any other means I have here to persuade you to tell me the truth. And you know what that means, I suppose? That means that I can put you in our special cell, you know the one we call 'Little Ease.' And do you know why it is so called? No? Well, I'll tell you anyway. Because it is so small and cramped that's all you'll be getting there. Little ease. See? And of course, if that doesn't suit you, we can always accommodate you with the 'scavenger's daughter.'"

At this point Waad's assistant chuckled loudly.

"And do you know who this young lady is? No, she's not your usual pretty wench. She's a particularly small cage lined with manacles and she doesn't let you stand up, sit down or do anything. Not very pleasant. No, not indeed." He rubbed his hands. "And so Mister Guy Fawkes, I'll leave you with this thought for the night, that is before you say your prayers. Tomorrow, unless you are forthcoming with the truth, that is, all the truth, it will be either the rack, the 'scavenger's daughter' or 'Little Ease.' Now which one is it going to be?" And leaving Guy Fawkes with that grim choice hanging over him for the night, the Lieutenant left.

As he promised, he returned the following morning accompanied by his assistant, four soldiers and another man. Ordering the soldiers to wait outside, Waad and the other two entered the smelly cell. Guy Fawkes was still lying on the floor, his face drawn and pale.

"Now, what is it to be, Fawkes? A quick and simple confession, or a session with the rack, eh? We'll not use the 'scavenger's daughter' or 'Little Ease.' They take too long and my Lord Cecil wants answers now. So let's be on our way. Oh, by the way, please excuse my bad manners but I have not yet introduced this man to you. He is the rackmaster and he is very good at his work. I have never known him to fail yet."

Guy Fawkes said nothing. He looked as if he had not heard anything. Waad was not perturbed by this.

"Now, listen Mister Fawkes and listen well. You are not a stupid man, so think on what I have to tell you very carefully. I have witnessed many a man who has been racked and not a single one of them was able to hold out. In the end, they all told the truth. Catholic and non-Catholic, traitor and all. They all confessed in the end. Now which is it to be?"

The prostrate prisoner looked straight up at his jailer, spat, but said nothing. Waad looked unimpressed.

"Fawkes, if you think those manacles hurt you yesterday, think again. They were like ...how shall I describe it?.. ah yes, the tickle of a swan's feather under the armpits, that is, in contrast to what you'll feel with the rack. So I'm giving you your last chance. Are you going to confess now or not?"

Fawkes spat again and said nothing.

"Well, if that's how you want it, on your Catholic head be it. And it will be on your head, believe me. Now you men, take the prisoner below to the racking room. And you," he pointed to another guard. "Take this message to the Privy Council. It will inform those members who are present that Mister Fawkes has lost his tongue, but will find it soon enough. Now let us be about our business."

Escorted by three burly pikemen and the Tower's leading officials, Guy Fawkes was marched downstairs to the most dreaded room in the Tower of London. As they descended deeper into the bowels of the Wakefield Tower, the air became noticeably thicker and one could easily hear the dripping of the water as it seeped through the walls or dripped from the low stone ceilings. It was as if the Tower was crying for the pain and anguish that it had seen inflicted there. The small group stopped at the end of a long and gloomy corridor and one of the guards pushed open a heavy door.

The dreaded rack. The only one of its kind in England lay on the floor in the centre of the room. Standing between it and the back wall were several members of the Privy Council who had been sent over on the Earl of Salisbury's instructions in order to witness the scene. None of them really wanted to be there. Several had witnessed previous rackings, and the cries and pain of the victim had been too much for their sensitivities.

Guy Fawkes looked at the rack. It was as he had imagined it, if not a little larger. It consisted of an oblong frame with a wooden roller at each end. At the end of the rollers were square holes in which the rackmaster and his assistants would insert poles to move the rollers round a notch or two, as Lieutenant Waad deemed fit and ordered accordingly. The prisoner's arms and legs were to be spread-eagled and tied to the rollers with strong ropes. There was no point in racking someone if the ropes snapped. Guy Fawkes, or anyone else in fact, did not need much of an imagination to picture what would happen next.

Within minutes, Guy Fawkes was stripped of his outer clothes and laid down within the wooden frame. His arms and legs, still aching from his previous torture with the manacles, were immediately tied to the two rollers. Two men checked that the knots were tight and two others tested the tautness of the ropes. As far as the Lieutenant was concerned, the rackmaster could now proceed. He had received written permission from the king and his Principal Secretary, and now all that remained was to see how long it would be before his prisoner surrendered to the pain. And surrender he would. No-one had ever resisted to the end. That is, if one didn't consider dying on the rack as resisting to the end. The art of it all, was of course to rack someone until they would confess everything. A dead prisoner who took his confession with him to his miserable grave was of no use at all to the authorities.

In a quiet tone, as if he were in his room asking someone a favour, Sir William Waad almost whispered, "Tell me Fawkes, who was involved in this plot with you?"

No answer. The members of the Privy Council held their breath and waited. They were hoping that Fawkes would confess and so save themselves from witnessing the terrible scenes that were bound to follow.

Waad repeated his question again. Still quietly, but now more insistently.

"Tell me, Fawkes, who was involved in this cowardly plot with you?"

No answer.

Without saying a word, Waad indicated with his hand to the rackmaster that the rollers were to be turned through one hole each. The ropes took the strain and Guy Fawkes winced as the hot and sharp needles of pain raced up his arms and legs. His body had broken out in cold sweat.

The Lieutenant leaned over to his prisoner. "Fawkes, you miserable plotter. Do you know why the rack is so called? No. I don't suppose you do. Well, it comes from the Dutch word 'recken' which means 'to stretch.' And that is precisely what I intend to do to you. Stretch you until you tell me the truth. And by the way, some wits working in the Tower think the word rack comes from the word 'wreck,' for that is what you will be in an hour's time. So think on that one too."

Fawkes did not react. He was gritting his teeth against the present pain, and against the pain he knew would follow very quickly.

"So now I'll ask you again. Who else was involved in your stinking plot?"

Fawkes just stared at him and watched as Waad signalled the rackmaster to turn the rollers round yet one more hole. The shooting pains were unbearable, and Fawkes could feel his whole body break out again in sweat, especially as the central roller under his back meant that the pressure on his already aching joints was maintained at the same level.

"Is this really necessary Lieutenant?" one of the Privy Councillors asked as Waad was about to order his men to continue with their gruesome task.

"I'm afraid it is, sir. As I told you earlier, I have received specific instructions from the king and the Earl of Salisbury, that until this man tells us what we want, we must continue."

And continue he did. For two days Guy Fawkes held out against the combined power of the rack and the will of Sir William Waad, but finally he collapsed. His half-broken body with its torn and dislocated limbs and joints surrendered just as the king's chief jailer had predicted. In the end, Guy Fawkes was forced to divulge the name of Francis Tresham and of five other people, people he claimed that he did not know personally. He also admitted to the name of a minor priest in addition to admitting that Hugh Owen whom he had met in Flanders had also known about the plot. He was also forced to tell about the plans to proclaim Princess Elizabeth as the next Queen of England.

Waad did not waste any time. He had a scribe record all of what his prisoner coughed out of his broken body and then have his wrecked prisoner sign at the bottom of each page of the confession.

"Do you notice," the Lieutenant remarked to a Councillor as he studied the written confession, "how his signature becomes progressively weaker. See here. On the first page it is quite legible. Look, Guido Fawkes. But here on the last page, I can barely make it out. It looks like an undecipherable scribble. Look G something, then a scribble followed by a D and an O. And as for the name Fawkes, he's just written two lines. I must say, that rack really does something to the human body, no? It's probably stretched him another two or three inches in length."

"If not more."

"True. And now I need a copy of this confession for the court. I will also show it to his fellow-plotters and see what they will say about it. I wonder if they will need racking too?"

"But where are they, Sir William? It's all well enough for this Fawkes man to tell you that they exist, but you will need them here in the Tower if you want to question them."

"True. But did not the Earl of Salisbury inform you," Waad answered with a smile, "that another one of them will be here soon? The earl gave orders that

Francis Tresham is to be arrested. I will then put him in a cell next to Fawkes', and once he sees the state Fawkes is in and hears what happened to him, I am sure this Francis Tresham will start talking very soon. It happens like that every time. The first one suffers and the rest of them cannot start talking fast enough."

Waad and the Councillor smiled.

"And if this Tresham is made of sterner stuff, or is even as tough as Fawkes, something I do not think he will be," Waad was forced to admit, "then I'll place him in a cell next to the racking room and that will persuade him to talk. Of that I have no doubt. The cries of a man being racked really work wonders on his fellow criminals. It often saves me a lot of work," he added cynically. "But now, let us go and report these events to our master. I am sure he would like to read this document and hear how his daughter, the Princess Elizabeth was about to become the Queen of England in his stead."

As a result of the Lieutenant's report, King James gave a twenty-minute speech in Parliament on 9 November, and while referring to the plotters as 'these wretches,' he did not wish to condemn all of his Catholic subjects because of some 'wayward members of the Romish religion.' He continued, "Not even the Turks, Jews and pagans, indeed, not even those of Calcutta who worship the devil have ever done this - to assassinate princes and destroy people over differences and controversies of religion." He concluded his speech saying, "That many good men seduced by some, only of the errors of Popery, can be good and faithful subjects. While on the other hand, not one of them who knows truly and believes fully all the principles and scholastic doctrines of that teaching could ever be a good Christian or faithful subject."

While the king was recovering from what was at least the third attempt on his life, his loyal ministers and servants were working hard to establish the scope of the plot. Had Guy Fawkes told the truth or not, they asked, despite the excruciating torture he had suffered? Had he similarly managed to keep certain details secret? A list of questions was dispatched to Sir Richard Walsh in Worcestershire and as a result, he asked his Holbeach prisoners, "Who was the principal person of quality in the Catholic church involved, and on what grounds or reason?"

This was followed by: Did you not consider it necessary in the action of blowing up the king and Parliament, of having care for the preservation of some noble persons, and if so, who were they? Walsh was also instructed to ask his prisoners if "any noble persons had undertaken to join with them and the Catholic party?" and "Who should be the head of your faction afterwards?"

All of the prisoners remained silent. All except Thomas Wintour.

"Ah, so you do admit that other Catholics were involved in this plot?" the Sheriff asked triumphantly after Wintour had agreed to answer some of his questions.

"Only so far as we expected other English Catholics to join us," Wintour replied vaguely, and hurried on to add, "But we did not expect any help from our Catholic brethren in Spain or the Spanish Netherlands."

"But you did want their help?"

"Yes, sir."

"And who was to be your leader, a lord or a plain man?"

"Neither sir. We did not have a general head. Of our company, we looked to Robert Catesby and Thomas Percy as our chiefs."

"Oh, and how unfortunate that they're both dead," Sir Richard said cynically. "So now I cannot question them, can I?"

As Thomas Wintour was being taken back to his dark and dirty cell, Sir Richard gave orders that his captives were to be sent to London. That night, while dining with his kinsman, Sir Henry Bromley, the two men divided up their tasks. The Sheriff would remain in Worcestershire in order to track down any more plotters, and check out the recusant properties at Grafton and Huddington, while Sir Henry would be responsible for escorting the prisoners to London.

A day or so later, Sir Richard received a somewhat grim request from the authorities in London. Would the Sheriff have the bodies of Robert Catesby, Thomas Percy and the Wright brothers exhumed and quartered? The request was quite specific, and closed with the final instructions: Make sure the heads are to be dispatched to London where they will be placed on public display.

And so, in mid-November 1605, the remaining members of the original core of plotters, except Robert Wintour who was still in hiding with Stephen Littleton, together with about forty other suspects, were escorted to London, in order to be investigated by a special commission. Their escort consisted of a large troop of armed militia, who apart from its obvious mission of guarding the prisoners, was to impress upon all who saw this procession that the government meant business when it came to dealing with Catholic plotters and the like.

The commission, under the supervision of Sir Edward Coke, first had to solve a delicate and logistical probe. They had to separate the suspect Catholic lords and 'men of gentle birth' from the 'lesser prisoners.' Thus, as men of 'gentle birth,' John and Thomas Wintour, Sir Everard Digby, Robert Keyes, Ambrose Rookwood and John Grant were sent to the Tower to be 'reserved only for the Lords Commissioners.'

Thus, two weeks after Parliament was supposed to have been blown up, Sir Everard Digby was escorted from his cell to face the Commission. After the preliminary questions, he was asked how he had been treated in the Tower.

"I have been treated well, my lords," he replied, his head held high.

"You have not been subject to torture or anything else unpleasant?" asked Sir Edward.

"No."

"Well, not as yet," interjected Sir Walter Cope with a leer.

Sir Everard ignored this and looked straight ahead at Sir Edward who was sitting at the centre of his prosecutors.

"How long had you known about this plot?"

"Not long. A mere two weeks. From about the middle of October."

"Then why did you become involved with it at such a late stage?"

"Because I am a true Catholic."

"But Sir Everard, you were not born as such," Sir Edward commented.

"No. It is true that I was born a Protestant, but I was received into the Catholic Church some years ago after the death of my first dearly beloved wife, Mary."

"Why did you do this?"

"Because I heard and became convinced that they were good and honourable people."

At this point, Sir Edward Coke almost exploded! His face went bright red and he threw his cap to the floor. He stood up, shaking.

"Good and honourable!" he said at last. "Good and honourable. Here you are, on trial for your life, and for doing what? For trying, together with your good and honourable Catholic conspirators, to blow up your anointed king and his Parliament! And then you have the gall to call yourselves good and honourable! I'll see you all hanged for this! Good and honourable indeed!"

And he sat down heavily as a goblet of wine was passed over to him to help calm his nerves.

"While Sir Edward is recovering from his shocking description, 'good and honourable,'" Sir Walter said with an oily grin, "let me ask you a few pertinent questions."

Sir Everard turned to face his new interrogator sitting at the far end of the table.

"When you were asked by Sir Richard Walsh in Worcestershire about details of the plot, you refused to answer him, yes?"

"Yes."

"So now, here you are in London, lodged, in fact, imprisoned in the Tower with many of those involved in this cowardly plot, and now I would like to ask you, how many people were involved in this plot altogether?"

The prisoner said nothing.

"Come, come Sir Everard. Surely you must know. No man joins such a venture, a venture that could result in the losing of one's head, without asking questions about his fellow-plotters, now does he?"

The ex-courtier remained silent for some time. It was obvious that he was wrestling with his conscience. All that could be heard was the wind and the muffled sounds of the traffic on the River Thames. At last Sir Everard spoke.

"Gentlemen, I was only involved in this venture, as you call it for two weeks. It is true that I knew Robert Catesby and Thomas Percy, but they unfortunately are dead."

"Fortunately for them, but less so for us," muttered Sir Edward Coke.

Sir Everard looked up at the fine woodwork on the ceiling, pointedly ignored him and then continued.

"During those two weeks I admit to meeting with Robert Catesby and Thomas Percy, but I believe I was more useful to them for my stable of horses and for my money rather than for anything else."

"Ha! So they used you!" Sir Edward Coke couldn't help himself from interrupting. "They were not interested in you, but in your horses and your money. They exploited you, and these were the sort of villains with whom you were dealing."

"That is not true. That is a lie. I joined this venture with my eyes open and..."

"Well let us move on," interrupted Sir Edward, now fully recovered after his outburst. "Sir Everard, this commission would like to know what caused you to be involved in this plot."

"Well, first and foremost, because I am a Catholic and I feel that I am bound to the Catholic cause."

"Yes, yes," Sir Edward cut in sharply "We have heard all about your Catholicism already. Are there any other reasons?"

"Yes. I could no longer see my fellow Catholics suffer the unjust laws that had been and were being passed. That is, the laws regarding recusants and the fines and..."

"And is there anything else?" Sir John asked dismissively.

"Yes. My fellow Catholics and myself have been sorely disappointed by His Majesty's attitude to us. When he came to the throne we expected him to behave towards us, well, in a way that we thought the son of Mary Queen of Scots, a beloved Catholic lady and a martyr..."

"She was no martyr!" thundered the Earl of Northampton, the 'court Catholic'."

"You had no right to expect promises or the like from His Gracious Majesty. Just because he was the son of a Catholic mother, a lady tried for treason, and not religion, I may add, you..."

Sir Edward stood up to interfere. He laid an authoritative hand on the aristocrat's shoulder. "Thank you, the Earl of Northampton, but we are not here to discuss why Mary Queen of Scots was executed. Now Sir Everard, do you have anything to add?"

"I do. What I have mentioned are general reasons. A more personal one is that I had much respect for Robert Catesby, and I was much saddened when I heard of his death. This country, and my religion hath lost a great man."

"More your loss than ours," muttered Sir Montague.

"Thank you, Sir Montague. So tell me, Sir Everard. You were prepared to blow up the king and his Parliament as well as kill several Catholic lords who were to be present there that day, true?"

"I did not know all the details of this plot, as you call it. For on that day, I was supposed to be, and indeed was, at Dunchurch, where I met the late Robert Catesby."

"Very late," muttered Sir Edward Coke, cynically.

Sir Edward ignored his fellow commissioner's remark to ask Sir Everard, who remained upright in the centre of that large room, questions about Spanish and foreign participation in the plot.

As before, the 'exploited' plotter stated that he was ignorant of such knowledge and that the only thing he had heard about such things, was that Guido Fawkes had served as a soldier in the army in the Spanish Netherlands.

"Yes," muttered the incorrigible Sir John. "And in whose army?"

"That is for him to tell you," Sir Everard answered somewhat haughtily. "Not I."

"He already has," Sir Edward said.

"Yes, on the rack," Sir Henry Montague couldn't help adding.

Sir Everard went pale and clutched the rail tightly. This was the first time that he had heard that Guido had been tortured.

"And did he tell you that?" the prisoner asked quietly.

"Oh yes. He told us everything. People always do. How do you think we know about you, eh? Think on that one."

Sir Everard did. He staggered for a moment and gripped the rail in front of him for support. Regaining his composure, he continued.

"Gentlemen, I have an idea. If you would allow me, as a past courtier, a personal interview with His Majesty, I am sure that I would be able to explain everything to him. I would be able to tell him about my part in this, as a loyal subject who was knighted by him at Belvoir Castle two years ago, and as a courtier who..."

Sir Edward held up his hand to stop the 'past courtier' and interrupted his flow of words.

"Please save your breath, Sir Everard. His Majesty has absolutely no desire nor reason to speak with you, and nor indeed with any of your fellow-plotters. To that end, he has appointed us as his commission to learn the truth, and that is just what we intend to do. Now do you have anything else to add to these proceedings?"

Sir Everard hung his head. He had shot his last bolt and it had missed. The former courtier, the well-connected man-about-town and the consort of royalty had counted on his charm and charisma to escape this fatal situation. Now, he saw for the first time that his good looks, personality and cultured background were for nought.

That night, he wrote a letter which was later smuggled out of the Tower. Among other things he wrote:

For some good space I could do nothing, but with tears ask pardon at God's hands for all my errors, both in actions and intentions in this business, and in my whole life, which the censure of this contrary to my expectations caused me to doubt: I did humbly beseech that my death might satisfy for my offence, which I should and shall offer most gladly to the Giver of Life. If I had thought there was the least sin in the Plot, I would not have been in it for all the world: and no other cause drew me to hazard my Fortune, and Life, but Zeal to God's religion. For this design had taken place, there could have been no doubt of other success.

For the next six weeks, the commission investigated all the remaining members of the plot. Torture was threatened or used in varying degrees and by January 1606, the authorities felt that they had enough information to try the eight conspirators in public. There were supposed to have been nine of them, but on 22 December 1605 Francis Tresham died in the Tower, ostensibly of a strangury, an acute and painful inflammation of the urinary tract, but many did not believe this. It was rumoured that he had been removed from the scene since he knew too much about his kinsman Lord Monteagle, as well as about the letter that bore his name. It was also rumoured that Tresham knew too much about the Earl of Salisbury's alleged part in the writing or dispatching of this document. Apart from Guido Fawkes, he was the only one of the thirteen plotters who did not flee London. He was captured a week later and immediately imprisoned.

A weak Guido Fawkes heard this latest piece of grim news while lying on the floor in the cell he was sharing with Sir Everard and Ambrose. The cell door was pushed open and a white-faced Ambrose was pushed in by one of the guards.

"So tell that to your traitorous friends," the guard mocked as he slammed the heavy bolts into position.

"Ambrose, what's he talking about?" Guido asked. Ambrose lowered himself heavily to the floor and spoke slowly. "Tresham, Francis Tresham is dead."

"Killed? Torture?"

"I don't know. The guards said he died of some illness in his gut, but I don't believe them."

"And when did this happen?" Guido asked in a tired voice. His racked and dislocated body barely supporting itself against the Tower's damp and rough walls.

"A few days ago. The guards said his wife Anne was with him almost to the end, but then she left as she could not stand to see him suffer so."

"And then he died?" Sir Everard asked.

"That's what the guards said. They said that he dictated some sort of confession to his servant..."

"William Vavasour?"

"Yes, that's him. And then he died in the night."

Guido tried to sit up. "What did they do with his body? Did they let his wife take it?" he asked.

"The guards said no. They told me that they cut off his head as a traitor and then buried the rest of it in a hole within the grounds of the Tower."

For the next few minutes none of the three men in that stinking cell said anything. If that was how the government would treat a minor member of the plot, how then would they deal with the others?

At last Sir Everard spoke up. It was clear from what he said that he had been thinking of his wife Mary and his two sons Kenelm and John.

"And what happened to Tresham's wife and family?"

"I didn't hear anything about them. But I suppose all his lands and goods were confiscated. That's what usually happens to anyone who is accused of being a traitor."

"True," Sir Everard agreed dismally as he imagined his wife and sons being roughly turned out of Gayhurst, their Leicestershire country home, by government troops. "And did he...?"

"And did he say anything about that letter Monteagle received?" Guido suddenly asked.

"Why?" asked Ambrose. "What's that got to do with this?"

"Well," Guido said, "Since I was captured, I've been doing a lot of thinking and I think that it must have been Tresham who wrote it."

"How so?"

"Well it seemed to me a very strange coincidence that I was discovered and arrested a short time before I was going to light the gunpowder. And later that night, when I was brought before the king and his council, the question of that letter was thrown in my face."

"Please explain yourself."

"I remember asking myself, who could have written it, or if it were a genuine letter or not. I know there's been some talk of it being a forgery and..."

"Do you mean that Salisbury had known about us all the time?" Ambrose asked in a shocked voice. "That he'd known about us all the time and then had us arrested, or at least had you arrested Guido, when it was the right moment and politic for him to do so?"

Guido nodded his head wearily. He had witnessed how the Spanish had worked in Flanders and now he guessed it wasn't only the Spanish who used such devious means to achieve their aims. "Yes Ambrose. That thought has passed through my mind many times in the past few weeks. I really think that we may have fallen into a trap that that cunning Salisbury had set a long time ago."

"But why should he have done so?" Sir Everard asked in disbelief.

"So that he could use our group as an example of Catholics traitors. This would then give him reason enough to persecute the rest of the Catholics in England. You know, more and more fines..."

"imprisonment..."

"...and banishing priests and confiscating Catholic lands and property."

"Yes, that's right, "sighed Guido. "I'm beginning to think that our plan to rid this country of its Protestant and Puritan tyrants has turned on itself and now our fellow Catholics are going to suffer even more so. And that my friends has been one of the hardest thoughts I've had to bear while I've been lying here."

This grim reflection sat heavily on the three men. It was true that they had debated this question in more than one of their tavern discussions, but not one of them had thought that this situation would ever really happen.

And now all that lay ahead of them was their trial. What they said and how they conducted themselves would affect the Catholic community of England. Would they, the remaining plotters be held responsible for even more government inspired anti-Catholic legislation? It was not an easy thought for the failed conspirators to live with. Would they die with it too?

Chapter Thirteen
On Trial

There was a steely grey, cold wintry sky hanging over London as seven of the plotters were led out of their cells onto the small pier adjoining the Tower of London. None of them were wearing clothes that were suitable for the English winter. In fact, after having lived in them for the past few weeks, their thin, worn and stained clothing looked even less suitable than normal. Guido shivered with the cold as he stepped, or rather, was half-pushed onto the river-barge that was to take him and the others for their trial at Westminster Hall.

It was the end of January, to be precise, Monday 27 January 1605, and Robert Cecil, the Earl of Salisbury had arrived at the conclusion that he had gathered enough evidence by now to bring the Gunpowder conspirators for a public trial. By doing so, he would show the people of England, that is, especially the Catholics, what would happen to them if they attempted to disturb the peace of the realm in the future.

Salisbury was feeling particularly self-satisfied as he sat in his elegant dark wood-panelled chamber in Westminster Hall. He had all the information he wanted; his royal master, His Majesty King James was exceptionally well-pleased with him as were many of the leading Protestant aristocrats. Also many of the Catholics, that is, those who were more than willing to demonstrate their loyalty to the state and its king were similarly pleased with the way things had turned out. Indeed, some of the most vociferous advocates of the use of torture and the confiscation of property had been the Catholic lords who were supposed to have been blown up that November night.

Salisbury smiled to himself. That document, now known as the Monteagle letter, had served him well. So far he had not divulged who had initiated and written it, and he never would. Not even on the rack, he thought to himself grimly, and smiled.

"It would serve no useful purpose to let that particular cat out of the bag," he had admitted one night in November to his wife. "Just let us say that this particular cat caught some very useful mice, and with that, we'll have the Catholic population of this country just where we want them."

"But wasn't it you, my dearest Robert, who had that letter forged and dispatched to Lord Monteagle?" Salisbury's wife asked. "At least, that's what I heard."

The only reply she received was when her husband put a rather gnarled finger on her lips and smiled his enigmatic half-smile. "As that playwright fellow, Shakespeare says at the end of his play, *Hamlet*, 'The rest is silence.'" And with that he left the room to check some state papers.

Now, as he was sitting in his chamber, he was looking forward to the trial. The outcome was a foregone conclusion. The plotters would be found guilty and would pay the grisly penalty that all such traitors pay. On that point there was no discussion. What would be interesting would be was to see how they behaved. Would they become hysterical as they pleaded for their lives, or would they act in a quiet and dignified way? In a way, Salisbury wanted them to make a noise, because a scene of quiet and restrained dignity might give the Catholics of England a new group of respectable and heroic martyrs. Noise and histrionics would show them up to be would-be assassins of kings, ministers, Protestants and even of fellow-Catholics.

As he sat there, in his large leather chair musing, he heard a knock on the door and one of the Council's minor officials entered.

"Yes?" Salisbury asked, even before the man could say anything.

"The prisoners will be here very soon, sir. The sergeant-at-arms wants to know what is to be done with them in the meantime."

"Have them placed in the room below the Star Chamber until we are ready to deal with them."

"Yes, sir."

"And tell the sergeant-at-arms to make sure that they remain under heavy guard. We don't want any heroic attempts made to rescue them, and we certainly don't want any of them to escape now, do we?"

"No, sir. And permit me to say, sir, that I doubt if any of them are in such a condition that even if they did escape, they would get very far, sir."

"Very true. Now go."

As these last minute arrangements were being made, the river-barge with its seven heavily guarded prisoners was making its way westwards through the choppy waters of the Thames. Passengers on other boats may have been impressed by the massive size of Old St. Paul's Cathedral, still without its steeple which had been struck by lightning in 1561, or the spires of the hundred lesser churches, but not Guido and the other plotters. Similarly, other travellers on the river may have enjoyed the sight of London Bridge, topped by its many-storied buildings and shops, but the plotters' thoughts must have been elsewhere as the barge headed towards Westminster. And as they did not see the Thames-side palaces, wharfs and other river traffic, so neither did they pay any attention to the sounds of the ferrymen shouting, "Eastward Ho!" and "Westward Ho!" as they plied for hire. The only thing that the plotters were aware of was that they were rapidly approaching Westminster, and with it, the end of an inexorable judicious procedure that had lasted for almost three long and often painful months. Most of this period had been spent in their cells, in the lower regions of the gloomy and forbidding Tower of London.

As their boat pulled up to the small Westminster pier, they were escorted off; a sorry looking group of men in worn and dank clothes, surrounded by over twice their number of brighter clothed pikemen and halberdiers, who were led by a noisy and nasty-faced captain. Marched into the basement below the Star Chamber, they were forced to wait for half an hour while the final preparations were being made in the adjoining site for their trial, Westminster Hall.

An ominous quiet fell over the plotters. Their movements were slow and deliberate. They hardly looked at each other at all. It was as if none of them wanted to display his thoughts and feelings to the others. Suddenly this false calm was broken, as amid the loud noises of heavy boots and the sharp thuds of pikes and halberds striking wooden floors, Thomas Bates was escorted into the basement. His grey looking pallor matched the colour of his somewhat dishevelled appearance.

"Thomas. What happened to you? Where have you been all this time?" Guido asked.

"Yes. We haven't seen you for nearly three months," Ambrose added.

"Well, there's not much really to say," Bates said slowly. "I was captured somewhere in Staffordshire, probably about the same time you were caught at..."

"Holbeach."

"Yes, and then they put me under guard there in some sort of gaol. I was only there for a few days before I was brought to London."

"To the Tower?"

"No. To the Gatehouse in Westminster."

"And were you tortured? Racked?"

"No, but I was hit a few times at the beginning, mainly by my guards, but it was nothing serious." He stopped and looked at his fellow-plotters. "But pardon me, sirs, but some of you don't look too healthy yourselves. Especially Guido, Ambrose and John Grant. What happened to you?"

Tom Wintour explained. "Well, Guido has been racked, terribly and the other two were badly burnt when some of our gunpowder suddenly exploded while we were at Holbeach."

Thomas Bates nodded his head sympathetically. It seemed that although the authorities considered him still to be a servant of Robert Catesby and had therefore imprisoned him separately at the Gatehouse due to his lower status, his fellow prisoners were treating him as an equal, which indeed he was.

"And have you all been together since the beginning of November?" Bates asked, thirsty for information.

"Most of us have been but..."

"But I was brought here only recently," Robert Wintour interrupted, feeling somewhat proud of the fact that he had managed to elude the king's soldiers for two months. "I was only brought to the Tower about three weeks ago."

Bates looked around the basement. "Well anyway, it's good to see you all again, although it saddens me to think of what befell Robin, Thomas Percy and the Wright brothers."

They were silent for a minute, in memory of their dead friends.

"Did you know," Bates said at length, "that one of the guards told me that the heads of Robin and Thomas Percy, Kit and Jack have been placed on display on spikes outside the Parliament?"

By the way the others nodded, it seemed that this particularly grisly piece of news had filtered down to them too.

The silence was gently broken when Sir Everard asked Robert Wintour to help him relight his pipe, and Robert Keyes took the opportunity to light his.

"Why are you smoking now?" Bates asked. He had never taken to the new fashion, probably due to his status as a gentleman's servant.

"It helps to calm the nerves," Robert Wintour explained.

"And it annoys the king," Sir Everard added. "It's a known fact that he hates to see men smoking."

"How do you know that?" Bates asked.

"Don't you know? He wrote a pamphlet against it last year. He called it a *Counterblast to Tobacco*. He said that smoking was self-destructing and an iniquity."

"Yes, and that it's a 'stinking torment' too."

"Maybe he was right there," Keyes said pragmatically. "But he's not here now to see you smoke now, is he?"

Thomas Bates looked around carefully. "Well I heard from a couple of the guards that he is going to attend our trial, but he will either be in disguise or be hidden from view."

"What do you mean?" Guido asked, leaning heavily on a stick.

"Well, I overheard some of the guards talking about a few chambers that have been reserved for the special use of the king and the royal family, as well as a few people who would prefer to remain in the shadows."

"So if that is indeed true," Robert Wintour said defiantly. "I'll make sure that he sees me smoking. But hush, something's happening. Look, there's another group of guards coming in here. There, by the door."

Within a minute or so, the plotters found themselves being escorted into Westminster Hall and placed on a platform which had been specially erected for the occasion.

The ancient Palace of Westminster had first been built by Edward the Confessor during that fateful year of 1066. William Rufus and Richard II had later enlarged the Hall, the latter being responsible for the addition of a superb hammer-beam roof. Although the Hall usually served as a meeting place for booksellers and the king's courts-of-law, it was used occasionally for state trials. Knowing that, the plotters would not have drawn any comfort from the fact that the secret lovers of Anne Boleyn and Catherine Howard, two of the wives of Henry VIII, had been tried there, as had the king's good friend and Chancellor, Sir Thomas More. All of these unfortunate people had been found guilty. More had been beheaded, while the royal lovers had been hanged, drawn and quartered.

The buzz of low voices and speculation of the spectators was cut short as a halberd-bearing captain, with a booming voice, called out for silence. Following this, the Lords Commissioner entered. They included the Lord Chief Justice, Sir John Popham, the Lord Chief Baron of the Exchequer, Sir Thomas Fleming and the Attorney-General, Sir Edward Coke. Two Justices of the Common Pleas as well as the Earls of Devonshire, Northampton, Suffolk and Worcester were also present, while naturally, Robert Cecil, the Earl of Salisbury made sure that his presence was recorded by everyone. After all, he, more than anyone else had caused this whole plot to be discovered, which had then led to this impressive setting and trial. Finally, Sir Edward Phillips, otherwise known by his title of Sergeant-at-Law was also present, in his official capacity for making sure that order and decorum were preserved in that ancient Hall.

Knocking on the floor three times, Sir Edward Phillips ensured there was complete silence for the Master of the Rolls, who was to open the trial.

"Are the following of the accused in this Hall at present this morning?" he called out in a loud voice.

"Thomas Wintour?"

"Present."

"Guido or Guy Fawkes, otherwise known as Guido or John Johnson?"

"Present."

"Robert Keyes, yeoman?"

"Present."

"Thomas Bates, also yeoman?"

"Aye."

"John Grant?"

"Present."

"Ambrose Rookwood?"

"Present."

"Robert Wintour, brother to Thomas Wintour?"

"Present"

"Francis Thresham?"

Salisbury leaned over to where the Master of the Rolls was standing. "Lately died in the Tower," he said quietly and dryly.

"And Robert Catesby, Thomas Percy, Gentleman Pensioner, Jack Wright and his brother Christopher Wright I have been informed are no longer with us."

"That is true," Salisbury said. "They are indeed no longer with us."

"Excuse me sir," a junior scribe at the table asked, "but what about Sir Everard Digby, Knight of the Golden Spur?"

"He will be tried separately, on account of his title and status."

The scribe noted this down and the trial started.

"The matter before this court today, this Special Commission," Sir Edward Phillips said in a clear voice, "is not just one of treason, but treason of such a horrible and monstrous nature that any sensible man cannot easily comprehend the foulness of which the conspirators here today are being accused. As the Scriptures say, to murder any man is an abomination, so how much more so is it to murder God's own anointed king, His Gracious Majesty King James I, lately King James VI of Scotland. And," the Sergeant-at-arms added, looking around the packed Hall, "how much more monstrous was it to plan to murder not just His Majesty, but also his sweet and innocent wife Queen Anne together with his son, Prince Henry? And all of this is of course in addition to the fact that these conspirators, these men who are to be seen standing in front of you today, men who had also planned the murder of His Majesty's true and honest government as they were to sit in Parliament in order to conduct the noble and legal affairs of this realm."

The silence that greeted this opening statement was palpable. It seemed as if the world had stopped for a moment as all the officials and spectators pictured their king and his royal family, together with his Parliament all being blown to smithereens in one huge and deathly explosion.

Sir Edward broke the silence. "And if that were not terrible enough, these men, these Catholic conspirators you see before you now, were even prepared to murder their fellow Catholics who were to sit in Parliament that November day last year. So let me inform you here, that the Earl of Worcester and the Earl of Northampton who are present now in this honourable court are also Catholics, albeit, noble and loyal ones, but they too would have died had this execrable act been carried out as these monsters of men had fully intended it to be."

Hearing this indictment, most of the plotters looked down. Only Sir Everard, Robert Keyes and Guido Fawkes looked up defiantly at the Attorney-General.

The Sergeant continued. "And so it remains for me to state here, that the aforementioned men are hereby accused of plotting treason against their king, the royal family, the state and its officials. I now call on Sir Edward Coke, the attorney-general to continue with these proceedings."

Seeing the Attorney General take up the central position in the Hall cannot have boded well for the accused. They had heard how this harsh Justice had served as the prosecution at the trial of Doctor Roderigo Lopez in 1594, a man who had been accused of planning to murder Queen Elizabeth. Being a secret Jew had not helped the poor physician who had been found guilty and executed.

Similarly, the Earl of Essex did not have an easy time at Sir Edward's hands. For after the failure of his rebellion, he too had paid the price for treason just four years previously. If all of this were not enough to establish the Attorney General's harsh reputation, one could also see how he had dealt with Sir Walter Raleigh in his treason trial. Luckily the explorer and initial importer of tobacco into England was granted a last minute reprieve while waiting to be beheaded, but now he was 'awaiting His Majesty's pleasure' in the Bloody Tower.

"My Lords Commissioners, gentlemen and others," His Majesty's chief prosecutor said in a loud and clear voice. "I fear that what I am about to say will be long, detailed and copious, but fear not. All of this is being done in the name of justice, especially that of His Majesty, whose life could have been extinguished, together with the lives of several other persons who are present here in this ancient Hall today."

Pausing just long enough to catch his breath, Sir Edward continued.

"This plot, this gunpowder plot is an example of the greatest treason that has ever been carried out, or rather attempted to have been carried out in this country since such acts have been recorded. It is not unique in that other such acts have been devised in the past to harm His Majesty, but they, and the Lord be praised for this, have always come to nought and failed. These include such piteous acts by Lambert Simnel and Perkin Warbeck who tried to harm His Majesty Henry VII just over a hundred years ago, while more recently, there were such conspiracies as the Bye and Main plots which were directed against Her Majesty Queen Elizabeth. The same could be said for the Babington plot which aimed, not only to harm our dearly beloved former queen, but to replace her with a Scottish queen instead."

Here Sir Edward was very circumspect with his language knowing that her son, the present king was hidden in the Hall, listening carefully to every word.

Bowing slightly in the direction where the king would be sitting, hidden from public view, Sir Edward continued. "And my Lords Commissioner, Gentlemen and others, what is common to all of these three last-mentioned plots? I will tell you. They all came about and were inspired by the Roman Catholic Church. Indeed, I have heard it said that these men, these monstrous men, these plotters," and here he pointed to the men on the platform with a sweeping gesture, "these men are exceptions to the normal Catholic population in this country. These men are *sine religione, sine sede, sine fide, sine re, et sine spe,* or to those of you who have forgotten their Latin, 'without religion, without habitation, without credit, without means and without hope.' But is this true of the monstrous men we have before us today? No! Certainly not! For these men are men of wealth and substance who did not act out of financial desperation like some petty cutpurse or thief born of poverty. No! They acted out of their misguided hopes to bring this country back once again under the authority of the popes of Rome!"

He paused to let the significance of his words sink in. Everyone present in that impressive Hall, bar the plotters was either a Protestant, and if not, then a Catholic who had sided with the present Protestant establishment.

"In all my years of service to the Crown," Sir Edward continued, "whether it be our past queen or our present king, and either as Solicitor-General, Speaker of the House or as in my current position as Attorney General, I have never encountered treason without a Romish priest or co-religionist being involved. And if that were not bad enough, we have today before us, a plot that involves at least eight Catholics such as these."

He stopped again, readjusted his magnificent red robe and continued.

"And to compound these matters, in fact at the beginning, more than eight of these Romists were involved, but today, several of their number, at least five of them are no longer with us. No doubt they are burning in the fires of everlasting damnation for thinking and conspiring to carry out this terrible plot, which has already been referred to today; the crime they had hoped to perpetrate on this Protestant and peaceful realm of ours.

"In other words ladies and gentlemen, these Catholics, these Romish Catholics and Papists had resorted to the laws of gunpowder and not to the laws of this sovereign state. And if all of this were not wicked enough, not evil enough, then these cruel men had planned to do even more."

At this point, many of his listeners leaned forwards to catch the attorney-General's next words. Many of those present had heard about the gunpowder plot and how it had failed, but they had not realized that even more was involved.

"My Lords Commissioner, gentlemen and others. Let me now inform you. Not only had these conspirators hoped to blow up His Majesty, his family and those members who were to be in Parliament that November eve, but they had also planned to usurp the royal order of life and set the king's daughter, the innocent Princess Elizabeth on the throne. This act was to have acted as a patch to cover up their treasonous and nefarious activities."

A few gasps of unbelieving horror were heard as various spectators rapidly speculated on the implications of this terrible deed. What? Remove the king from his throne through violence, and then exploit his daughter, the sweet Princess Elizabeth, not yet ten years old, to be queen in his stead? Impossible! Absolutely impossible!

"And," continued Sir Edward Coke when he was satisfied that everyone in the Hall had understood the fullness of his last statement. "If all of that were not evil enough, these evil conspirators had even planned to implicate their equally wicked Spanish Catholic co-religionists as well, under the guidance of their wayward Papist priests. These foreigners were to provide all manner of help and succour to these traitors. These seducing Jesuits were to supply help in any way they could, especially with men, money and arms. However, I am happy to add, that the King of Spain, King Philip III was not involved in any of this gross act of malfeasance to which I have just referred."

The Attorney-General had been instructed to stress this last point so that no offence would be given to the Spanish ambassador who was secretly following the trial from a small adjacent chamber. Salisbury was well-aware that the Anglo-Spanish peace treaty had been signed the previous year and he did not wish for this treasonous plot to be the destruction of one of the cornerstones of his foreign policy. Peace meant trade and trade meant prosperity. With prosperity came a feeling of satisfaction. Riots and rebellion did not thrive in the soil of prosperity. Therefore the differences between Protestants and Catholics on an international scale were to be reduced to the minimum, although at home, such differences were to be exploited to the full. If the majority, Salisbury reasoned cynically, had a common enemy, then their national anger would be vented against it. Once the Jews had been the scapegoat for the country's ills, but since Edward I had banished them from England in 1290, their place had been taken by the Lollards. However, this religious minority had later seen the light and as a result had merged with the Protestants. Now it was the turn of the Catholics to be the national scapegoat, and Salisbury was more than willing to exploit this situation as much as he could.

"And so, the Roman Catholics in this country, believed in the two D's; the deposing of kings and the disposing of kingdoms. Let me tell you, these vile traitors, quiet and respectable as they may look now, carried out their plans, right up to the moment one of their leaders (although he strongly denies this title) was caught in the act of preparing to blow up our gracious king, his royal family and our Parliament. For this deed, he and the rest of his Catholic band received the blessing and encouragement of their priests. In fact, it may be said, that these men who stand in front of you in the centre of this chamber today had duped many otherwise good souls, and it is only through good luck and the Lord's Providence that their vile and evil activities were discovered in time. I dread to think what would have happened to this gentle and peaceful realm if this had not been the case.

"And so my Lords, Judges, Commissioners and gentlemen, I wish to conclude my lengthy and detailed opening remarks by telling you a short fable."

Once again, the spectators and even the aristocrats at the top of the Hall leaned forward. The latter knew what line of attack the Attorney-General would take, but his use of a fable in court was new. The tough Sir Edward Coke was not known as a raconteur of imaginary tales.

"Once upon a time," he began, looking around at his captive audience, "a cat who was king of a country had slaughtered most of the rats and mice in a certain country. All those rats and mice who were fortunate enough to have survived were forced to stay in their holes and in their burrows. One cat who noticed this, then disguised himself as a priest and proceeded to lure the frightened animals out of their places of hiding. The cat then promised them that as he had forsworn his kingly role, he would behave in a most Christian manner from henceforth. Alas and alack! The poor rats and mice soon learned otherwise as they discovered to their cost, that their new priest was as cruel and as bloody as their king had been."

The sound of subdued laughter was heard in the Hall as the prosecutor concluded his fable. Only the plotters on their platform looked even more uncomfortable.

"I am sure that I do not have to interpret the meaning of my fable to you," Sir Edward said. "But I feel it is my duty to show you all that this court is fair. We will give the accused the opportunity to speak in their own defence, or at least an opportunity to ask for forgiveness before sentence is passed, or why a sentence of death should not be pronounced against them."

Returning to his seat, Sir Edward sat down, a grim smile on his lips.

Thomas Wintour then moved to the front of the platform and indicated that he wished to speak.

"My Lords Commissioner," he began in a low voice, "all I can say is, is that I will take this opportunity to plead for the life of my older brother Robert

Wintour, who stands before you now, a condemned man. The only thing I can say is that he, Robert, was little involved in our plans and those whom he knew were only those that I had told him. He instigated nothing and only intended to execute instructions that he had received."

Thomas Wintour looked straight at the Lords Commissioner on the bench opposite him to see if his words had any affect. Not noticing any, he continued.

"If I were able to ask for the sentence of death twice, I would do so. Once for myself and once for my brother. But since I know that this is an impossible request, I call upon the mercy of the Lords Commissioners, to show mercy and punish only me, and to spare my brother who I had led astray." Hanging his head low, he awaited their lordships reply. He received none.

"And you," the sergeant-at-law called out to Robert Wintour. "Have you anything to say?"

Thomas' brother stepped forward.

"No, my lords. I just ask for mercy and ask this court to remember the words from the Book of St. Matthew, 'Blessed are the merciful for they shall obtain mercy.'"

He stepped back and did not hear Sir Edward Coke mutter to the Earl of Salisbury, "And how much mercy would he have shown had their dastardly plot succeeded?"

In the meanwhile Guido was called on to speak on his own behalf.

"Guido Fawkes or Johnson," the sergeant-at-arms said dismissively. "Will you tell this court why you entered a plea of Not Guilty, when we who are assembled here today think otherwise?"

Guido leaned on the side of the platform and looked up wearily at his accusers.

"I entered such a plea for indeed I did not do anything. I caused harm to no man..."

"Because you were caught just in time," Sir Edward Coke interrupted.

"And," continued Guido ignoring the Attorney General, "and as such I should not be tried for intending to carry out any action, even if the state deems such actions harmful."

"Enough! Enough!" the Attorney-General called out imperiously. "We have heard enough."

But Guido would not be silenced and held his ground. "In addition I entered the plea of Not Guilty since one cannot be charged with meeting fellow citizens at night in hostelries and taverns and for the other charges that were brought against me, about which I know nothing."

"Knows nothing, huh!" Sir Edward snorted. "Since when does ignorance of the law mean you are innocent? Let us hear the next man. We have heard enough of this man's prating."

Guido was about to say something else, but a soldier pushed him to the back of the platform and Ambrose began to speak.

"My lords, since I was a child I have been brought up to fear the Lord. I was educated in the Catholic faith, and as such, when I was approached by Robert Catesby, I naturally thought that this was the right path to follow."

"Naturally," Sir Edward muttered cynically leaning over to the Earl of Salisbury.

"I know that I cannot expect any mercy from this court, but I would just ask you to deal kindly with my wife and two sons. They are truly innocent and knew absolutely nothing about my part in this plan."

At this point the Earl of Salisbury leaned over to Sir Edward Coke and remarked, "Have you noticed that these plotters always say plan when they mean plot?"

Sir Edward nodded his head in agreement. He too had noticed. "Yes, you're right. It just seems to me as if they haven't really considered the magnitude of their actions."

And he leaned forward to hear Ambrose continue.

"I ask that mercy be shown to my family, since I alone was induced to join with Robert Catesby, and that it was only my tender feelings for this man that persuaded me, perhaps unwisely, to join him."

"Perhaps unwisely!" the Attorney-General blurted out. "Very unwisely I would say. Are there any more of you who wish to say anything? You there, John Grant. You have been silent throughout these proceedings. Don't you have anything to say in your own defence?"

The accused man faced the bench of the Lords Commissioner. He had a look of complete disdain on his face for all of them.

"You may know me as a man of few words," he began.

"Too true," Sir Edward couldn't help himself from muttering out aloud.

"But," added Grant, thrusting his head back in defiance, "I may be guilty of being a conspirator, but as you know, this conspiracy was never effected, and so *ipso facto* I am innocent."

"Very well," the Attorney General replied. "If we are to bandy Latin phrases around, *Veritas temporis filla*, or as the old Latin proverb states: Truth is the daughter of time. And it is only because you were stopped in time, before your miserable act could be carried out, that it did not happen, and not because you intended it that way. And so, *ipso facto*, as you say, you are guilty as charged."

King James, ever the academic scholar and now hidden from public view, looked at Queen Anne, his Danish wife, and smiled at the use of the Latin phrases.

Robert Keyes then stepped forward.

"All I can say in my own defence is that by this action..."

"Action, he calls it!" Sir Edward guffawed.

"...by this action, I had hoped to promote the common good and..."

"Common good!" Sir Edward repeated, unable to restrain himself again.

"...and bring this country back to the old faith of Roman Catholicism." Before the Attorney-General could interrupt him again, Keyes hurried on. "What motivated me and my fellows was the continual persecution of our fellow Catholics. This had reached such depths, we could no longer be silent. Had the authorities of this government and of this country been more liberal and just with my fellow Catholics, then I am sure none of this would have happened. I have tasted persecution before and have lost my worldly goods as a result. To me, it would be the lesser of two evils to die rather than to continue living amidst so much tyranny and persecution.

"Finally, I would just like to say that I am ready to die for this cause, in fact more so for this than any other."

Sir Edward did not react to the remainder of Robert Keyes' defence. He just sat there with a look of complete disbelief on his face. When Keyes had finished, the Attorney General said, as if bored by the whole procedure, "You, Thomas Bates, do you have anything germane to add to all this litany of unconvincing half-truths and distortions we have just heard here?"

Bates shook his head. He had seen how his superiors had been treated and he did not wish to face the strident Attorney General.

"If that is so," the sergeant-at-law said, "Will Sir Everard Digby step forward to hear the indictment against him.

The slim and trim prisoner-knight moved to the front of the platform. He looked better dressed than the others and was wearing a clean black doublet and hose. His neat deckle-edged collar gleamed white and he clearly looked out of place with the others on the platform.

Sir Edward Coke moved from his bench to the centre of the Hall and faced the ex-courtier, now on trial for his life.

"Sir Everard Digby. You are hereby charged, together with the other plotters here, of conspiring to harm our gracious king, His Majesty King James I of England and latterly King James VI of Scotland, in addition to harming his royal family and his servants, namely his Parliament. You are charged with being party to a plot whose aim was to murder the aforementioned persons through the explosion of many barrels of gunpowder placed under the Palace of Westminster at the beginning of November, 1605."

The Attorney-General paused, looked at the Earl of Salisbury and continued.

"In addition to the above, you are charged with aiding and abetting the aforenamed plotters, specifically by providing them with much material support, namely money to the sum of six thousand crowns, together with horses, arms and other sundry equipment. Equipment, I must add, which was considered essential for the successful carrying out of this wicked plot."

Sir Everard looked up at his accuser, his body straight, stiff and proud.

"Well sir, how do you plead? Guilty or Not Guilty?"

"Guilty."

"Good," replied the prosecutor, smiling. "I am glad that, unlike your fellow conspirators, you still have the decency to recognize the evil of your deeds."

"Not at all, sir," Sir Everard replied sharply. "By pleading Guilty I am allowed to say a word or two in my own defence as is my right, and not as a favour as you granted my companions here."

Sir Edward gulped, recovered his breath and retorted. "So, speak Sir Everard and see what becomes of it."

The titled conspirator pretended to ignore this last remark and proceeded with his defence.

"First of all, I cannot deny that I have been involved in this affair, and in fact, neither would I wish to do so, for our activities were nothing but noble and pure."

The Attorney-General spluttered onto the back of his cuff, and feeling a restraining hand on his arm from His Majesty's Principal Secretary, said nothing.

"We intended to do nothing that would offend our Lord, and I for one would have gained nothing material from this affair had we succeeded. The good

Lord hath blessed me with lands and riches and I had no need for more. In addition, I was not motivated by revenge for personal injuries, but I must admit to this court that I was indeed motivated by the injuries the Catholic population of this country of ours have suffered in the past. We have been afflicted and persecuted like the ancient Hebrews in Egypt, and it was surely the aim of this government to cause us to leave this country in the same way the ancient Jews left Egypt as described in the Book of Exodus."

"And His Majesty is Pharaoh, I suppose," the Earl of Worcester whispered to his counterpart from Devonshire.

Sir Everard, who did not hear this remark, continued. "I therefore joined this venture as a way of correcting the wrongs that I saw were being perpetuated here and as such, joined with my fellow Catholic Robert Catesby, a man I deeply respected, and whose friendship I sought and found."

"I see," muttered the Attorney-General. "Robert Catesby and Moses the Israelite."

This time Sir Everard heard the cynical remark but chose to ignore it.

"Therefore, in the name of the Catholic religion, I forswore my name, my lands and my estates and all my worldly goods to help my brother Catholics. Indeed, all of my material goods seemed trifling and immaterial when I matched them with what I had hoped to gain for my brothers in religion."

"Very noble," commented the cynical chief prosecutor. "And pray tell me sir, do you think that this is still true?"

"Yes sir. In fact, even more so. For if you are to kill us as it seems you are bent on doing, then you will be supplying the Catholics of England, nay, of Europe with a new number of martyrs to the cause."

Ambrose lifted a hand and patted Sir Everard on the shoulder in support.

"Finally, in my defence, I would like to take this opportunity to state that even if I am to die for my actions, that I wish to plead for two things. The first is that His Majesty and his Parliament will ease the cruel laws that are now being directed against the Catholics of this realm, so that they will no longer need to live a secret life of fear as recusants and so that they can donate all that they can to the well-being of this country and..."

"And secondly?" Sir Edward cut in.

"That since I alone of the Everard family was involved in this affair..."

"Plot man! Plot! This was a plot!" the Attorney-General exploded.

"And since I alone of the Everard family was involved in this affair," Sir Everard repeated, "that I call upon the mercy of this court not to punish my wife Mary and my family in any way or form. They were, and still are to this day, completely innocent and have never had anything to do with this," and he looked at the Attorney-General straight in the eye, "affair."

Leaving the red-faced Sir Edward spluttering again onto his sleeve, Sir Everard smiled and stepped back a pace.

The Earl of Salisbury stood up, but the prosecutor indicated that he would continue as intended.

"Sir Everard Digby," he almost barked. "What I have heard from you, sir, is one of the most misguided speeches I have ever had the misfortune to hear in all my years as a Speaker in Parliament, Solicitor-General or Attorney-General. Your friendship and devotion to Robert Catesby, sir was based on folly, as is your Jesuit or Papist religion, which can only be described by true Christians as myself as heresy. And then, after all this, you make a plea for His Gracious Majesty to be liberal and lenient with you Catholics, so that you will not, in your words, be forced to lead lives of recusancy. Well, let me tell you sir, if you Catholics and your wives had ever thought more about the treasonous acts in which you were involved, together with their grim and terrible results, then you would not have even contemplated your participation in these nefarious plots. And now, I must repeat to you sir, the word is plots, and not ventures or affairs, as you and your fellow plotters insist on calling them.

"And now see where your behaviour has brought you. You now stand here, charged in this ancient Hall, with treason, a crime so heinous, that it hath only one punishment, and a just and fair one it is too. Death. And that be a traitor's death too. The situation is now that only your gracious and generous king can save you. And that is only if he hath a mind to do so.

"Similarly, you talk about your children's innocence. Well I ask you, what about the innocence of His Majesty's child Prince Henry who would have died as a result of your plot? What about him, eh? Wasn't he innocent? Did you consider that sweet child, a mere boy of only eleven years old? No sir. I am sure you did not. My only reply to you is a quote from our Holy Scriptures, namely: Let his wife be a widow, and his children vagabonds, let his posterity be destroyed, and in the next generation let his name be quite put out."

And with that, he turned his back on the defendant, and with a flourish of his black velvet cloak he resumed his seat between the Earls of Salisbury and of Devonshire.

All that remained now was the passing of the sentence. No one present in that great Hall that January day, be they prosecution, defence or spectator expected any verdict other than 'guilty.' And 'guilty' here was synonymous with death. The only remaining questions were when would that fatal punishment be meted out and would it be meted out to all of the plotters? Had Thomas Wintour's plea for his brother carried any weight and would Sir Everard Digby's knightly status and his separate hearing, together with his close connections to courtly circles help him in any way?

Just as the sergeant-at-law was about to say something, the Earl of Salisbury tapped him on the arm and indicated that he wished to address the court.

"Fellow Lords, gentlemen and others. Throughout these deliberations I have sat here on this bench and remained silent. I feel the time has come for me to say a word or two. I would also like to take this opportunity in order to clarify one major point that several of these plotters have insisted on making here in this Hall today.

"On several occasions today, we have heard how disappointed the Catholics of this country were when they claimed that His Majesty had broken his promises to them. The men you see before you, here in the centre of this Hall today have claimed that the gracious sovereign whom I serve as dutifully as I can, had promised to alleviate the alleged suffering of the Catholic population of this country. This is not true. No promises of this sort were ever made. I repeat, His Majesty, despite what we have heard said here several times today, never made any such promises to the Catholics of England. The king had merely stated at the beginning of his reign some two or three years ago, that he hoped that all of his subjects would prove to be law-abiding and keep the king's peace. There was never an occasion that he promised to alleviate any alleged suffering of the Catholics, or indeed of any other minority living in this realm. And as His Majesty's Principal Secretary of State, I am indeed qualified to issue such a categorical statement like this."

The Earl of Salisbury turned towards the lords seated at the top end of the Hall who all nodded their heads in agreement.

"And now that I have clarified that point, I will permit the sergeant-at-law to continue as he intended, that is, before I interrupted him."

He resumed his central position as Sir Edward Philips rose to speak.

"My Lords Commissioner, gentlemen and others. I will be brief. Today we have heard much talk and alleged justification for a vilely plotted act of murder and treason. But was this just one act? Oh no! It was many acts. We have also heard very few words of sorrow or regret. It is true that we have heard several of these plotters say how sorry they are for their wives and children, but none of them have expressed true regret for having been involved in this terrible plot. This by the way, as it has already been pointed out, has been referred to by these monstrous men as an affair or venture. And so, all it remains for me to do, after consulting with the Lords at this bench, is to call upon this honourable court and demand the rigours of the death penalty for the plotters who pleaded Not Guilty. And of course, a similar sentence should be passed on Sir Everard Digby, who by his own cognizance has admitted that he too was guilty of taking part in this hellish plot."

He stopped and looked scornfully at the plotters on the platform. They showed little reaction. The end of this dramatic scene was rapidly drawing to its inexorable close.

Sir Edward Philips continued. "I therefore call upon the Lord Chief Justice, Sir John Popham."

The sergeant-at-law stood aside as Sir John took up his position in the centre where all could see him.

"We have had a long day here today and I will not waste any time, especially as I have to perform a most distasteful task. And so I say to you all, all of the aforementioned plotters, all eight of you who are standing here before us today, that this inquiry, this court has found you guilty of high treason." He stopped, looked around, had a sidelong glance at where it was assumed the king was sitting behind a heavy curtain, and continued.

"Therefore, you shall return to the place from whence you came, there to remain until the time comes when you shall be drawn through the open City of London upon hurdles to the place of execution. There you shall be hanged and let down alive, and your privy parts cut off. Your entrails shall be taken out and burnt in your sight. Your heads shall be cut off and your bodies shall then be divided into four parts. These shall be disposed of at His Majesty's pleasure. That is all. May God have mercy on your souls."

None of the plotters visibly reacted. There were no surprises here.

As the lords began to step down from the bench, there was a sudden shout from Sir Everard.

"If I may hear but any of your lordships say you forgive me, I shall go more cheerfully to the gallows!"

The lords stopped moving. There was a sudden silence in the Hall. Everyone was looking at the condemned young aristocrat who was still standing tall and erect on the platform in the centre of the hall.

Suddenly a reply was heard from the bench, "God forgive you, and we do."

It was not recorded who said this.

Chapter Fourteen
Execution of the Sentence

Now that the sentence had been formally handed down, it did not take long for the Council to make all the necessary arrangements for it to be carried out. It was decided that the eight men would be executed in two groups of four; the first on Thursday 30 January 1606, that is, within three days of the trial, and the second group would be executed the following day. The Lieutenant of the Tower, Sir William Waad was informed of this decision and it was with a vicious feeling of glee that, escorted by four guardsmen, he descended to the cells to inform the condemned men.

They were in two cells: Sir Everard, Robert Wintour and John Grant in one, and Guido, Ambrose, Keyes and Thomas Wintour in the adjoining one. As befitting his lower social status, Thomas Bates had been returned to the Westminster Gatehouse. Perhaps several of the words that Ambrose Rookwood had used in his defence had hit the mark. For the Council had decided not to carry out the sentence with all the attendant public coverage that had usually accompanied such events in the past. The Earl of Salisbury and his advisors did not want the sight of the eight men, sentenced to being hanged, drawn and quartered to arouse public feelings of pity. In contrast, the crypto-Catholic Earl of Northumberland believed that 'justice should be seen to be done,' and argued that the sentence should be carried out at the traditional site at Tyburn. He was overruled and it was decided that the first group would be executed at the western end of St. Paul's Churchyard, and the second group would meet their grisly end at the Old Palace Yard in Westminster.

This in essence was the news the Lieutenant of the Tower was in a hurry to tell the seven men. Gathering them into the larger cell, he looked at them closely. Sir Everard still looked clean and almost fresh, but John Grant and Robert Keyes looked particularly haggard. It was clear that Guido had not recovered from his hours of torture on the rack, causing Waad to speculate if the would-be lighter of barrels of gunpowder would be able to scale the ladder to the gallows in a day or so. Hanging sick men might provoke unwanted cries and acts of sympathy from the crowds. That was all the Council needed, the Lieutenant thought cynically: sympathy for the Catholic plotters. He made a mental note to discuss this that afternoon with the Earl of Salisbury and Sir John Popham, and then dismissed the thought from his mind.

The two Wintour brothers, Tom and Robert sat huddled in a corner, Tom with a protective arm around his younger brother. Ambrose Rookwood sat a little apart from the others and appeared to be lost in thought.

The Lieutenant tapped his wooden staff on the floor for attention and the men looked up at him, that is all of them except Ambrose who continued to stare at his intertwined fingers or at the dirty straw-covered floor.

"You conspirators," Waad said without any sort of introduction, "prepare yourselves to die."

"We are prepared," answered Sir Everard evenly, looking at their gaoler in the eye.

"Good. For you are to die quicker than you thought. You..."

"You mean we are just to be executed, and not hanged and quartered?" Robert Wintour asked hopefully.

"Oh no. I mean that you are to be executed tomorrow. At least, some of you are. This Thursday and Friday, and early in the morning too," he added with relish. "So don't forget to say your prayers and 'Hail Marys' and all the rest of your miserable Catholic mumbo-jumbo, because for where you will be going, you'll be needing all the help you can get."

One of the guards standing next to him made a sickly grin, while another made the traditional sign of death, drawing his finger across his throat, topped by a grimace of a smile.

"And will we be able to see a priest beforehand?" Robert Keyes asked.

"Oh, that I don't know. But if you do, I doubt if he'll be able to help you much," Waad replied with a leer.

Keyes persisted. "But will you call for one?"

"Yes," added Guido. "Now that we've been condemned, what difference can it make?"

"Well, I'll see the Council and see what they decide. Now those of you who were in the other cell, get back there and I will return later in the day."

He did not return and no priest was forthcoming.

That night, Guido and the three others in the cell with him began to question themselves. Ambrose Rookwood stopped staring at the opposite wall, pulled his cloak about him to keep out the damp and opened the debate.

"In the last few hours, all I've been doing is asking myself, were we right to do what we did, or at least what we intended to do?"

"What do you mean, right?" Thomas Wintour asked.

"I mean, we had planned to kill the king and his family, as well as many members of Parliament, no?"

Guido pulled himself into a sitting position. Since he had been racked, nearly three months earlier, any physical movement sent white hot needles of pain through his joints, but it also pained him to remain in the same position for long. So he really had no choice but to move every so often. Wincing as a particularly sharp stab of pain shot up his right arm, he faced Ambrose.

"Ambrose, my dear friend. When we began this venture, or at least when you joined us, you knew it would be fraught with danger, no?"

Ambrose nodded his head thoughtfully.

"We all knew that there would be a possibility that the authorities would be watching out for us, or that there would be spies, or that maybe one of our number would report on us. This we knew, yes?"

Ambrose nodded again.

"Well, did Francis Tresham send that warning letter to Monteagle?" Keyes asked suddenly. "For that is a question that I have been racking my brain for the past two months. To me, it is too much of a coincidence that the one of us who was closely related to Monteagle,- he was his brother-in-law, no?- and was also related to Lord Stourton, should be imprisoned separately from us. We have also heard that he was racked and then died from a disease in the guts. Maybe all of that isn't true. Maybe he was secretly spirited away. Such things have happened before you know. I personally think he died on the rack. And think about this. Was it not Tresham who tried to dissuade us from carrying out our plan, and when he saw that we were determined to go through with it, then suggested that we warn some of the Catholic lords about attending Parliament that night? I am telling you, it's just too much for me."

"That's what I mean," Ambrose said. "For what he had planned to do in fact was, to murder some of our fellow Catholics who were innocent of any persecution and..."

"But Ambrose, they were not innocent," Guido said sharply.

"Why not?"

"Why not? Because they were working together with Salisbury instead of standing up to him and trying to get him to rescind those terrible laws."

"But Guido, they couldn't. They were always in the minority. Don't you see, if they had made too much noise, Salisbury would have trumped up some excuse to have them sent to the Tower. Queen Elizabeth and Henry VIII were always doing that. If you remember, the queen even sent Essex, and he was her lover, to the Tower for a while."

"So in other words, these Catholics lords had become part of the Protestant establishment," Guido said.

"Yes, I suppose so."

"So?"

"So they had to die for that?" Ambrose asked, shrugging his shoulders.

"Yes," Guido replied flatly.

"And what about the queen and Prince Henry?" asked Robert Wintour. "Would they have had to die too?"

"Of course," Guido replied. "They too are part of the establishment."

"So therefore all Protestants would have to be killed?" Ambrose stated.

"I didn't say that," Guido said testily. "I just meant that all Protestants who are in authority and who have the wherewithal to prosecute Catholics, must be destroyed. If we do not destroy them, they will destroy us."

"But surely the queen and Prince Henry weren't in a position to hurt us Catholics,"

Ambrose said.

Guido conceded that maybe Ambrose was right about the queen, for how much power and influence did Queen Anne of Denmark have?

"But," he asked, looking at Ambrose. "How long would it be before he became king in his turn, and how would he have treated us Catholics then, especially having been brought up in this particular court?"

Ambrose looked at Guido. It was clear that this answer was not good enough for him.

"But what about Christian fellowship and brotherhood? Is not that part of our religion too? Should we live according to 'an eye for an eye' or should we 'turn the other cheek?'"

Guido looked at Ambrose somewhat wearily. "Ambrose, my dear friend. Maybe because I am older than you and maybe because I was a soldier for many years, I am telling you that I tend to believe in 'an eye for an eye.' And my friend, this is especially so if it means that unless we look after ourselves, the king and his ministers will continue to persecute us Catholics for ever, or even drive us out of England. That is, in greater numbers than they have done so far."

Ambrose said nothing. Much of what Guido had said was true. But he still did not feel comforted. Tom Winter put his hand on his shoulder for support.

"Fear not, Ambrose," he said. "Soon we will be in a far better place than this."

"I know that Tom. That does not worry me. It's just the journey there that does. I just hope that I'm strong enough, that's all."

"Amen to that," replied Guido and Tom, crossing themselves fervently.

That night the condemned men fell into a fitful sleep. Guido probably slept better than most of them as he was more convinced of the righteousness of their cause than either Ambrose or the Wintour brothers. Tom Wintour's conscience continued to prick him for having involved his younger brother in the plot. Only Thomas Bates, separated from his fellow-plotters in his small cell in the Westminster Gatehouse hardly slept. He had no-one with whom to share his thoughts, the only human company being a couple of half-drunk and taunting guards who tormented him into the late hours with graphic descriptions of his imminent execution.

Thursday 30 January dawned cold, heavy and grey. The sun was barely visible through the wintry London sky. By the time the guards had unlocked the heavy and creaking door of their cell, the plotters were well awake. Pushing the guards aside, Lieutenant Waad entered their cell.

"Ah good. You're up," he said beaming. "No need for a long sleep now, is there? You'll have plenty of time to rest later on, won't you?"

Guido and Ambrose said nothing and Sir Everard deliberately turned his back on Sir William and adjusted his doublet and collar.

"Oh, I wouldn't concern yourself about that Sir Everard, at least not for where you are going. But don't worry gentlemen, I have some good tidings for you."

"The king's reprieved us?" Ambrose asked quickly.

"Oh no. This news isn't as good as that. It's that you are not going to be dragged to the site of execution by horses. You'll be placed on hurdles instead. You know, those long straw ones"

The prisoners looked at each other apprehensively. The Lieutenant noticed their expressions.

"Now don't you worry yourselves. The hurdles are waiting outside near the Green. So let us be on our way. Guards, take up your positions."

As the three prisoners, surrounded by pikemen and halberdiers started to make their way down the gloomy passageway, they suddenly heard shouting from the cell next door.

"Be strong, men."

"Be of good courage."

"The Lord be with you."

But before the first group to die could react, they were hurried on by Sir William and his guards.

Outside, the three men shivered in the cold and grey dawn. Apart from their recent journey to their trial in Westminster Hall, this was the first time, except for Robert Wintour, that they had been outside since their capture three months earlier. As the men were being bound to the hurdles, feet towards the horses, Sir William felt that an occasion like this could not pass without him having his final say.

"In the past, traitors like you would have been executed here on Tower Green or on Tower Hill, but the Council, for whatever reasons, have decided to have you executed at St. Paul's, so that is where we're going. So guards, check they're securely bound. We don't want any of their heretic Catholic friends coming along and rescuing them, now do we? So let's be going. It's nearly seven of the clock."

Within minutes the grim procession set off. Even though the plotters were bound on the hurdles, the bumpy route meant that they were jostled about and bounced about like sacks of vegetables on their way to market. Each man in his own way had made his own preparation for the rough journey and grim death that lay ahead. John Grant closed his useless eyes tightly and concentrated on his prayers. Robert Wintour gripped his rosary and prayed, as did Sir Everard Digby. As they passed on their bumpy way, bouncing over the cobblestones, they tried to blot out the cries of 'Papist traitors' and 'Catholic heretics' that the bystanders shouted at them. Suddenly Sir Everard felt a stone hit him in the chest. He saw the child who had thrown it receive a cheer and a pat on the back from someone in the crowd, before running off. He hoped there would be no more, but even if there were, there was nothing he could do about it.

On arriving at St. Paul's Churchyard, Sir Everard was the first to be cut free from his hurdle which had stopped at the foot of the scaffold. "You're lucky, Sir Everard," Sir William said with his usual grim prison humour. "You are going to be first. You're the lucky one. You'll be spared seeing what happens to your friends, won't you? Anyway, you'll all be together soon enough, so cheer up and off you go."

Sir Everard looked around. The whole area was surrounded by pikemen and soldiers with drawn swords. The authorities were taking no chances. Sir William had not been joking when he had mentioned the possibility of the plotters being rescued. Slowly he climbed the steps up the scaffold and looked around again. Saying that he wished to say a few words, he cleared his throat and took his final look at the crowds below. It might have been early in the morning, but the word had got around that the plotters were due to be executed at this early hour and many people had turned out to watch the gruesome spectacle which was about to take place.

"My friends," he called out in a clear voice. "I just want to declare that even though I have broken the law, I have committed no moral offence since I have acted according to the dictates of my own conscience and according to my Catholic beliefs."

"Boo! Hang him!"

"Hang him now and be done with it!"

Ignoring the shouts, Sir Everard continued.

"However, since I have broken the laws of this land, I beg forgiveness from God, the king and the people. Now, before I depart this life to meet my Maker, I pray that all will be well with my dearest wife and two sons for they are innocent of any part of this. I now ask you to pray with me for a moment." Saying this, he turned his back on the Protestant clergy who were waiting in attendance and bowed his head in silent prayer.

"Come on! Hang him!" a raucous voice shouted out.

"Yes! Now!"

Sir Everard Digby then raised his head to show that he had finished and, well-mannered courtier to the end, he shook hands with the executioner and the other officials, and waited calmly for the hangman to do his duty. Very soon after being hanged, his still live body was cut down, and still breathing heavily and unevenly, his heart was cut out of his body. As the executioner was holding up the bloody organ to the crowd, he shouted out the traditional cry, "Here is the heart of a traitor!"

The writer and philosopher Sir Francis Bacon who was standing nearby later reported to a friend, that at this point Sir Everard had cried out, "You lie!" and then died.

Later, his head would be chopped off, and be impaled on a spike high on a tower on London Bridge. From here, this aristocratic head, together with those of his fellow-plotters would stare out blindly over the capital. This was to act as a public and official announcement of death as well as a grim warning to any other would-be plotters.

As soon as the executioner had finished with Sir Everard, Robert Wintour mounted the scaffold. Standing there, at the foot of the ladder that would lead to the noose, he said nothing aloud but was just seen moving his lips in silent prayer. Within minutes he too was half-hanged, had his head cut off and his body quartered, the parts of which were shown aloft to the appreciative and noisy crowd.

Perhaps fortunately for John Grant, his sight had been so harmed by the accidental explosion of gunpowder at Holbeach House that this taciturn plotter could not see what grim death awaited him. After having been helped to the top of the scaffold, he too turned his face in what he thought was the direction of the crowd and indicated that he wished to say a few words.

"Good people! I confess nothing! I have done nothing wrong. All I have done was to try and right the many wrongs that have been perpetrated against the Catholic population of this country. I..."

"Boo! Hang him!"

"Finish him off!"

John Grant continued regardless. "I would have preferred to die old and peacefully, but..."

"I bet you would!" a wit in the crowd called out.

"...but this king, this King James who is a traitor to his mother, the saintly Mary, Queen of Scots would not allow us to go our way in peace. And so our plan to rid this country of this man was not wrong. I..."

"Boo! Traitor!"

"I am now ready to meet the good Lord and so I die as a true Catholic!"

Immediately on crossing himself, the rope was placed around his neck and he too was beheaded and quartered while still half-hanged and choking. As with the others, his quartered body was shown to the cheering crowds.

"God save us from all Catholic traitors!" yelled a hysterical woman in the crowd.

"And God save the king!" yelled another and the crowd began to disperse. The show was over for the day and, after all, the people had to go to work.

"Wait! Wait! Here's another!" someone called as the straw hurdle bearing Thomas Bates was dragged to the foot of the scaffold. In a co-ordinated effort, the authorities had decided to execute whom they considered the less important plotters on the first day and leave the others for a 'grande finale.' Since Thomas Bates was merely a servant, he was automatically thought of as of lesser importance. The crowd returned and once again took up positions from where they could get a good view.

Just after the executioner had cut Catesby's servant's arms free, a flushed looking woman pushed her way to the front of the crowd.

"Let me through! Let me through!" she cried.

Those standing in front of her in the crowd were so surprised at this, that they stood aside and let her through to the front. Gathering up her heavy skirts, she ran up to the remaining plotter who was still lying on the hurdle, his eyes tightly closed. She bent down over her husband.

"Tom! Tom!" she cried. "O Lord help us! What am I to do?"

"Peace woman! Listen!" And he quickly told her where he had buried the hundred pounds he had hidden after he had fled Holbeach House. He was about to embrace her with his freed arms when two guards pushed her roughly aside.

"She calmed down quick enough," someone in the front of the crowd noted as Martha Bates pushed her way back through the crowd. She did not want to see her husband suffer, as suffer he would.

"I wonder what he said to her," a fat man asked

"Probably that he was truly innocent or..."

"Quiet man! He wants to say something."

"People of London! I was wrong. I know this now today. What I did, I did for the love of my master, Robert Catesby. My love for him made me forget my God and how to serve my king. And so good people, I beg your forgiveness and I pray that the Lord and Jesus Christ our Father will forgive me too."

Two or three women in the crowd started weeping but a rough voice shouted out, "Silence, you women! He wanted to blow up our king and queen!"

"Yes, and Parliament too! Hang him!"

"But he begged for forgiveness," cried out one of the women between sobs. "Does he still have to die? Haven't enough died today?"

"'Course he should die. He's a traitor! Now come on hangman. Do your duty!"

And within minutes the hangman and his assistants had 'done their duty' on the poor half-dead body of Thomas Bates. His head was placed near those of Sir Everard Digby, Robert Wintour and John Grant, while his body parts too joined the bloody pile near the foot of the scaffold.

Seeing that the grisly butchery was over for the day, the crowd began to melt away. After all, today was a working day, not a festival and the crowd still had to earn their daily bread.

"But I'm coming back tomorrow to see the rest of them hang," one loudmouthed man said.

"Yes. I'm coming with you," replied another. "You know, they're hanging their leader tomorrow."

"Who? That Guy Fawkes fellow? The one they caught with the gunpowder?"

"Yeah. That's 'im."

"Oh, then I'm coming back tomorrow as well. 'Bye. See you. Hope it doesn't rain."

"Me too."

The bloodthirsty man's hopes were not disappointed. Although the weather remained as it had been, if not a little cooler, the crowds turned up as before. Perhaps there were even more in the Old Palace Yard at Westminster than there had been the day before at St. Paul's Churchyard. Obviously the word had got around the crowded and cramped city of London that the authorities were providing a good spectacle. There was no reason to miss it.

As before, the remaining plotters had spent much of the night in discussion and prayer for themselves and for their poor dead and mutilated friends. They were awake when Lieutenant Waad noisily entered their cell early that morning to supervise all the arrangements for their final journey. His sense of humour had not changed.

"Now, don't you all worry yourselves," he said with his usual leer. "We're taking you to a clean place today. Not all bloody from yesterday. You're going to be at Westminster, not St. Paul's."

As usual, his fat assistant laughed at the lieutenant's black sense of humour. "Aye, you're right there, Sir William. It'll be very clean there. Well, at least for the first one. I wonder who that will be?"

"Don't you worry, man. We'll know that soon enough, won't we?" Sir William said, eyeing his silent prisoners. "And so will they."

Within minutes, the four men had been led outside and tied to the hurdles. Seeing that everything was going to plan, Sir William gave orders to the guards to take them away.

"Now that your cells are empty, we've got more room for more of you Catholic traitors, haven't we? That is, if anyone will do anything after seeing what you're going to look like soon," were his final words to them.

Although the place of execution was different, the proceedings were the same. As were the witticisms heard from the crowd. As Tom Wintour mounted the scaffold, the jokesters in the crowd did not waste any time.

"'e don't look very 'appy, does he?"

"Sort of pale I'd say."

"Well 'ow'd you feel, eh?"

"Me? Don't think I'd 'ang about long enough to find out."

"'ang about,' he said. 'ang about. Oh very funny."

"Will you two shut up? He's going to say something."

Tom Wintour looked around and opened his mouth to say something out loud. Then he thought the better of it. "Now isn't the time to speak," he half-muttered to the executioner and the priests who were standing nearby. "I have come here to die and I just pray that the Lord and the king will forgive me and my fellow Catholics. Now I am ready."

He crossed himself and bent his head forward to receive the hangman's noose. As on the previous day's proceedings, he was quickly cut down before he was dead and the diabolical ritual of beheading and quartering was expertly performed.

Ambrose Rookwood, whose turn was next, had done his best to look away. He tried to look brave to the end. In fact he felt better than he had expected to. On his hurdle journey to the Palace Yard, his much-beloved wife, Mary, had pushed her way through the crowds and had called out to him, "Ambrose, be of good courage!" But like Martha Bates, she did not stay to watch her husband's fearful end.

At the top of the scaffold, Ambrose placed a hand on the hangman's arm. "Stay. I wish to say something."

"'Tis your right sir. But just don't go on for too long 'cos I've other things to do today, that's all."

Ambrose faced the crowd below.

"Good people of London. My last words to you are that I have sinned. I have sinned grievously in wanting to improve the lot of us Catholics by bloodshed, by trying to spill the king's blood and that of his family. For that I am going to die. All I can do is ask and pray that His Majesty will reign over us..."

"Over us man, not you!" one of the wits in the crowd called out.

"...in peace and happiness. But I would still wish, with all my heart..."

"You won't 'ave that for long!"

"...that our Blessed Lord makes the king a Catholic."

"Boo! Hang all Catholics!"

"God save our Protestant king!"

These must have been the last words that Ambrose Rookwood, the 28-year-old bon-vivant from Suffolk ever heard. Soon, like Tom Wintour, his still warm body was separated into a head and quartered body and then placed next to his fellow plotters hacked up body near the quartering block.

"Only two of 'em left now," said one of the crowd.

"Yeah, this next one and their leader, Guy Fawkes."

"But he wasn't their leader. He was just the one what was going to light the 'powder, wasn't he?"

"Well, it doesn't matter now, does it? Look here he comes. The next one."

The 'next one' was Robert Keyes.

"Will you see how quickly he's climbing up that ladder. Look at that."

"Yeah. Seems like he wants to die. You know, get it over with."

"True. No point in 'anging about, is there? Get it? 'anging about?"

"Will you keep quiet! You've already made that joke."

"Hey look! What's he doing?"

"He's jumped off the top! Poor bugger. Wants to finish it off quickly. But look!"

"Yeah, he's on the ground. The rope must 'ave snapped or something."

"Well 'e's still alive, poor soul."

"So he didn't escape the chop, did he?"

"Oh no."

"Poor sod's still alive."

And so he was. Robert Keyes attempt to escape 'the chop' had failed, and like the other plotters before him, his still warm and breathing body was brutally cut up, ready to serve as a warning to any other Catholic conspirator.

The last one to mount the scaffold was Guy Fawkes. Unlike the others, his racked and broken body had to be helped off the hurdle and on to the scaffold. Now the crowd could see the effects of racking and torture. Each step up the ladder to the raised platform sent red-hot stabs of pain searing through his body. His legs could hardly bear the weight of his body and more than once he slipped and missed his footing. Gripping the sides of the ladder with his hands, he gritted his teeth to prevent himself from crying out with pain, as he slowly mounted the scaffold. Doing his best to remain steady, he raised his head and faced the bloodthirsty crowds. He was about to speak, but then he stopped himself. All he could do was to cough weakly. The racking had beaten him. Instead, he looked around and made the sign of the cross several times.

"What? Isn't he going to say something?" someone in the crowd called out.

"Don't look like he can, does it?"

"Yes, but he was their leader, no?"

"Shush! Be quiet! He is trying to say something."

Those at the front were pushed forward as those behind strained to hear what Guy Fawkes had to say.

"What's he saying?"

"Can't hear properly. Something about forgiveness from the king, I think."

"Are you sure? Well it's too late for that now, isn't it?"

"Anyway, look. He's climbing up to the top now."

"Yes. And he's very slow about it, isn't he?"

"Well, you wouldn't be any quicker if you'd have been racked like he was."

"Look, he's made it to the top bar anyhow."

"Aye, with the 'angman's help."

"And look, they've put the rope around his neck. Shouldn't be long now."

"Hey! What's he doing?"

And just then, with his last ounce of strength, Guy Fawkes, the soldier-plotter from York, the would-be exploder of King James, the royal family and his Parliament, threw himself off the scaffold and broke his neck. By the time the executioner and his men had pulled in his swinging body, cut him down and taken him to the quartering block, the 'chief plotter,' the plotter whose name would live for evermore was dead. Guy Fawkes, the man whose name and conical-hatted and bearded image would forever be associated with gunpowder, fireworks, explosions and dark underground passages in Westminster had defied the excruciating pain of the axe and of the executioners' knives. He had cheated the king, Salisbury and the Council. He had had his final revenge. Now, he was beyond them all.

Epilogue

The barbarous execution of eight of the plotters at the end of January 1606, some three months after Guy Fawkes was first arrested did not signal the end of the Gunpowder Plot. King James I, ably assisted by Salisbury and a mixed group of Protestant and crypto-Catholic lords worked hard to round up and serve their idea of justice to all of the conspirators' inner and outer circles of friends and supporters who, in the eyes of the authorities, would serve as other potential plotters.

On 7 November 1605 John Wintour, step-brother to Thomas and Robert Wintour, fled Holbeach House, probably feeling that he should not have been there in the first place. He made his way south to Robert's place, Huddington Hall, a large Tudor mansion house. There he surrendered and was arrested by the Sheriff of Worcestershire's deputy. He was moved to the Tower of London from the Midlands and accompanied the other plotters to be tried at Westminster. Despite his plea that he was ignorant of the plot, he was condemned to death for conspiracy and treason, and a few weeks later was transferred back to Red Hill, Worcestershire. There, on 7 April 1606, he was hanged drawn and quartered. Unlike the plotters who had received this treatment in London, his remains were not put on public display as a warning and he was buried in the churchyard at Huddington Court.

John Wintour was not the only Catholic associate of the plotters to be executed at Red Hill that spring day. He was joined by 'Red' Humphrey Littleton, a recusant who had become involved in the plot at the very end. He and Stephen Littleton had joined the plotters in the Midlands and their aim had been to raise a force of men who would reinforce the regiment of Catholic troops in Flanders. At first, the authorities were not interested in Humphrey Littleton. However, later they changed their mind when his servants Daniel Bate and cook John Finwood betrayed the fugitives, Stephen Littleton and Robert Wintour who were then hiding at Hagley House. Humphrey managed to escape, but did not get far and was captured at Prestwood in Staffordshire. In a last desperate attempt to save his life, he revealed the names of two other Catholic priests involved in the plot, Father Edward Oldcorne (another of Guy Fawkes' school friends) and Father Henry Garnet. They were discovered soon after, hiding out at Hindlip House, a huge building in Worcestershire which belonged to a Catholic supporter, Thomas Habington.

Despite this act of betrayal, Humphrey was tried and executed on 7 April 1606 together with Father Oldcorne, John Wintour, a farmer named Parkes, who was accused of helping the fugitives and Ralph Astley, a lay brother who was associated with Father Tesimond.

Humphrey Littleton's nephew, Stephen, was also executed at about this time at Stafford for aiding the plotters and 'for rebellious acts.' He had fled Holbeach House after the explosion with the dispirited Robert Wintour and the two of them were to remain on the run in the West Midlands for two months before being betrayed. Stephen Littleton was executed together with Henry Morgan who had joined the conspiracy very late in the day and who had also been badly burned in the Holbeach House explosion. Of the executed men, Father John Gerard recorded that Littleton "showed great resolution and devotion, to the satisfaction of all (presumably the Catholic part) the country."

Henry Garnet, (sometimes spelt Garnett) a Jesuit Father and member of the 'outer circle' of Catholics who suffered the traditional bloody and grisly end death as a condemned traitor was an English priest who had spent some time in Italy. At first he had actively opposed the Protestant establishment by becoming involved in the Bye Plot of 1603; a pathetic plot devised by Father William Watson. This had involved kidnapping the king and keeping him in the Tower of London until he had promised to grant full toleration to the Catholic population of England. Watson was hanged, drawn and quartered and Garnet, despite his being persecuted by the authorities, succeeded in keeping one foot ahead of the law, while gaining many converts to the Catholic cause at the same time.

His relevance to the Gunpowder Plot is, that as a religious and spiritual authority, he was consulted by Robert Catesby and Francis Tresham on the question of the morality of killing innocent people in order to kill the king and other anti-Catholic lawmakers. Garnet replied that such an action was justified and many of the central core of the plotters drew much moral support from this decision. Using his Continental connections, Garnet was also involved in trying to persuade the Spanish King Philip III to invade England and thereby help the English Catholics resume their former role as in the days of Mary I (1553-1558).

Shortly before 5 November 1605 Garnet was informed by Father Oswald Tesimond about the whole plot. Tesimond recorded that his confessor was then completely shocked and said that he would do his best to prevent the execution of the plot.

Since then, Garnet's role in the Plot has been seen as a controversial one by both Protestants and Catholics. On the one hand, this influential priest advised Robert Catesby, the initiator of the Plot, against any violent action, but on the other hand he appears not to have taken a positive stand in trying to stop the plotters from carrying out their mission. In fact, in December 1605 he wrote a letter to the Lords of the king's Privy Council stating that he abhorred 'the late most horrible attempt' with reference to the Plot

However, whatever his true position was, on 20 January 1606 Garnet was discovered hiding in a priest's hole at Hindlip House and arrested by Sir Henry Bromley, the Sheriff of Worcestershire. At first he was held in the sheriff's own home and then sent to London where he was incarcerated in the Gatehouse Prison. He was first interrogated by the Council in mid-February and soon after transferred to the Tower. He remained here for six weeks and was finally sent for trial at the Guildhall. At his trial he had to face Sir Edward Coke as prosecutor, the same man who had harshly conducted the case for the government against the original plotters. The court took only a quarter of an hour to find him guilty of treason, and once again the Chief Justice, Sir John Popham ordered another prominent Catholic to be hanged, drawn and quartered. The date for his execution was set for May 1, but this was changed as this was a public holiday, and the government felt that the holiday crowds might prove to be in sympathy with the condemned man. Garnet was therefore given a two-day reprieve.

At the scaffold, when asked if he had anything to say, he said that the third day of May was a good day to die as the Cross of Christ was allegedly found on this day. He concluded his last speech in public, saying, "I thank God I have found my cross." Such was the spiritual reputation of this man, that when he was half-hanged, several people in the front of the crowd rushed forward to grab his legs and pull him down. This was to ensure that when he was cut down, he was dead and would not suffer the additional pain when he was beheaded and disembowelled. Thus died one of the most influential Catholics who was involved in the Gunpowder plot. His actions and decisions regarding the conspirators still provoke discussion in Catholic circles, some seeing him as a saint, while others see him as a coward and turncoat.

Another important Catholic to fall into the hands of the authorities was Father John Gerard. Like Garnet, he seems to have been a very charismatic person, for during a term of imprisonment in 1594 he even managed to convert his gaoler's son to Catholicism. His relevance to the Gunpowder Plot is that it was Gerard who converted Sir Everard Digby to the Catholic cause and it was the latter's activities who caused Gerard to suspect 'his most loyal friend' regarding the Plot. The following extract of a letter Gerard wrote demonstrates the priest's suspicions.

> ...and there urge you to tell me what was the reason both of that sudden alteration in your house and of divers other things which I had observed before, but did not until then reflect upon them so much, as, for example, the number of horses that you had not long before in your stable, the sums of money which I had been told you had made of your stocks and grounds, which (said I) in one of your judgment and provident care of your estate, are not likely to be done without some great cause, and seemed to think you had something in hand for the catholic cause.
>
> (Original syntax and punctuation)

After the Plot was discovered, and with the authorities looking for him, Gerard went into hiding before fleeing to Europe disguised as an ambassadorial assistant. He became the British Penitentiary in Rome in 1607 and two years later was sent to Flanders where he worked at Louvain and wrote his *Autobiography*. He died in 1637 at the age of 73 after having fulfilled several ecclesiastic posts in connection with English Catholic institutions.

The third important Catholic priest involved with the 'moral' aspect of the Plot is Father Oswald Tesimond (sometimes known as Greenway.) He also showed great respect for the plotters, especially Robert Catesby and Francis Tresham and was spiritually involved with Father Garnet. After the Plot's failure he was 'tailed' by the authorities, but one dark night managed to throw off his pursuers and quietly escape from London. He then travelled south and sneaked aboard a ship bound for Europe, bearing a cargo of dead pigs. Like Father Gerard, he eventually reached Rome and remained in exile for thirty years.

His importance today is that he wrote a record of the Plot, which, in terms of history is very important as it is one of the few contemporary Catholic records of this event.

In connection with Catholic exiles on the Continent, Sir William Stanley, the soldier who had been involved with Guy Fawkes during the Flanders chapter of his career, realized that the Catholic cause had completely failed in England. Like Father Gerard, he helped to establish a Catholic centre of education in the Spanish Netherlands and died quietly in Ghent in 1630.

Interestingly enough, the ancestors of both of the prominent and dissident Catholics Sir William Stanley and Robert Catesby had fought on different sides some 130 years earlier during the reign of Richard III. Sir William Catesby was one of the king's chief advisors who paid for his loyalty with his life after Richard's defeat at Bosworth Field, while Lord Thomas Stanley betrayed this same king at Bosworth, and so helped usher in the Tudor era by aligning himself with Henry VII. In fact, as tradition (and Shakespeare) have it, that it was Stanley who crowned Henry of Richmond as the first Tudor king on the battlefield immediately after the battle.

Moving from a minor aristocrat, exiled in Europe, we move on to one of the major and all-important aristocrats in England, Robert Cecil, the Earl of Salisbury. Between the coronation of his master, King James in 1603 to the Gunpowder Plot of November 1605, Salisbury had spent much energy in putting down various Catholic plots such as the Bye and Main plots. These plots were either intended to kill the king outright or kidnap him in order to improve the conditions of the English Catholic community. The chief plotters were arrested and tried, the most famous being Sir Walter Raleigh. He and several other nobles were granted a last minute reprieve, but some of the less fortunate plotters, that is those of less than noble status, were executed in a similar fashion to Guy Fawkes *et al.* In keeping with Salisbury's devious *modus operandi*, one of the plotters, Sir Griffin Markham had his life spared so that he could be exiled and become one of Salisbury's chief spies on the continent. It was a network, parallel in style with Sir Francis Walsingham's in England twenty years earlier which kept the English authorities on the look-out for many of the Catholic anti-government plots.

One of the major results of these plots is that King James, who had good reason to be worried about plots, (having been the object of at least two attacks on his life in Scotland as King James VI,) reintroduced several very severe laws regarding Catholics, recusancy and fines for non-attendance of Protestant church services.

In the years following the Gunpowder Plot, as the minister responsible for financial affairs, Salisbury's reputation became besmirched as he was accused of obtaining money deceitfully. However, during the remainder of his life he did manage to acquire much wealth and property, but when he died in May 1612, he left over thirty thousand pounds in unpaid debts.

Today, many historians question the role Cecil played in the Gunpowder Plot. Did he initiate much of it through spies and agents-provocateurs, in order to exploit it to attack the Catholic population of England, or did he just jump on the band-wagon and use the plot once it had been discovered?

It is known that he had close relations with Lord Monteagle, the recipient of the warning letter, the 'tip-off' about the imminent execution of the plot, but does this mean that the wily Earl of Salisbury was actually responsible for the writing or forging of the letter? In an article in *The Observer* (November 1967), Joan Cambridge analyzed samples of both Salisbury's handwriting and the writing of the Monteagle letter and wrote in conclusion:

> *So on aggregate there is sufficient evidence to support an opinion that in all probability Cecil himself wrote the Monteagle letter.*

She based her conclusion on a detailed study of such graphological points as serifs and handwriting movements.

As for William Parker, 11th Baron Morley, 4th Baron Monteagle himself, what happened to him? After delivering the aforementioned letter to the Principal Secretary, he became intimately involved in the final playing out of the plot. After the major plotters had been executed, Monteagle was granted an annual pension of five hundred pounds for life. This was an extremely generous reward. The question is, did the government award him this prize and protect the noble lord so much in order to protect him from contemporary rumours? These stated that he, Monteagle, was responsible for having his brother-in-law Francis Tresham poisoned in the Tower before he could be tried with the other plotters and possibly give away state secrets, or at least divulge Salisbury's nasty ways of obtaining information.

Running counter to this is the argument that it was Francis Tresham who wrote the warning letter as a means of appeasing his conscience. However, even though Monteagle did nothing to help Tresham after his arrest, the aristocrat did step in to help save the life of Thomas Habington, his sister's husband after he had been accused of hiding priests in his house at Hindlip.

In 1617 Monteagle was honoured in a popular woodcut illustration. It showed King James sitting on the throne, with an eagle delivering a letter to Monteagle, who is obviously happy to pass on this missive to his king. Underneath it says:

The gallant *Eagle*, soaring upon high:
Beares in his beake, *Treason's* discovery.
MOUNT, noble EAGLE, with thy happy prey,
And thy rich *prize* to the *King* with speed convey.

However, despite his part, great or small in preventing the Gunpowder Plot from being carried out, Monteagle continued to support the Catholic cause and his daughter even became a nun. According to various rumours, when he died in July 1622, he received the last rites as a Catholic.

As for the principal target of the Plot, King James, what did he have to say about it? He made a pointed comparison of the Plot with the Scottish Gowrie conspiracy to murder him in August 1600. Since both plots were organized to take place on Tuesday 5 August 1600 and 5 November 1605, the king claimed that the plots were destined "to teach me, that it was the same devil that still persecuted me, so it was one and the same God that still mightily delivered me."

As a result of the plot he demanded a new Oath of Allegiance be sworn and that this would stipulate that Catholics who attended Anglican services must also take the sacrament at least once a year in their local parish churches. In addition, Catholics were forbidden to enter the legal and medical professions. These laws remained on the statute books throughout the 17th century but were not strictly reinforced.

Later Acts which harmed Catholic interests were actually aimed at Protestant Nonconformists. Such measures as the 1673 Test Act declared that the holders of official positions in the state must take the sacrament according to the rites of the Church of England. Then, in 1700 William III was forced to pass an Act forbidding Catholics to inherit or purchase land unless they took the oaths of abjuration which meant in effect that they were renouncing their religion. In addition, priests were forbidden to carry out their various religious duties, while other Catholics were barred from teaching.

Again, the laws were not very strictly reinforced, but it was not until about 1770 that the English Catholics began to agitate for their complete removal. Eight years later, several of the above laws were indeed removed from the statute books and by the end of the 18th century, fines for not attending church services were abolished. In addition, Catholics were allowed to enter the professions and to buy and inherit land. Catholic schools and places of worship were legalized, but this was only part of the problem as they saw it. In 1829 the Catholic population was granted full emancipation under the law and were also admitted to both houses of Parliament. They were also allowed to run for all civil and political offices, except those of Regent, Lord Chancellor and High Commissioner for the Church of Scotland. As a footnote to the granting of all of this religious freedom, even today, a Catholic (or a Jew, Muslim or Hindu etc.) cannot become the Prime Minister of Britain, this post only being open to a member of the Church of England.

A more popular result of the Gunpowder Plot is Bonfire night. This tradition started on the original night itself, the night of 5 November 1605, and it has continued unabated since. Perhaps the most significant Bonfire night occurring in 1688 when the Protestant King William III landed at Torbay in Devon. He arrived in response to Parliament's desire to replace the unpopular and despised Catholic King James II, who was to live out the remainder of his life as an exile in France.

Today, bonfires are still lit on a wide scale, and thousands of 'Guy Fawkes' are burnt in effigy. However, if you were to ask the man-in-the-street about the historical background to all this, you would probably receive an answer something on the lines of, "Guy Fawkes was a man who tried to blow up the king and his Parliament a long time ago, but who was caught just in time." Nevertheless, despite this ignorance of the details, Guy Fawkes' or Bonfire night still remains a popular night of celebration. Pennies are collected for the guy, fortunes are spent on fireworks, huge bonfires are lit, much rubbish is burnt and fire-brigades and hospitals probably record November the Fifth as their busiest night.

Ironically, King James I, despite the Catholic attempt on his life, and indeed upon the life of his family adopted a more pro-Catholic stand when it came to foreign policy. He wished to be known as the 'Rex Pacificus' and as such, encouraged dealings and trade with Spain, an attitude the extremist Plotters could not possibly stomach. He also made sure that his dealings with Protestant Europe were placed on a sound footing and in 1613 his oldest daughter Elizabeth married Frederick V, King of Bohemia. This pragmatic attitude to foreign policy reflects the king's own axiom: Between foolish rashness and extreme length, there is a middle way.

Finally, the question must be asked, were the plotters a group of bad and evil men who conspired to kill the ruling elite and take over the kingdom through extremely violent means, or were they just a bunch of misguided extremists whose plan never really had a chance of succeeding? The basic cause of their desperation was the constant persecution they suffered. They were acutely aware of the fact that they were a Catholic minority in a newly formed Protestant country and that the establishment led by the king and the Earl of Salisbury had reasons to fear a Catholic return to power.

Today, such a group of men would quickly and clearly be labelled as terrorists. They would be equated with those who had hijacked airplanes in the 1970s or who have murdered politicians and businessmen in Ireland, Germany and Italy, or who blew up the World Trade Center in New York on '9/11,' or London transport trains and a bus in London in July 2005. All of this was done of course to keep their stories on the front pages of the world's press or to be the major item on the television news.

At the end of her excellent book *The Gunpowder Plot: Terror and Faith in 1605*, Antonia Fraser raises this point and quotes the 19th century historian S.R.Gardiner who described the plotters thus in his pro-plot work *What the Gunpowder Plot was* (1897).

> *Atrocious as the whole undertaking was, great as must have been the moral obliquity of their minds before they could have conceived such a project, there was at least nothing mean or selfish about them. They had boldly risked their lives for what they honestly believed to be the cause of God and their country.*

I do not think a modern judge would grant the existence of 'honest belief,' or of the lack of meanness or selfishness on the defendant's part as extenuating circumstances in a trial, especially if human life were at stake.

Even though their action was certainly terrorist in scope, today, some four hundred years later our attitude to the plotters may be gentler, especially if the element of time is combined with the fact that happily they failed to carry out their explosive plans. Today it may seem that it was the king and his ministers who through their brutal and contemporary laws of the 1600s appear to be the cruel, vicious and barbarous actors in this play.

And while talking of plays, one of the most famous contemporary plays of the time - *The Tragedy of Macbeth* contains several references to the Gunpowder Plot.

According to most experts, Shakespeare wrote this play in about 1606, or at least after the Plot had been discovered. It may be readily assumed that the Bard, who had a very well developed political and social conscience, and who referred to other contemporary events in his other plays, would not have ignored the Gunpowder Plot.

First of all he shared a geographic connection with many of the central core of plotters. The instigator, Robert Catesby, was born at Lapworth, just north of Stratford-upon-Avon, while the three members of the Wintour family, John, Robert and Thomas came from Huddington Hall, a little west of Shakespeare's hometown. Their brother-in-law, John Grant's grandfather, had been involved in business deals with Shakespeare's father, while Catesby, the Wintour family and Francis Tresham were all distantly related to Shakespeare's Catholic mother, Mary Arden.

When drawing a Gunpowder Plot - *Macbeth* connection, many literary critics and editors have referred to the Porter's scene in Act II, where the porter drunkenly calls out in response to Macduff's midnight knocking on the castle gates:

> *Knock! Knock! Who's there, in the other devil's name? Faith, here's an equivocator that could swear in both the scales against either scale; who committed treason enough for God's sake, yet could not equivocate to heaven.*
>
> *O, come in, equivocator.*

This quotation is usually considered to be a direct reference to the Jesuit plotter, Father Henry Garnet who became well-known through his use of the word 'equivocator.' He was also one of the authors of *The Defence of Equivocation*, a publication which claimed that persecuted Catholics were justified in lying, presumably for political and/or pragmatic reasons.

Incidentally, if any of Shakespeare's audience did not make the connection at the beginning of the play, he used it again at the end when, feeling weary and resigned before the final battle, Macbeth says:

> *I pull in resolution and begin*
> *To doubt the equivocation of the fiend*
> *that lies the truth.*

Similarly, when the Porter in Act ii says:

> *Here's a farmer that hang'd himself on the expectation of plenty.*

Shakespeare was not only referring to a current joke, which was also used by his fellow dramatists Ben Jonson and Joseph Hall, but that 'farmer' was also an alias used by Father Garnet during his trial.

The play *Macbeth* of course takes place against the backdrop of a nobleman successfully stabbing his (Scottish) king, as opposed to the Gowrie plot where the would-be murderers were unsuccessful. Both acts were also supposed to have been conducted stealthily in the dead of night.

Even if Shakespeare's allegedly earlier pro-Catholic sentiments had not been shaken by the Gunpowder Plot, then the fact that his 22 year old daughter Susanna was reported by the church-warden and sidesmen of the Holy Trinity Church in Stratford-upon-Avon to the authorities for not receiving the sacrament at Easter 1606, cannot have caused him to have positive feelings towards the Catholic church.

In general, although the mainstream Catholics did their best to disassociate themselves from the extremist Gunpowder Plotters, they still continued to suffer from a bad press until well into the 19th century when Britain's Catholics were finally and officially emancipated.

When the Great Fire of London broke out in 1666, loudmouths quickly spread rumours that it was part of a Catholic plot. Similarly a few years later in 1678 a disreputable anti-Catholic loudmouth and trouble-maker called Titus Oates similarly spread rumours that he had discovered a Popish plot to murder Charles II and re-establish the Catholic church. His lies were believed by the authorities and many innocent Catholics were executed before Oates was exposed for the disgusting person he was.

Seven years later in 1685, rumours began to circulate that it was the Catholics who were responsible for the death of the 'Merry Monarch,' King Charles II. Those accused included the Catholic servants of the Duchess of Portsmouth, while others accused the Duke of York, a known Catholic, of poisoning his older brother.

These sordid rumours did not prevent the Duke of York from succeeding his brother as King James II. However, his blatant Catholicism, together with the fact that his Catholic wife, Mary of Modena had just given birth to a son, and therefore another potential Catholic king, proved too much for Parliament and the people. He was forced to abdicate in 1689 and seek shelter in France, his place being taken by his Dutch Protestant son-in-law, William of Orange.

A century later, the Gordon Riots of 1780 showed that anti-Catholic prejudices were still a very relevant aspect of life in Britain. These riots which began as an anti-Catholic demonstration, rapidly degenerated into widespread disturbances which lasted for a week. They were instigated by Lord George Gordon who was protesting the Roman Catholic Relief Act. Leading a mob of 50,000 Protestants, they destroyed much Catholic property and 300 people were killed before law and order were restored.

Even in recent history, in Lewes in East Sussex, effigies of the pope have been burnt, although the organizers of this event state that the effigy is of a 17th century holder of that office, and that no connection should be made with the current pope.

And so, ironically perhaps, all that remains to be said is that the Gunpowder Plot, despite it being a terrorist (and extremely naive) episode, has come down to us, some 400 years later wrapped up in a pale aura of misguided heroism. Is this because people tend to side with the underdog; the poor persecuted Catholics taking on the mighty Protestant establishment of King James and Salisbury *et al*, or is it just because of the sheer drama of this story? For this story contains it all: the secret plotting, the use of explosives, the discovery and chase, all of which were followed by the final use of the grisly and bloody forces of Stuart law and order. And after all has been said and written, these were the basic ingredients of the Gunpowder Plot of that fateful Fifth of November of some four hundred years ago.

* * * * * * *

Printed in the United Kingdom
by Lightning Source UK Ltd.
115488UKS00001B/103